Books by Wendi Zwaduk

Heart Attack

Over My Head

Haunted By You

Miss Me Baby

Immortal Love

Until the Night

Wanton Witches

Candlelit Magic

Jolly Rogered

Ruined by the Pirate

Clandestine Classics

The Phantom of the Opera

Lust Bites

Must Be Doing Something Right
Love Remembers

Sexy Snax

Firelit Magic
Sunshine of Your Love

Anthologies

Treble
Switch
Bound to the Billionaire
Wild After Dark
Over the Knee
Boots, Chaps and Cowboy Hats

Single Titles

Learning How to Bend
My Immortal
You'll Think of Me
Tangled Up
Careless Whisper
Please Remember Me
What Might Have Been
Ever Fallen In Love
Savin' Me
Someone Like You
When You're With Me
Still The One
Play to Him
Whip It Up
Honey and Decadence
Lasso Lovin'
Tying One On
Taken In
Silk and Decadence
Her Man
Between Us

Her Man

ISBN # 978-1-78651-362-5

©Copyright Wendi Zwaduk 2016

Cover Art by Posh Gosh ©Copyright 2016

Interior text design by Claire Siemaszkiewicz

Totally Bound Publishing

Published in 2016 by Totally Bound Publishing, Newland House, The Point, Weaver Road, Lincoln, LN6 3QN, United Kingdom.

HER MAN

WENDI ZWADUK

Dedication

Logan and Cass wouldn't stay in my imagination forever and now they've got the chance to shine once again. For JPZ because you're my man and you're right where I need to be.

Chapter One

Trouble. That's what most women were—too much trouble! When Logan Malone's last movie had ended, so had his love life. He'd decided women weren't worth the effort—not right now.

Well, no, that wasn't the case—not entirely. Red-hot American blood still charged through his veins and he needed a woman, someone soft in all the right places, tough as nails and unafraid to fight to warm his bed. Why not go for totally impossible?

Logan shifted in his seat. The olive-colored plastic creaked and scratched against the ceramic tile floor. The other three men in the drafty room glared as though he'd ruined their concentration.

"Quiet," the blond man to his right growled.

"Sorry," Logan muttered. He caressed the worn cover of the book jacket as he convinced himself he could play the romantic lead better than the rest of the competition sitting in the drab hallway. Who else could embody the sexy, romantic boy-next-door role better than Romeo Malone, the hunk of the silver screen? He smiled, but quickly lost faith. He faced the biggest roadblock of his career—convincing the directors, producer and author that he was the man for the job. Yeah, another impossible task.

He sighed. Was he the man? Logan took a deep breath to relax before another glance at his competition. Mark Lanigan stood hunched in the corner with his index finger in his ear as he spoke on his cell phone. *Shit.*

Logan flexed his jaw and turned away. His heart dropped to his stomach with a sickening thud. Mark Lanigan wasn't a slouch in the looks department. His baby blues melted even the iciest of hearts with ease. Romance publishers begged for his services as a cover model and Mark had the honor of being selected the 'Sexiest Man of the Decade' according to *Delish* magazine. Last year the man had won an award for his performance of a baseball phenom in love with a farmer's daughter in *Flowers in the Outfield*.

Logan ground his teeth. He should've had that role, but no! He'd spent the two-week casting call screwing around with Katrina Butterfield, romping in the Virgin Islands, answering her darned booty call and living up to his womanizing Romeo image. When he realized he'd forfeited his chance at the part of the year, he'd just about wrung her pretty little neck. He sighed. At least he'd learned from his misstep.

Logan gripped the unforgiving black rubberized armrests. He had to get his career in order. Andrew Speedle exited the conference room through the thick wooden auditorium door. Logan's heart plummeted to the floor. *Great.* More competition he didn't need. Andrew's crooked smile could be both sinister and sweet at the same time. His rumpled, straight-out-of-bed look graced the covers of countless magazines. And he was only twenty-seven! Not only that — he had three supporting roles under his belt, with a lead coming up at the end of the year. Audiences had flocked to see his last film, making it the third highest grossing movie of the year. Andrew could play the sexy hunk-next-door role in his sleep and Logan hated him for it.

Logan pinched the bridge of his nose. Shit. Another part down the drain and he hadn't even tried out yet.

Please let them turn him down. I can do this.

"Malone? Are you giving in already?"

Logan's gaze met Andrew's glare. "They laughed at your sappy credits, didn't they?"

Andrew gave him the finger. "Piss off, Malone. Once she finds out you've screwed the producer and the director, that writer will have your balls in her pocket. Go home and try for a fitting job, something you can handle without dialogue. This ain't the role for you."

Logan's eyes narrowed. "Thanks, asshole."

Andrew sauntered away. Jealousy crashed in Logan's body like a tidal wave. What did that man have that he didn't? He mentally tallied his own assets—broad shoulders, six-pack abs, toned legs and tight buns. Women drooled over his hazel eyes and perfect grin, and he looked hot with any hairstyle. So what was the issue? He was the man for the job without a doubt—case closed.

He sighed. That line of reasoning worked, but Andrew had roles and money, lots of money. A tight ass meant nothing without dollars in the bank.

He thumbed through the book. There were no answers in the battered pages, but simply holding the paperback gave him comfort. He could identify with the hero who wanted true love and honesty with no pretensions. He shook his head. That wasn't possible in Hollywood. Maybe not even in California. Possibly not the world.

Logan flipped to the black and white picture of the author on the inside back cover of the book. Her dowdy professional clothing covered her figure and she smiled sweetly over her shoulder. He'd stared at her so many times and dragged the book around so much over the past three months that the edges of the paper had ruffled. He wondered if she was the actual writer or a model meant to trick the reader. Women that beautiful didn't write romance. Or did they?

Desire curled in his stomach. If she weren't a model, he'd love to tangle his fingers in her dark hair, kiss her lips raw and make her scream with pleasure. Did her skin feel as soft as it looked? Logan guessed it would and she'd do just fine as his arm candy for the premiere. Hell, he'd love to love her for quite a long time.

Love? Too bad it was all a load of crap and nothing more than an act of foreplay involving fictitious emotions. Who actually believed in love? Logan drew a deep breath and let it slide between his lips. He'd never meet a woman who could change his mind and his heart. Women like that didn't exist. Not that lasting relationships mattered much. Paying the bills—that was important. Keeping up the movie star lifestyle had drained his already dwindling bank account. Another flop would mean the end of his career. Career over before the age of thirty-three, hard to envision...but it looked like a very real possibility.

Maybe it was time to go home. No, he'd begged too long and hard to get the chance for the audition. He couldn't back down now. *I will earn this role.*

"Malone?"

Jostled back to reality, Logan looked up. His throat constricted at the sight of another ex. Perfect. "Well, hello, Nikita. It's a pleasure to see you again. Is it my turn, or did you fill the role? I saw Speed walk out earlier."

Nikita Cline pushed her black-rimmed cat's eye glasses back up the bridge of her nose. "It's your turn. We haven't made a decision, yet, but you might do."

Logan felt her heated gaze travel the length of his body. He shivered. He should switch to a different production—one without Nikita. He pasted a wolfish grin on his face and stood to meet her in the doorway. "Well, I'd better dazzle your socks off, then, shouldn't I?"

She grabbed his arm before he entered the room. "You could dazzle other things off instead." Her lips grazed his ear. "I miss you."

Logan shivered again as her perfume wafted to his nose, demanding his undivided attention. He didn't miss the arguments, the accusations, the experimentations she loved so much. She liked to play the field with multiple partners, toys, role-play and whatever she could find for kink. He liked a little kink, but she wasn't his style. "How about I just pass the audition, huh?"

He spotted the women at the table and pasted on his most wicked smile. His voice caught in his throat and a ripple of excitement ran the length of his spine at the sight of his audience. The writer? Was she really there? Or did she moonlight as a screenwriter? Maybe a friend of the producers? *Oh, my, my, my.*

Nikita gestured to the table. "I'd like to introduce the heads of this production. This is Maggie Bowles, our associate producer." She shrugged a shoulder to the woman on the right. "And this is the writer, Cass Jensen."

Logan forced a nod. Maggie had worked on *Break* and co-directed *Maia*, both mega box office hits. She had a reputation for fairness and impartiality with her actors and crew. But the other woman — oh man. He blinked. Cass Jensen penned *Wrong Turn, Slingshot* and toyed with his fantasies from the safety of a black and white photo. Crossbeam Studios had translated three of her earlier novels into box office hits. Now she sat across the room, in living color and completely unaware of his innermost desires.

Had the heat just kicked on? He licked his lips. Something had happened and not just between his legs.

It seemed as if everyone else in the cavernous conference room had evaporated except him and Cass. She wasn't his normal blonde model-type, quite the opposite. She had curves and porcelain skin. Her dark chocolate-colored hair glittered slightly under the harsh glare of the fluorescent lighting, and she brushed the silky strands off her face, revealing her lack of a wedding ring.

Score!

Her mouth curled into a faint smile, accompanying the sparkle in her startling blue-gray eyes. Color rushed into her pale cheeks.

Oh man.

Logan's eyes slipped greedily over her body. Would she flush during sex? The light scent of her perfume muddled his brain. Lilac? Rose? Whatever it was, it was enticing. Logan swallowed hard. Tightness invaded his chest. Such a rapid reaction to a woman knocked him for a complete loop. Cass was the kind of woman who ended up being a cherished lover, not a plaything. He glanced at her once more. His throat went dry. Damn, if she blushed too much longer, he'd be in trouble. If he got time alone with her, he'd be a goner. How would her hands feel gliding along his body? Heaven, probably.

Maggie spoke and interrupted his visual grope session. "You'll read with Tiffany Dufraine. She's agreed to play the part of Sophie. Turn to page nineteen. I want to see what you'll do with the initial love scene."

His shoulders slumped and he bit back a growl. Love scene? Why not the track dialogue or the buddy scene with the crew chief? Logan cleared his throat. He could do a love scene. He had heartless down to a science. But something foreign curled around his brain. He didn't believe in love at first sight, yet looking at Cass in the flesh… He needed air. No, he needed Cass. Right now. He couldn't shake the overwhelming feeling. Heat thrummed in his belly. He didn't understand why, but he wanted to find out whether she wanted heartless or if she was a forever kind of girl. He wanted her body writhing under his, screaming his name in sheer ecstasy.

"Logan? Are you ready?"

Wide-eyed, he turned back to the blonde actress and flipped the script open. "Sorry." He scanned the page and rolled his shoulders. The vertebrae in his neck cracked. He closed his eyes and swallowed a groan.

Way to act totally unprofessional.

He opened his eyes and focused on his reading partner. "This isn't your dream," he began. "You don't want this life, Soph."

Tiffany reached out to him. "You're my other half. Don't leave me," she pleaded. "I can't walk away from you, Jonathan."

Logan squeezed his eyes shut and wrapped his arms around her waist. He wondered how it would feel to hold Cass. No, this was Tiffany portraying Sophie. This was a major audition. Focus. "Babe, racing is my life. I don't have money to offer and my heart's been broke too many times to count. Is that the kind of man you want to pin your hopes and dreams on?"

Tiffany tipped her head and brushed her lips against his. "You're the man I want to pin my life on. Money never was important. As for your heart, that'll mend over time."

Logan cast a quick glance across the room. It felt wrong. All wrong. "Soph, can you handle being second fiddle to a race car?" He wondered about Cass. Could she handle being second fiddle to his career? Or would she want him to change?

He clenched his jaw. Enough! He needed the part and the money and couldn't possibly need Cass. Why? He didn't know her. Besides, why couldn't he think straight? She wasn't a stunner. She was sort of plain and average, with a heart-shaped face and soulful eyes...soft, innocent and beguiling. Cass smelled good. No, better than good—intoxicating. Damn it!

Tiffany snuggled into his arms and raked her nails down his back. "I'll learn to drive the damn thing just to be with you. All you have to do is say the words."

Logan stumbled, only for a moment. "Uh, well, then babe, you got a deal. I love you." God, he sounded stupid and clumsy. "I'm sorry." *Another blown opportunity. Shit.*

Cass's grin blossomed exponentially and Logan completely forgot about the role. His heart pounded like a bass drum in his ears. Everything focused on the angelic woman scribbling notes on a yellow legal pad. He needed to see that brilliant smile again and to taste her kiss. How else could he make her bloom?

"Do you have the DVD of clips we requested?"

He frowned. Cass looked away. If she hadn't spoken, then who had? Logan turned to face Nikita as she poked his biceps with her sharp fingernail. Oh, her. Damn it, he had no idea what she'd said. "Huh?"

Her pale blue eyes narrowed. "Your DVD. Did you bring one?" She held her hand open. Her long acrylic nails flashed and clicked as her fingers waggled. "Don't tell me you forgot. You forget everything, like returning phone calls."

Logan stole another glance at Cass before digging in his backpack for the disc. She'd turned to conference with Maggie. Damn, had he lost her attention already? Did he have it to start with? Probably not. And Nikita brought up his lousy personal skills. His heart sank. He zipped the bag closed. "Here." He placed the disc on the table. "Thank you for considering me for this role."

Maggie looked up. Her smile was cold and thin. "Thank you. You did well." Her words sounded trite. Logan's shoulders sank. Maggie wasn't impressed, which meant Cass wouldn't be either. Strike one.

Nikita rubbed his arm with the case of the DVD. "You did very well," she purred a little too close to his ear for comfort. Logan forced a tight-lipped smile. An icy chill skated up his spine. Great. Nikita was impressed for all the wrong reasons. Strike two.

Slowly Cass met his gaze as she brushed another pesky lock of hair away from her face. The nervous but very sexy gesture sent blood rushing below his belt at warp speed. Holy shit, he had an erection. Fuck. He needed to hide the boner. He moved his backpack in front of his groin.

When Cass smiled, his insides melted. He liked her lips— full, but not too full, with a hint of coral—and her dark lashes framed her eyes perfectly. He tried to think about baseball stats, the president, the economy and anything else that would derail his growing lust. Too late. His erection pressed tight against his zipper. Thank God for the backpack.

"You don't look like my vision for Jonathan, but I think you've got the heart for it," Cass said.

Nikita laughed and covered her mouth with her hand. "He has no heart."

Cass forced a tight-lipped smile and glared at Nikita before returning her attention to Logan. "My guts tell me you'll do the best job. I think I've found my Jonathan," she announced. "Are you available for filming on Monday? I know it's extremely short notice. We had an issue with our previous choice and problems with the production staff, so to speak."

Logan stepped close, ignoring the fact that he wasn't their first choice. He knew that already. Alan Gottfried had turned the project down when he landed the role of Anderson in Myra Kelly's action blockbuster. Thank God for his foresight to grovel and the poor planning on Alan's part.

He took her hand in his. A spark shot through his body. It felt like the air surged out of the room. Heat engorged his dick to damn near painful proportions.

His ears burned. Would she notice his predicament? Would she care? He didn't. He needed the part more than his next breath. Correction, he needed Cass more than his next breath. Whoa, better tamp that down. He didn't deal in feelings like that.

"Thank you, Ms. Jensen. My calendar's free if you want me." Wow. Talk about babbling. He sounded like a green actor indeed!

Logan caressed the back of her hand with his thumb. Cass's skin reminded him of silk. His mouth watered. How did she turn him inside out with just a touch? Enough, enough! This was crazy — and so sexy. Someone grabbed his arm and Cass's gaze fell.

No, no, no! Wait…

Nikita dragged him away from the table. "We'll get back to you." He nearly stumbled on the uneven tile floor. Strike three! End of game. Erection deflated. He wriggled free from Nikita and waved before exiting the room.

"I'll tell you what I think, later," Nikita hissed and slammed the door in his face.

Logan stood dumbfounded on the other side of the thick wooden barrier. He'd never thought of himself as a man with a heart, especially not with Nikita acting as she did. Romeo Malone never let women take him for a ride. Cass was just another meaningless encounter, right? Her words rang in his ears. She had faith in him. She wanted him —

well, for the movie.

In the brightly lit hallway, he slung the backpack over his shoulder. Mark Lanigan shoved forward, knocking Logan into the rough brick wall. "My turn. I'll show them what real acting looks like."

Logan stood stiff and glared. "Asshole number two." He'd turned to exit the foyer when a voice halted him.

"Mr. Malone?"

Cass Jensen, in the flesh. Her lips curled into a slight but pleasant smile. Her eyes sparkled with an intensity he felt throughout his body. The bounce of her ample breasts caught his attention, bringing the erection right back and then some. Standing, she wasn't much more than five-two, which put her at least six inches shorter than he stood and exactly chin level—perfect for kissing. Nice.

Logan nodded and stuttered. "Ummm, yeah." He wasn't a stuffy Mr. Malone. He was just Logan. "That's me." He felt clumsy. Not at all the Romeo façade his agent worked so hard to cultivate. "How can I help you?"

She licked her lips. He wondered what she tasted like. He'd have to masturbate tonight to get her out of his system. Cass's perfume tickled his nose.

Her smile grew. "I want you to play Jonathan. I don't care what Nikita says and I can convince Mags. You are Jonathan."

"I'm glad we agree."

Her soft expression faltered to a slight frown. "Maybe I made a mistake in selecting you." She massaged her forehead with her left hand. "I knew Nikita would cause trouble. Mags tried to warn me that you two were something and it would be a problem. Okay. I just thought..."

He shook his head. "No mistake. I thought I left a lot on the table, but not now."

Cass's gaze met his once more. Her blue-gray eyes calmed his jittery nerves and heated his body. She brushed her hair away and covered her growing smile with her petite fingers. Logan wished he was that hand pressed to her lips.

Oh man, he had it bad for Cass Jensen.

She cocked her head. "I thought you looked like Jonathan felt. You're stuck in a tricky situation and unsure of the outcome. I was touched. You portray edgy quite well."

Logan needed her to stop explaining. She touched him in places he thought were dead, like his heart. "Well, Ms. Jensen, I'm honored that you want me and hope our relationship continues."

Cass arched one brow. A playful smile curled the corner of her mouth. "Oh?"

He clasped his hands together and dipped his head. "I mean, I'm glad I'm your choice for the part — in the movie."

Cass pursed her lips, stuck her hand out. "Well, congratulations. I'll let Nikita and Mags know. And you can call me Cass. Everyone does."

Logan couldn't help but smile. "And you can forget all that Nikita nonsense. We dated for a couple of weeks, but I didn't want her attention." Why did he tell her that? It wasn't like she demanded a dating history.

Cass raised both brows. Pink tinged her cheeks, bringing out the blue in her eyes. "I see. Thanks." She withdrew her hand and tucked her hair behind her ears, revealing three hoops in each lobe, plus one in her cartilage. "Well, then come back tomorrow at eight and sign the contracts."

Instinctively, he pulled her into an embrace. "No — thank *you*." Bank account back in the black, ego intact, and Cass in his arms. Damn she felt good there. Despite the upswing in outlook, inwardly he cursed. Money wouldn't bring her affection. Unlike the other women who floated in and out of his life, she cared about character. His ego wasn't important to her. He had to be himself. She held the power to make him a better man. Could he handle it? For her, he'd try.

Her body relaxed. Her sigh, like the mew of a kitten, thrust him into a new dimension. He wanted more, way more. He rubbed her back and trailed his fingers up her soft body to cup her jaw. His eyelids drooped. He wanted to kiss her.

Cass tilted her face to look at him. "What do you think you're doing?" Her no-nonsense tone jarred his common sense back into play. What was he doing? "Just because I liked you for the part Logan doesn't mean I like you." She wriggled out of his grasp. "I'm not a notch on your belt. If that's your inclination, then I'll give the role to Mr. Speedle."

He felt like she punched him in the stomach. She should've. "Cass, I'm not used to women walking away."

Cass straightened her spine and squared her shoulders. "Then turn around so you don't see me leave." With that, she spun on her heel and left.

Logan pinched the bridge of his nose. He didn't want her to go. Quite the opposite. Should he shout? No. He decided to run. "Cass?" He hurried to catch her. "Cass?"

She slipped silently into the meeting room. Too late.

Logan stared at the cream-colored drop ceiling tiles. "I'll get you to change your mind before this is over. You'll see."

Chapter Two

Cass leaned against the door and tried to catch her breath. She ran both hands through her hair. Was it possible to calm down enough to look professional? Logan Malone came on to her. Could his smooth lines be a joke? She replayed his words. *I'm honored you want me.* Probably a load of BS. Why had he tried to kiss her? *Her.* It had to be a desperate plea to get the role. Cass closed her eyes. She still felt the warmth of Logan's strong and steady embrace. Too bad the relationship wouldn't happen.

"Why are you so flushed?"

Cass opened her eyes slowly. "Huh?"

Nikita stood a mere foot away with her crimson lips pursed. She waggled her finger. "Your face is red, Chunks. Did he come on to you? Don't take it personally. He comes on to everyone. It doesn't make you special."

Cass averted her gaze to the colorful abstract artwork decorating the bland beige walls. She hated the nickname Chunks and she wasn't fond of Nikita. She smoothed her hands over her blouse. God, she had sweaty palms. She could still smell the enticing scent of Logan's cologne. Damn, he smelled good. "Mags, what do you think of that last guy?"

Maggie folded her arms and sat on the leading edge of the folding table. "Mark? He was good. But I take it you don't agree?"

Cass faintly raised one shoulder. How would she know about Mark? She hadn't seen his performance.

Maggie shook her head and shifted her sandal-clad feet. "Lanigan wasn't sincere, but he had the look. Speedle

19

nailed the lines and Malone had the attitude, but in truth? I didn't favor any of them."

Cass winced. Just as she thought—Logan was a sinfully sexy man with an attitude. She kicked at the floor tiles with the toe of her boot.

"If you want looks, go with Lanigan," Nikita snapped. "Not that my opinion counts. If you want used, go with Malone. He's a wolf in designer clothing."

Cass' stomach lurched. "But he looks good doing it," she whispered. Women around the world met decent guys all the time. She attracted jerks. No more. She refused to fall for a wolf in designer clothing.

"I want Speedle. He's sexy and I heard he's available," Nikita said, butting in once again. "Then again, so is Malone, if anyone's interested." She cackled. "He's taken a shine to you, Chunks. Probably to get the part. Won't last."

Cass shot her a dirty look. Who cared if the man with the chiseled body, boyish face and bedroom eyes was available? She didn't. Not any time soon. Correction—never would.

Maggie put her arm around Cass's shoulders. At least she had friends to turn to when all else failed, like her sanity. "You favor Logan, don't you?"

Cass shrugged again. Favor? Not a chance. Want so badly that her body quaked from a scorching glance? Yes. "He's got something going for him—I'm not sure what, but the more he read through the lines, the more I saw him as Jonathan."

"Oh no," Nikita gasped. "No, no, he's way out of your league. Leave him to the pros."

Maggie stepped away and held her hands open. Her heels clicked on the tiles. "What? She wrote the character. If Logan fits and wants to do it, then he's it."

Cass shivered. *If he's it, then he's it.* Why did that make her toes curl? "He's coming in tomorrow morning to sign his contract. I'm going back to Crawford tonight, so, Mags, you're in charge."

"Me?" Maggie rolled her eyes. "Sure, why not? I've

always wanted to babysit a pack of brats."

Nikita's eyes lit up and her hands clasped together. "I'm sticking around for that. I want to see that tight little butt once more. Too bad you're giving up, Chunks. Logan Malone is grade-A meat."

Cass sighed and pushed her hair from her face. *Chunks.* Damn that stupid nickname. Men with tight little butts didn't pay attention to women nicknamed Chunks. They fell for skinny, statuesque women in spiked heels and short skirts. Besides, she didn't trust her instincts when it came to men. All she managed to find were the liars and cheaters of the world. Her heart felt raw. She liked Malone. She left her chair and grabbed her purse. It was time to collect her thoughts. "You can stick around, Nikita. I've had enough of California. I'm going home."

"Can I have him?"

Cass spun around. Jealousy hit like a swat to the nose. Nikita had had Logan once and let him get away. Why did she deserve a second chance when Cass wouldn't have a first? She shoved thoughts of Logan to the back of her mind. "More power to you, Nikita," she said, although it hurt. She left the room and forced herself not to care. Logan wasn't her problem.

Cass' footfalls sounded hollow on the tile floor in the empty hallway. Then again, everything in her life sounded pretty hollow. Nothing felt right except for her writing. True, her literary career paid the bills and kept her secluded, but it didn't warm the dark nights. In her world, very little warmed the nights.

She pushed the heavy steel door open to the waning rosy sunset washing over the parking lot. Streams of amber, mauve and periwinkle sparkled on the cars dotting the concrete landscape. She adjusted her shoulder bag and pressed the button on the key ring to unlock the rental car. She frowned. The navy blue Charger didn't suit her personality at all. Fussy wasn't her style. Rugged and dependable was. She liked full-sized, slightly beat-up trucks.

"Cass."

Reflected in the window, piercing green eyes stared back at her. She closed her eyes and ground her teeth together. She drummed her fingers on the roof of the car. Dex. What did he want? How did he know she was in California? She turned slowly and pretended to be tough. "What do you want now, Dex?"

A contented smile curled his perfect lips and tightened his chiseled jaw. He caged her body with his bulky, muscle-corded arms. "Chunks... Why, can't I say hello to my wife?"

Cass bristled. She felt the venom in his voice all the way down to her toes. The bruises, the broken bones, the scars and the names flashed across her memory. "That's not my name, Dex, and I'm your ex-wife. I have nothing to say to you, so please leave me alone." She shook her head. "Your Pleasure 45 cologne is overpowering. Did you douse yourself in the entire bottle?"

Dex braced his hands on the window frame and pushed his crotch into her belly, painfully reminding her of what she divorced. "Now is that any way to speak to the man who loves you?"

Cass closed her eyes and swallowed hard. Her hands fisted against his solid chest in an attempt to shove him back. "You don't love me."

Dex patted her cheek with his palm. "I never stopped loving you."

The endless parade of women strolled through her head. All the cheating. The lies. "You did it with everyone but me." If she recalled correctly, he'd cheated on her more times than she could count.

His groin pushed farther into her, squashing her bottom and back against the car door. "Don't tell me what I did, Chunks. I invited you to join in and you declined."

Cass winced as his hand connected with her cheek in an earth-shattering crack. That was his style. Hard enough to matter, but light enough for no lasting marks. He bashed her head against the glass until she saw stars. "You walked away from me, but I'll never leave you, sweetheart."

A male voice came from behind Dex. "I think you should."

Cass's stomach did flip-flops. She knew that husky voice. Her head ached. More trouble she didn't need. Logan Malone.

"Who the hell?" Dex spun around. "Oh, it's you, Malone. Why aren't you off sparring with my sister? She's still got a thing for you."

Cass rubbed her temple. She didn't look forward to nursing an injury during the flight home. She looked at Dex and then to Logan. Like a schoolgirl, her heart fluttered. Any more of this hero stuff and she might fall for him. No way. She was too strong to fall for such a womanizer. Well, she hoped she was.

Logan braced his feet and stood firm. Hate flashed in his soulful eyes, making them a deeper, darker shade of hazel. His jaw clenched, reminding her of an old Roman statue. "I think the lady told you to leave her alone."

"I wanted to see my wife before she left for Ohio." Dex took a step toward Logan. "I won't let her leave without seeing me. You can wait."

Cass felt a momentary catch in her throat. Could Logan really care? Or did he really want that stupid role? She pushed past her ex and gripped Logan's arm. Thick, with the right amount of muscle—just the way she liked it. "I can handle this, Logan. You'd better go. He'll only want to rearrange your face." Her heart clenched. She didn't want Logan bruised on account of Dex. "Logan, please. If you let me deal with him, nothing will go wrong." Cass couldn't mistake the wild look in Logan's eyes. She'd imagined it a million times before with her fictional heroes. Seeing it for real sent fresh shivers down her spine.

Logan glared at Dex. "I needed to speak to you." He wrapped his arm around her body. "And I'm not leaving you alone with this monster."

Dex shoved her away from Logan. A lock of her hair caught

in his thick watch, ripping it from her skull. "Sweetheart, I still love you. I think we can work through our problems. Give me another chance."

Cass shrieked and massaged her scalp. "Dex, that hurt!"

Logan stroked the injury, turning her pain into an odd pleasure.

Dex flicked the dark strands onto the concrete. "Oh, how cute! Romeo Malone wants to speak to you. He only wants in your pants, Chunks, or he's trying to get a part in one of your movies."

Logan spoke through clenched teeth. "Go home, Dex."

"This isn't over," Dex snapped.

"It never is," Cass muttered. Logan crushed her against his broad shoulder. His fresh, right-out-of-the-shower scent tickled her nose and she took a deep breath, loving the safety she felt in his arms. A tiny moan escaped her lips. Even his narrow waist felt delicious in her hands.

"Her name isn't Chunks, but as her ex-husband, you should know that," Logan growled.

How could he know about her past? She hadn't told him, but she liked that he stuck up for her. Maybe he could be her strong warrior, ready to protect her from the evil clutches of her former husband. That thought sent a fresh rush of heat coursing through her system.

Dex raised his hand and slapped her arm, making her cower. "Keep your hands off my wife, Malone. I'll have something to say about it if you don't."

"Get out." Logan spoke through clenched teeth. His dark brows bunched, creasing his forehead.

Dex strolled over to his BMW and yanked the door open. "I'm not through here." Burned rubber floated in a thick fog as Dex peeled out of the parking lot.

Cass finally gulped the gritty air. "I'm sorry you had to witness that, but it's...he's part of my life."

Logan's grip never failed. In fact he held on until Dex was long gone. It made her heart beat so loud she knew he could hear it. The man made her knees weak. At thirty-six, she was too old for weak knees.

Cass swallowed a sigh. His hazel eyes were devastating from a distance and up close... Damn his sexy eyes. She could easily lose herself in their warmth and sensuality.

"Can I steal a moment of your time?" he asked.

Something new uncoiled in her body — safety. She ran a shaky hand through her hair, buying time to process the situation. He wanted to protect her. Her mouth pursed to a tight smile.

No. Don't fall for this guy. Never fall for the devil in soft blue jeans. "Fire away."

Logan loosened his grip, but didn't let go. He looked deep into her, like all the way to her soul. The twinkle in his eye, mixed with the guilt on his face, showed his honest, but odd desire. "I'm sorry," he said finally.

"For what?"

"I see you heard the rumor."

Cass nodded. Rumor? Make that plural. Logan could have his own five-book series full of lies and innuendoes. "Romeo Malone scores in every picture and in every state," she said in a singsong fashion. "Who is he gonna do now? It's all over Hollywood, but that doesn't mean I believe it." Although she did believe he'd had more than his fair share of fun.

Logan pinched the bridge of his nose with his free hand. "You know that's a load of crap, right?"

Cass yanked the car door open, forcing herself to ignore the words her heart believed. She slipped out of his hold. If she stuck around any longer, she might fall victim to his charms. "Why should I believe anything coming from the master of the female form, Romeo Malone?"

He gripped the window frame. "Is that a challenge? I love a challenge."

Cass put her hands on her hips. The urge to throttle the man came to mind. Then again, so did the idea of kissing him senseless. She noted the lack of stubble on his tanned cheeks. His lips made her mouth water. Full and supple without being girly. He shuffled his feet and her gaze was drawn to his scuffed shoes and tapered legs, then inexplicably to his groin. Oh, God! He had an erection or a damn thick cock. The cars in the parking lot suddenly became extremely interesting. "How about we keep our relationship professional?"

Logan folded his arms. "Professional? You'll need to examine my style on a personal level to tailor the part to the man I am. We could do that tonight...all night long."

Cass scrunched her brows and shifted her weight behind the open door, hoping he didn't see the extra cellulite on her hips, or anywhere else for that matter. "So, what's your point?"

"I'm an ass."

Cass nodded her head. A lock of her hair obscured her view. "That's one way of saying it. Frustrating works too."

"Touché," he replied and brushed her hair from her eyes. His touch felt like fire licking her skin. Cass shivered and pressed her thighs together. Her nipples tightened. What did his lips taste like? What about the rest of him? She tried her best to shove the naughty thoughts from her mind. Men didn't have that effect on her, especially not gorgeous men.

Logan scrunched his nose and looked away. He rested his hands on his narrow hips and stepped two paces away before turning around. He slapped his palm on his thigh. "I wish you weren't at the audition. Because of you, I nearly blew it."

She forced a tight smile. She couldn't tell whether anger or amusement shone in his eyes. She'd bet anger, which pricked her fragile ego. "You mean to tell me I'm heinous? Is that it? One look and you'll die? Or better yet, one look and you lose hotness points?" She folded her arms, mimicking his combative stance. "I'd love to hear you talk your way out of this one, Romeo." She plopped behind the wheel of the muscle car and tugged the door closed. "We're filming *Broken Wheels* on my farm in Ohio, but don't you dare try to find me. No more talking to you...forever. I mean it.

Forever."

Logan held his hands up as if to stop her. "But…"

Confused by her bodily reaction, Cass engaged the ignition, backed up and sped off, leaving him dumbfounded in the parking lot. Good riddance. Males weren't going to use her as a stepping-stone any longer. Enough with guys who only cared about themselves.

"Don't tell me I'm the reason you screwed up!" Cass screamed to the interior of the car. "I know when I've been insulted and when I'm not wanted." She swiped the back of a hand at the tears racing down her face. "Why do the sexy ones know how to hit below the belt? Why do they think I have no feelings just because I'm not a size two?" Her voice choked in her throat. "Curvy girls are sexy girls, dammit!"

After turning down the wrong exit and circling the side streets around the airport for the better part of twenty minutes, Cass pulled into the parking lot for the airport in Burbank. The glass around the terminal reflected the stars sparkling in the night sky. She retrieved a tissue from her bag to blot her face before walking through the building.

Deep breaths. Deep, relaxing breaths.

She tried hard to keep her composure, but the long day had finally caught up to her. She forced a smile and waved to the girls behind the desk. The thunder of a departing jet engine blurred out her words of welcome. Cass held up her hand and mouthed, "Hi, girls," and continued on her way past the ornate displays of peonies, daisies and ferns decorating the waiting room. On the other side of the glass sat her one luxury—her Learjet. The gleaming white plane waited patiently on the slate gray tarmac. Two other planes filled the otherwise barren landscape.

Cass rubbed her arms. A shiver rippled through her body. She looked over her shoulder and around the tarmac once more. "Dex? If you're out there, just tell me. I'm tired of your games."

A musky, familiar scent wafted through the air. Cass closed her eyes momentarily to take it in. It smelled like home. She shook off the sensation and continued up the short set of steps to her jet. Once inside the plane, she settled a bit until she heard an annoying sound. The shrill beacon in her bag meant that she had a phone call. Instead of answering, she let it go to voice mail. She toyed with the silver letter C dangling from her shoulder bag. The charm was a silent reminder of simpler times.

She peered out the window at the landscape. Across the way, a dark convertible GTO sat parked under a faint security lamp. A man wearing jeans and a mocha-colored leather jacket perched on the hood. His dark hair, tinged with russet hues, draped over his eyes, obscuring his identity. It couldn't be Logan. He wasn't that interested. It had to be her mind playing tricks.

She shifted in her seat.

"Are you ready?"

Cass smiled and leaned against the captain's chair. "Yes, Scott. I'm ready to go home and never set foot in California ever again. Does that tell you enough?" No more fear. No more worrying about people in the shadows. No more piggish men playing games.

The pilot matched her grin. "It says plenty. Well, we're ready to go. I called Sandy to tell her I'm coming home. She'll wait with the car when we get to Crawford."

"Okey-dokey." Cass clapped his shoulder and returned to her seat, where she stared out of the window. Scott's wife, Sandy, and their two children, Seth and Emma, waited at home. Tad had his fiancée Meredith and Dopey, his Great Dane. All she had was a big, empty house. She leaned on the captain's seat to annoy the pilot. "Do you have any pets?"

He laughed. "You know we have three cats and four dogs. The kids can't turn down a stray. Why?"

"I don't know..." Cass said and trailed off. A playful, wide grin crossed her lips. Unwanted, unloved and looking for a home—a stray was just what she needed.

"I know where I can get you a mutt that looks like a cross between a Shepherd and a collie real cheap," Scott said.

"How about two?"

"House trained?"

"Yep. Eppie's dogs had pups and she wants to get rid of them. She's only got two left, a boy and a girl. They're fixed," he said and turned to deal with radio traffic.

A pair? Noise, accidents, excitement?

Scott spoke over his shoulder. "You want 'em?"

Cass grinned like a fool. Yeah, she'd love a pair of pups, trouble and all. "We'll call Eppie when we land and I'll pick them up tomorrow." She leaned back in the seat. Two dogs. At least she'd have energetic, slobbery company. "Hey, Scott? Let's go home to civilization. I need the rest."

Chapter Three

Logan stared at the planes leaving the airport. He could only wonder which one Cass was on. He flipped the empty can of soda over the windshield into the seat. It dropped onto the leather upholstery with a soft thunk. He leaned back against the windshield. It wasn't like him to pause on one particular woman. He'd been taught women were disposable, like the discarded soda can. Once their use was up, so was the so-called relationship.

Then again, Cass wasn't just some woman. She had tantalizing curves and a smile that could light up a small city. Her energy and devotion would weaken lesser men. He could still smell her perfume. So why sit on the side of the gravel road circling the airport when he should have a plan to add Cass into his life? Hell if he knew.

Another plane took off. Cass probably sailed across the sky. Did she see him? He ran a shaky hand through his disheveled hair. No doubt she'd forgotten about him by now. So what was he doing watching her from afar? He'd allowed himself to get caught up wishing for someone he could never have.

Logan slammed his fist into his thigh. It wasn't like he didn't have a bevy of beguiling women dying for his attention. He'd earned the honor of being one of Delish magazine's hottest bachelors for two years in a row. Okay, so that was last year. He was still a movie star and possessed the power to bed any woman he chose.

Except Cass. He felt a connection with her that extended beyond the character. She lit him up and turned him inside out. He wanted more. But he couldn't forget her nuisance ex-husband, Dexter Rose. That inconvenience dampened his sex drive.

Logan groaned. He had to get the vivacious woman with the devastating blue eyes out of his mind. His phone buzzed in his pocket. He felt the vibration and fought the urge to ignore it. No one needed him right now. Would Cass? He retrieved the device. It bleated with a new voice message. Damn. Before he could check the missed call list, the phone buzzed again. He stuck his finger in his ear to hear the caller. "Malone."

"Hey, Logan." It was Jade Weir, one of the sexy bit players from his last sitcom, Mending Fences. Jade oozed raw sex and sin. Her voice could melt butter. "We're going to Club 1000. Wanna come?"

Logan laughed. He knew her double meaning all too well. Jade's nickname was Plenty. She could give and receive plenty in bed, not that he had firsthand knowledge. She wasn't interested in him, although he had chased her all across the country to find out. He watched another plane take off. Maybe a Thursday night out with his girls would be therapeutic. "Did you invite the others?"

Jade giggled. "The dance crew? Well, I called Melinda, Davinda and Chandra. I think Chastity is going to be there. I know how much you like her. But tonight, maybe I could give you some special attention."

The taillights from a smaller jet disappeared into the clouds. The tail number caught his attention. 78 CJW. He processed the letters. Cass Jensen, Writer? Cute. Who knew what the seventy-eight meant. He waited for the roar to die down. "Let me think about it." He hung up without giving her the chance to answer.

Logan shoved his phone into his back pocket and slid off the hood of the GTO. The gravel crunched under his feet as he paced in front of the vehicle. What was he thinking? He had to stop chasing women who didn't want him. Romeo Malone indeed. He shoved that thought aside for the moment. "Women should be thrilled to have my company."

He said the words aloud, but somehow they didn't sound right. He kicked a large rock into the weeds. "What a load of crap."

As Logan drove to the studio, he dialed a phone number then switched the device to the speaker setting. "Maggie Bowles, please."

A couple of clicks later, the secretary connected the call. "This is Maggie Bowles."

He shifted in the seat. "Hi, my name is Logan Malone. I auditioned for the part of Jonathan Sherman for *Broken Wheels*. Cass Jensen told me to come in tomorrow morning to sign my contract. I have business to take care of and don't want to annoy my agent, Carmine Adell, at this hour. Can I take care of this matter tonight?" Carmine would be pissed when he found out tomorrow, but Logan didn't care.

"Well, I can get in touch with Carmine," Maggie replied. "Why now? I won't honor your decision to back out at this point in time."

Logan snorted. "Back out? I have no desire to back out. Actually I wanted to get a jump on the part."

Maggie sighed. "Fine. Can you be to the studio by ten?"

"I'm in the parking lot. I'm ready when you are."

"Come on up."

Moments later, Logan stood outside Maggie's office. Orchestral versions of soft rock hits serenaded through built-in speakers. Framed posters from her work lined the ivory walls. A handful of photographs littered the dark cherry coffee table. He leaned against a bright red armchair shaped like the letter P, but upside down. "Why don't they make chairs you can actually sit on anymore?" He saw fellow actors, a few musicians and a lot of people he didn't know. The one face he searched intently for wasn't there.

"Looking for Cass?"

He whipped around. Maggie stood with her arms folded. He couldn't quite read the expression in her vibrant green eyes. He righted his stance and shoved his hands into his pockets. "Say again?"

She took a step forward and frowned. No nonsense, through and through. "Are you looking for Cass? Because you won't find her up there."

Logan nodded. "I see. Too bad. She deserves to be up there with all the other greats." He attempted to smile. Cass deserved the moon and stars. He just didn't have them to give, but dammit, he'd like to try. "Soon, I'll be up there too."

Maggie narrowed her eyes, making her cheekbones more pronounced. "No lack of modesty. I have the contract in my office, but something tells me you aren't here for that. So, tell me, what is it you do want?"

Logan gasped. Cass, that's what I want, he wanted to say. Instead, his ego took over. "You know so little of me. I came to sign on for the picture. Anything else is mere speculation." He nearly choked on his words. Speculation? No, he had it bad for Cass. His ears burned and jaw tightened.

Maggie spun on her spiked heels and entered her office. Blonde curls bobbed as she walked. Logan followed obediently, unintentionally admiring her tapered legs. Not like Cass's soft curves. Nice, but he preferred Cass.

Maggie sat behind her enormous oak desk. Advertising posters for *Maia* and *Break* flanked her like silent sentries. A tiny fountain trickled water over rose quartz rock. "She likes you."

Logan stopped in his tracks, bumping into the caramel-colored oak office chair. Wait a minute. *What? Likes me?* Not Cass. Not possible. Was it? He swallowed his surprise. *Please, please, please.* "Who do you mean? Nikita? She's had a thing for me, but what we had is in the past."

Maggie slid the papers across the desk. She pushed a straw-colored curl behind her ear, revealing three large diamond studs adorning her lobe. "You know exactly who I mean and, no, not Nikita."

Logan glanced down and signed on the highlighted lines. He had to tread lightly. Cass? There was a God. "She just hopped on a plane back to Ohio. And no—she doesn't like

33

me. Speaking of those who don't like me, I met Dex." He dropped the pen with a flourish.

"Oh?" Her crushing grip on her writing utensil belied her confident exterior. "Tell me what happened."

Her reaction puzzled him. The pen was innocent. Apparently Dex wasn't. "He's a jerk, isn't he?"

With her jaw set, Maggie simply stared.

Logan shifted his weight and stuffed his hands back in his jeans pockets. "I went to apologize for being a dirtbag. Dex slapped her and I lost my shit. I couldn't let him hurt her like that. He called her his wife. I thought they were through."

Please let them be over.

Maggie closed her eyes and sank back in the large chair, rubbing her forehead with the pads of her fingers. "He may be a jerk, but he gave her Josh."

"Josh? Who's Josh?"

She opened her eyes, only to narrow them. "Forget I said that. Look, do you care about her?"

Logan shrugged. "I only talked to her for a few minutes." He sat on the edge of her desk and grinned. "But I'd like to get to know her a whole lot better." *And learn about this Josh person.*

Maggie leaned forward and toyed with the blotter. "Okay, dirtbag. What did you say exactly?"

Logan sighed and ran his fingers through his hair. The rage simmering in her eyes jostled his composure. "I told her she makes me nervous."

Maggie snorted. "Moron."

"Ha-ha," he said with a thin grin. Okay, now wasn't the time to show bravado, but he couldn't help himself. "I made a quarter million this summer for my appearance on *The Beach.* Those who watched my episode didn't think I was a moron."

Maggie tucked the documents into a folder and smoothed the top page of the blotter. Her bright red nails shimmered in the harsh office light. She cleared her throat. "She's my friend, so I'm only going to say this once. If you have any desire to break her heart, stop now, because if I find out that you hurt her in any way, I'll personally hunt you down and remove your balls with a dull knife. Got me?"

Logan's mind reeled. Romeo without his Malones? He'd never pegged the director as a sadist. He scrunched his brows and folded his hands over his crotch. "Wait. What—"

"I'm not saying another word." Maggie folded her arms. "It's just food for thought."

"I understand." Well, he thought he did. "See you on the set in a few days." He left the office and moments later stood in the parking lot, running his fingers through his hair. Though he didn't understand it, he yearned to comfort Cass. Every fiber of his soul wanted her in his arms, even if they weren't a good match.

"Cass needs a wicked ride with a hot guy." He wiggled his eyebrows. "Me." He strutted across the nearly empty parking lot, smirking at his cleverness. A pang of realization hit. He couldn't show up at her house unannounced. He had an image to uphold. He sat behind the wheel of the GTO, debating his next move. His cell phone beeped with an incoming text message, jerking him from his thoughts. The topless photo of Jade included a note.

U R missn this Cum clubbn!
Plz?

He massaged his forehead. Clubbing sounded fun. He liked losing himself in the music and sweat of the dance floor. He closed the phone without sending a return message. As much as he tried to ignore her, his thoughts returned to Cass. She probably wouldn't live for the noise and crazy atmosphere of the clubs. She seemed too quiet.

Logan sped through town, ignoring the bright neon lights advertising the clubs and bars. He drove along the ocean promenade, allowing the scent of sea salt to clear his senses. At the stoplight, scantily clad women skittered past his bumper, giggling, waving and tossing scraps of paper with their phone numbers onto his lap.

He winked, waved and played up to his audience. When the signal changed, he charged away. Suddenly the nonstop party and willing female escorts seemed dull. The neon blurred together, blotting out the palm trees along the roadway. The flora around him was real, but everything else felt unreal.

He pulled into a parking spot in front of an old, abandoned movie theater. Weathered plywood covered the doors. Many of the bulbs in the once majestic marquee were missing or broken. Still, it reminded him of the innocence and big dreams that had sent him to Hollywood in the first place. Life used to be simple back then.

He maneuvered the car back out into the street and headed through the evening traffic to Club 1000. The song on the radio reminded him of Cass. He hummed along with the melody. *You bring out the best in me with just a smile.* A grin tugged at the corner of his mouth. If she only knew the power she held over him. If only he could drive her beautiful image from his mind. They were opposites. She didn't even claim to like him, unless he believed Maggie. What did that really mean? He wanted to call Cass and hear the truth. Instead, Logan dialed Jade's number. He needed to do some heavy damage control. Jade could wait. Hell, he could wait—for Cass.

"Baby boy!" Jade cried over the thrumming techno beat.

"Shout, so I can hear you, sexy girl," he replied.

"Hurry up. I requested some Dizzy Jane. I can't dance to their tunes without you. The twins want to grind."

Logan rolled to a stop in the valet line. His normal freewheeling mood dissipated to a hollowness he couldn't tamp down. Jade wouldn't make him feel better and neither would the alcohol or the twins. He needed something homey and organic, something honest and logical. Oh, hell. He handed his keys to the attendant. "I'll be back within the hour."

The teen nodded. "Ah, a short night."

"Something like that." When he entered the club, a throng of girls crowded around him. "Hello, ladies," he purred and stretched his arms. A blonde tucked against his shoulder and a redhead curled around his right arm. Another blonde pressed her backside into his crotch. The strobe lights blinked on the group as they waded through the dancers. The girls grabbed drinks from passing waitresses and took turns enticing Logan. A couple of the ladies danced provocatively together in order to rouse his attention. He squeezed in between them. "Not in public, girls."

Just as the words passed his lips, he spied Speedle. He nodded to the other actor. "Andrew." The DJ released a fresh wave of sweetly scented fog to billow over the dance floor.

Andrew narrowed his eyes and waved the air to clear it. "I don't believe you."

"Jealous," Logan shot back and smacked the ass of the closest redhead. The girls disengaged from his body to dance together to tempt both actors.

"We know you got the part," Andrew snapped. He stopped dancing. "Why are you out clubbing? Because Kat didn't want to celebrate, or is Nikita your flavor of the month? You don't earn awards by partying preproduction."

Logan snagged a bottle of beer from a passing waitress and downed half in one draw. He didn't want to think about Nikita or Katrina. "Screw you. I can do what I want because I'm Logan Malone."

Andrew shook his head. "You're lame."

Logan snorted and finished the drink. He handed his empty bottle to one of his dance partners. "Lame? I got all these girls begging for my attention and you're calling me lame?"

Andrew folded his arms, making the tribal tattoos on his forearm bulge. "CJ's a helluva woman. Way better than Weir and her falsies."

Logan fumbled. Jealousy shot through him like a bullet.

He stepped close to Andrew. "What do you mean?"

Andrew narrowed his eyes and spoke through clenched teeth. "Stop thinking with your dick."

A sly smile curled Logan's lips as another woman ground her body against his. What else was there to think with? "She shot you down, didn't she?"

"That's not the point, dumb ass."

Logan laughed and grabbed another bottle of beer. "You can't have all the sexy women."

Andrew took the bottle out of Logan's hands and thrust it at the waitress. "He's finished." The server glanced at Logan before shrugging and disappearing into the crowd.

Logan squared his shoulder and took a deep breath. "What do you think you're doing?"

"Saving your sorry ass," Andrew bit out. A shriek from the dance floor behind them interrupted any further argument. He glanced over his shoulder and frowned. "Yet another of your harem. Go home, Malone, before you have something to regret."

The throng of girls whimpered in unison and withdrew to another part of the club. Logan sighed and rubbed his forehead. He wanted to melt into the floor or disappear under a rock—a huge rock.

"Logan!" Not the woman he wanted screaming his name. Jade twirled up next to him and grated her ass on his cock. Her overly processed blonde hair tickled his nose. "Touch me," she hissed in his ear. "I'm wearing my new Topher Azad creation. Like it? It shows off my best...assets."

"I thought you wanted to get a reduction." Logan held her anatomy in place. The rhinestones rubbed him raw. If he had five minutes alone with Cass, he'd do so much more than callously hold her breasts. Hell, he'd make her burn for him with a white-hot flame. He willed his dick to cooperate instead of giving the woman in his arms the wrong impression.

Jade twirled around to nibble on his neck. "I get better parts with the D-cup. Besides, I thought you liked big, bouncy breasts and blonde hair."

He did like generous breasts, didn't he? No, she was all wrong. He longed for the soft, supple feel of Cass. "I like real breasts."

Jade shrugged. "Same difference." She kissed his lips, snaking her tongue into his mouth. She tasted like stale cigarettes and Cosmopolitans. Logan curled his fingers around her bony shoulders. "Honey, we can't do this."

She licked her lips and pouted. Her eyes sparkled. "What can't we do? We always club like this. Hell, you chased me all over for a taste of my love. One of these nights, you'll finally get me into bed."

Logan bit the inside of his cheek. "Oh yeah?"

Jade brushed her hand over the zipper of his jeans, teasing his cock. "Let's go back to my place and make it happen!"

Any other night, Logan would've dragged her out of the club to have sex, but not tonight. He tipped his head back to consider her proposition. "No."

Her hand smoothed under his shirt to pinch his nipples. "Please?"

Begging? He took her wrist, to remove her anatomy from his. "Sorry honey. I have to call the airport. I'm flying out of state."

Jade hooked her fingers into his belt loops. "Take me with you."

He plastered his most winning smile on his lips. "I'd love to, but this is work." He leaned down and kissed her forehead.

Jade chewed the corner of her mouth. She ran her hands over her breasts. "Find us as soon as you come back."

"We'll see."

Logan rubbed his forehead left the club, then strode across the lot. He got into his car, willing away the pounding headache growing behind his eyes. He wanted sex. No. He wanted a woman. A certain special woman who wanted nothing to do with him. "I am lame," he muttered and drove away.

Back at his apartment, he packed a smattering of clothes. In the unpredictable Ohio weather, jeans and long-sleeve shirts would be the most practical. He grabbed his favorite leather jacket with the deep pockets and his wallet off the dresser. With the car securely parked in his locked garage bay, he called a taxi for the airport.

At four in the morning, he boarded the flight to Cleveland. For the first time since coming out to California, he felt like he'd made the right decision. He donned his favorite Cincinnati Reds ball cap to obscure his identity as he made his way through the bleary-eyed crowds. A couple of the soundtrack songs from his favorite movie, *Rust*, played. Why did the love songs remind him of Cass? Logan wanted her as his woman. Hell. Now he sounded lame, not like a stud of the silver screen.

During the early-morning flight, Logan ignored his fellow passengers and lost himself in the heavy metal playlist on his MP3 player. Music, like acting, was his refuge. It was a world where he could immerse himself without the constraints of outsiders. It was his safe haven, his salvation and a darn good stress reliever.

An hour before landing, someone nudged his arm. He turned to see a shapely redhead from the row behind staring at him. Her tawny-colored eyes sparkled and her blood-red lips pursed. A smattering of freckles dotted her cheeks. Her perfume, Radiant 1, clouded the confined area, making Logan's eyes water. He hated the fragrance on Jade and wasn't fond of it on a stranger. She touched his shoulder, lingering a bit too long for his comfort. "Are you Logan Malone?"

Logan saw the interest behind the woman's painted-on smile. Never one to skimp on details, he leaned in close to murmur, "Are you a fan of his?"

She shrugged, but her smile grew. The scarlet sweater hugged her generous breasts. The deep V neck revealed a lack of undergarments and too much tanned skin. Her eyes narrowed slightly. "I wouldn't turn you down," she purred.

He grinned and shook his head. "I'm an actor between jobs, but I know him well." It wasn't a total lie. He was between jobs and he was an actor. Above all, he wasn't interested.

The old Logan would've suggested a meeting in the lavatory. The new mature Logan knew better. Thank God for growing up.

"Got his number?" She stroked his arm. Her nails scraped the soft leather, leaving scars. "But then again, you're cute enough, you might work."

Logan laughed to mask his irritation and put the MP3 player away. "I'm spoken for, babe."

She switched to the empty seat across from his on the aisle. She reached out to examine his left hand and threaded her fingers through his. "I don't care if you're spoken for. I don't see a ring, so that makes you fair game." She fondled his thigh with her other hand. "I'd love to meet you for some acting lessons."

Logan grinned and leaned in close. His lips hovered inches from her ear. "Not a chance."

Not when I have a chance with Cass. I don't want to screw that up.

The woman shrank back into her seat. Her eyes narrowed to hate-filled slits. "Arrogant slime."

Logan fastened his seat belt and checked the time on his cell phone before shoving it back into his pocket. He winked and dipped his head an inch. "Your words, not mine."

Once the plane landed, he made sure he still had his phone. He left the plane and headed into the airport. He retrieved his overnight bag from the luggage carousel. The scent of frying sausage wafted through the air and drew his attention. At the fast food kiosk, he ordered a breakfast sandwich to calm his growling stomach.

Chomping on the egg, sausage and cheese biscuit combo, he strolled casually to the rental center on the other side of the facility. He tossed the empty wrapper in the waste bin and stepped up to the burgundy Formica counter. "Hello."

The clerk dropped her clipboard. Her eyes grew to the size of saucers. "Are you really him?"

Logan whipped out his California license. He pointed to the picture. "He is me."

She shrieked and clasped her hands over her mouth, reminding him of a scene from an old Jack Lemmon movie. The girl took a deep breath and fluttered her hands to calm down. "I am honored." She held out a blue ballpoint pen with faded white lettering. "May I?"

Logan grinned and nodded. This was the part he loved about being a celebrity. Genuine fans who were excited to meet him. He hated the hair-pulling, clothing-shredding, memorabilia hounds. "Here's an autograph." He glanced at her nametag. "Caroline, but please... I'm just a regular guy. No different than anyone else." He tucked a lock of her strawberry-blond hair behind her ear. "See?"

Caroline shook her head. "Not hardly, but meeting you is very cool. My friends will be so jealous!" she gushed, blushing a deep crimson. She produced her cell phone from her smock pocket. "Can I get a picture?"

He chuckled. "Absolutely. I'd hate to make you into a liar." He waved his arm and held the phone out to snap the shot. As the shutter opened, she turned and kissed him on the cheek. Logan felt himself blush. He remembered being young and bold, but it seemed like such a long time ago. Since arriving in California, the bold gave way to brash and the young weathered to stale. Maybe that's why he liked Cass. She wasn't jaded, stale or coarse.

Caroline clasped the phone to her breast. "Wow."

Logan winked. "Thank you, darlin'. Now, about the rental. I'm a former country boy. Got anything in a fifteen or twenty-five hundred model with a full-sized bed?

"Oh, yeah?" She clicked the mouse, printed up an agreement form and handed him a set of keys. "How about a jet-black Silverado fifteen hundred?"

He dipped his head. "You read my mind." He strolled

out of the rental office, leaving Caroline grinning from ear to ear at her post.

In the rental truck, Logan programmed the GPS with Cass' address. Good thing he'd done an Internet search on her before leaving his apartment. Then again, Maggie had the address as well. No matter. It was already one in the afternoon. By the time he made the two-hour drive, it would be three p.m. That didn't include food, restroom breaks and any unwanted phone calls. Oh well.

Logan started the engine, found a rock station on the radio and set off. He drummed his hands on the steering wheel in time with the current song blasting from the vibrating speakers. His thoughts turned to Cass. Based on their embrace, he knew they were very compatible. If Dex hadn't been there to screw up the mood, Logan probably would've kissed her in the parking lot.

"I've gotta slow down and think before I do something really stupid. If I show up right now, she'll just call the cops and have my butt arrested."

Logan turned off at her exit. A discount motel and two fast food establishments decorated the largely undeveloped wooded landscape. The towering maple and pine reminded him of a simpler time. He waited patiently at the traffic light. Pennsylvania wasn't such a bad place to live and neither was Ohio. He shook his head. "This is right where I need to be."

A quick pass through the drive-through garnered an unhealthy but satisfying burger 'n fries supper and adoring shrieks from the female counter attendants. Suddenly exhausted from more than twenty-four hours without sleep, Logan headed for the motel. He grabbed a hat and his wallet before heading in to rent a room. Fortunately an older couple ran the business and didn't recognize him.

Ten minutes later, with his truck secured, Logan tossed the overnight bag in the room. He locked up, choked down his food, showered and fell naked into bed. He'd deal with Carmine, Nikita, Jade and all the other stress in his life later.

Right now, he needed a good woman. He needed Cass.

Chapter Four

Two days after arriving home, Cass set out to tidy her property and get Logan out of her system. Hard work could cure anything. That's what she told herself anyway.

"I'd better get this done before the film crew gets here." She laced her grubby sneakers and adjusted the frayed ball cap. Her new dogs, Paula and Elliott—named after her favorite movie characters—followed along as she toted the watering can. She laughed. True, they weren't a substitute for a man's love, but darn close. Even with a few minor accidents on the living room rug, she still wouldn't trade them for the world. "You two could help me."

The dogs frolicked and nipped at her heels. She chuckled. It was like someone bred them with her in mind—easygoing, minimal shedding and fairly quiet, but totally devoted. They followed her everywhere.

"I'm going to put you on the run so I can use the tractor." Cass clipped chains to their collars. Elliott chewed on Paula's ear. She pawed his face and they both ended up rolling in the grass. "No barking when Les gets here."

The grass spread out in a deep green blanket before her. Cass loved the smell of freshly cut grass and how the lawn looked like a calm emerald sea after she mowed. In three hours' time, the yard would be perfect for the filming crew to mash down. Paula sat at attention, watching her. Elliott threw his head back and howled.

"Oh, hush," she said and laughed

"Cass! Calm your dog."

She turned to acknowledge the booming bass voice. Raymond Earl Russell was like her older brother, if she had one. "Hello. What can I do for you?"

"I needed to work on the engine for the championship race, but your dog won't let me near the house to get a drink. I forgot to restock the fridge in the barn."

She snorted. "He won't bite."

Ray clenched his jaw and folded his muscled arms. The skull and dagger tattoo on his right arm bulged. "You know I don't like dogs."

Ray wasn't like any man she knew. He hated dogs but kept at least three cats. He insisted on growing his own food, except during Christmas when he splurged on chocolate. His green eyes became electric when he strummed his guitar. Crowds surged to his stage. He was shy, considerate, looked sexy without a shirt and catered to her every whim. Perfect, except that she wasn't in love with him.

"Go through the garage, Ray. Elliott won't tear your limbs off," she said and engaged the mower blade. She bobbed her head to the music playing on her MP3 player. Though she couldn't hear over the music and rumble of the mowing machine, she saw the furious behavior of the dogs. They bounced and jumped to get attention. She turned to see her friend, Les, strolling across the lawn with her tool of choice—the weed whacker. Angeles 'Les' Miliron was the best girlfriend she could have. Understanding and blunt, Les could smile her way out of trouble and then turn right around and stir the pot back up. She pushed Cass to get out of herself once in a while. And man, could that girl put back the whiskey! But what was life if there were no friends to keep things light? A mile-wide smile graced her face. Les loved destruction almost as much as she loved to argue and dye her hair oddball colors.

As Cass spun the tractor around for another pass in the front yard, an unfamiliar black truck pulled into her driveway. Fans occasionally sought her out and ended up at the farm. Few drove shiny new trucks, though. She tugged the earbuds from her ears and considered the vehicle. Ray's sun-faded navy blue half-ton truck with dented front fenders sat by the barn. Who was this mystery person?

A man with faded blue jeans and boots stepped out of the vehicle and walked towards the mower. Cass drove across the yard to greet the visitor. She held her cell in her hand in case she needed to call the sheriff. "Hello," she called. Blood pounded in her ears. Something felt off. She willed her heart rate to dip back to normal.

Don't panic. Don't show fear. "Can I help you?" Ten feet away, she knew exactly who he was.

"Hey. I'm Logan Malone. I'm looking for Cass Jensen. Is she up in the main house?" He shoved his hands into his pockets and leaned against the side of the imposing vehicle.

Cass bit back a grin. Good thing she had taken the lawn tractor out of gear. Apparently, the hat, rangy T-shirt and dirt had him fooled. At the same time, panic skittered through her system. What did he want now? "I'll park the mower and let her know you're here," she said and bit back a giggle. She stopped the machine by the barn and strode over to the porch swing. A streak of desire curled in her belly. She tried in vain to tamp it down, but the notion remained. *He came to see me.* It seemed a little weird because he could have any woman in the world and he chose to annoy her.

"Who's that?" Les dusted the loose grass off her shorts and brushed dirt off Cass. "He's awful cute."

Cass allowed the giggle. "Logan thinks I'm the help. He wants to meet" — she hooked her fingers in the air — "Cass. Won't he get a big surprise in about ten seconds?" Her heart pounded.

Les rolled her eyes. "You're awful," she muttered with no malice as she walked away.

Cass laughed out loud, but quickly closed her mouth as Logan approached. He met her at the swing. "Is she coming out? I have some important business to discuss with her and it can't wait."

She forced a frown and accusing tone. "Wait a minute. I want to know what type of business. She never mentioned

47

a visitor."

Logan shifted his weight from his left to his right foot. "I called ahead. She knows I'm coming."

She stopped swinging. The liar. "No, you didn't. I man the phones." She held up her cell phone as proof.

His mouth opened and closed, but no sound came out. His eyes widened for only a split second before the sly grin decorated his lips.

"Being a high and mighty actor doesn't give you free reign to show up unannounced." Cass folded her arms. He looked even sexier when he got irritated. His nostrils flared and gentle color rushed into his cheeks. Flecks of gold and green lit up his hazel eyes. Cass shifted her body. She longed to feel his strong arms enfolding her once more, even if she really didn't want him anywhere within reach.

Logan tapped his foot nervously. "Okay, you caught me. So get your boss, okay?"

Cass's mouth watered. Logan's hair curled slightly around the edges of his ball cap. The heat of the August day made his long-sleeve T-shirt stick to his body like a second skin. Man, he had muscles to spare. His cologne — a combination of aftershave and man — lingered in the sticky air and toyed with her frayed senses.

"Put it back in your pants." She lifted her hat a couple of inches. "It's me. I do my own yard work, which includes sweat, dirt and filth."

Logan's grimace disappeared. He swayed with embarrassment.

Cass scooted over and patted the seat. "Sit down before you hurt yourself."

Logan studied her a moment before moving. "You're cute when you're sweaty. Beautiful, really."

Cass lowered her gaze. She the tips of her ears burned and not from the sun. Cute and sweaty didn't go together to label attractive women and she wasn't stunning covered in dirt. Why did he insist on describing her this way? She was neither sexy nor gorgeous, but indeed sweaty. "You're early. What's your business?"

"Why don't you hire someone to tend the grounds? I'm sure a teenage kid who needs gas money would love to do it." He eased down next to her, then propped his arm across the back of the swing. His hand skimmed her shoulder blades before resting on the top slat—away from her skin. "Not that I mind, I like the look."

She shook off the tingle. A niggling feeling of fear roiled in her brain. Was he making fun of her? She turned to look at him. "In my family, everyone had a job to do, so I'm used to it. It makes me feel like I've accomplished something." She shimmied to the opposite end of the seat.

Logan caressed her shoulder with his fingertips. "Can I help you finish? You and your friend should be sipping margaritas and ordering the lawn boy around, not sweating yourselves to death."

Cass wriggled away from his deft hand. "Excuse me." She wanted him to touch her, she really did, but on her terms. "Hands."

His eyes widened and his hand recoiled. "I thought..."

She raised her brows and stared at him. "You thought being a movie star meant you could do whatever you want. That's not how I roll."

Logan dipped his head. A wolfish grin curled his lips. A fresh rush of lust spiraled right to her core. He leaned in very close to her ear. "Maybe I want you to help me change the rules."

She closed her eyes and took a fortifying breath. She fought the urge to taste him. Damn that cologne. Her heart skipped a beat. She donned her best sultry smile. Two could play his game. "Really?"

He nodded. She shivered and licked her dry lips. How could one man be so irritating and damn sexy at the same time? She scooted close enough that her bare knee brushed against his denim-clad thigh. The man had firm muscles without an ounce of fat. Ooh, she wanted to explore that body. She whispered in his ear to distract her growing desire. "Do you want to explore?"

"Uh-huh."

Cass took his hand, teasing his palm with her fingers and caressing the creases in his skin. Logan nodded again. His voice went from friendly to sexy in an instant, making her thighs quiver with excitement.

"Cass," he murmured and closed his eyes. "Yes."

She bit her bottom lip and filled his hand. "Okay. Explore to your little heart's content."

His eyes opened wide before he scrunched his brows. "Keys?"

Cass grinned. "Yep."

His blank expression turned into a frown. "For what?"

She patted his thigh and stood. "The mower. Tell me when you finish. I've got an acre in the back that's got your name on it."

"But…"

Cass held up both hands. She crinkled her nose and stepped off the porch. "You said you wanted to explore and that I deserved a lawn boy. Hello, lawn boy. If you're going to annoy me, you're getting put to work."

"You got more than you bargained for!" he called.

She grinned to herself. *Looks like we both did.* Pride welled in her head. Maybe easing back into the dating world wouldn't be so heinous after all.

* * * *

Mid-morning, Logan wiped the sweat from his brow. A glance at the front porch revealed Cass sitting on the steps and laughing. A glass of something cold melted at her feet. A woman he didn't recognize sat on her left. Something about Cass…the way her honesty shone like a bright aura, or was it her genuine smile that warmed his heart? Maybe both, but he was falling for her. He turned off the blade and drove the tractor to her position.

Cass acknowledged him with a round of applause. "Look,

folks! He can act and mow a lawn in nice even lines!"

Logan cut the engine and jumped off the machine. He bowed. "And for my next trick, I'm going to melt into the grass from dehydration. That's one helluva yard."

The woman next to Cass stood. "I'll get you a bottle of water, but Cass, you better fess up first. Why did you hire him? He's all looks and no brains."

Logan wiped his sweaty hands on his shirttail. So much for clean clothes. "I'm Logan. Cass chose me to do all the manual labor around here. Some women find hard work sexy." He stuck out his less dingy hand. "And you are?"

The woman shook her head. "Smart enough to see through your charade, Romeo Malone."

Color rushed into his cheeks and it wasn't from the sun. He winked, overdoing his suave exterior. "So you *do* know me?"

Cass groaned. "Logan, meet Angeles Miliron. I call her Les. She's my closest friend and agent."

A smile tugged at the corner of his mouth. "An agent, eh?"

Les poked him hard in the chest and knocked him backwards a step. "Yes, I'm an agent and no, I'm not looking for any new clients. I'm not even sure you're good enough for Cass."

Logan cocked his head. His gaze vacillated between the two women. *So they did talk about me?* Cass smiled sweetly, confounding him further. How could such an innocent vibe come from such a sexy woman? He wiped the sheen of sweat from his brow, knowing it wasn't from the hard labor.

"I'll get your water, but know this, Logan Malone—don't hurt her or I will hurt you. That's a promise and a threat." With that, Les stepped off the porch and disappeared around the corner of the garage.

Cass propped her chin on her knuckles. "Care to sit? You did work hard."

Logan eased down next to her on the concrete step. He

bumped her shoulder with his own. "I know where I'd like you to sit," he mumbled.

Cass threw her head back and laughed. "You know how long it's been since I heard that line?"

Logan shared her humor. "You can't blame me for trying."

Her laughter subsided as she watched him. He liked the camaraderie building between them and bumped her shoulder again. "That was a dirty trick, you know."

Cass bit the corner of her mouth. "I know." Those two words resonated through his soul. She played his games with ease and intended to win. She brushed her hair away from her face.

"So where's the water? I'm parched." He grabbed his chest over-dramatically and slumped against her. "And fading fast."

Cass playfully punched his thigh. "You are not, drama king," she shot back. "We don't have valets here in Crawford so you're temporarily out of luck."

Logan laughed until his chest hurt. "I need to learn how to get what I want on my own. I think this was lesson number one."

She patted his knee, but her hand lingered a bit too long. "Good call." She glanced at him and then at the ground before standing up. He reached out to touch the perfect globes of her ass, but recoiled. *Don't scare her.*

"Cass?"

She paused without turning around. "I'm putting the tractor away. Do you need something?"

Logan opened his mouth. *You naked and in my bed* teetered on the tip of his tongue. "A shower?" Was that all he could muster? Wow. He'd lost his suave attitude somewhere between Ohio and California.

Cass hopped aboard the mower. "You do ask for a lot, but I owe you." She started the engine. "Les will show you where the guest bathroom is." Before he could answer, she drove off.

Yes. A shower gave him time in her house. Now...to

breach her defenses and melt her heart.

* * * *

Cass locked the barn door and rested her head against the weathered white wood. The man wore her out. "I'll let him clean up and then he's out." She smoothed her humidity-frizzed hair back under the ball cap and headed to the porch. Uneasiness slid through her brain. He was way too close for comfort, but totally out of her league. The silence heightened her anxious mood. The view around the corner of the garage validated her suspicions. Empty.

She ventured back to the driveway to see Les' vehicle nowhere in sight. Crap. "Les left me alone with him. Okay." She slid her phone from her crinkled shorts pocket and dialed her friend.

"Thanks for abandoning me when I could use backup." Les tsk-tsked. "Call it incentive."

"I don't need incentive. I need to shower and I could use a nap. I've had a long couple of days and I need to prepare for the public appearance tomorrow."

"After you make that poor man beg and orgasm."

Cass ground her teeth together. "Not going to happen."

"Fine. I'll meet you at eight and dress shabby chic. It's a boutique bookstore," Les replied. "Gotta go. Levi's on the other line."

Before Cass could retort, the line clicked dead. "Great." She sat on the tailgate of her truck long enough to fortify her defenses. She puffed out another breath and went into the house. The beep of the dryer caught her attention. A note stuck to the machine served as a silent reminder. *White clothes in here. Remember, shabby chic. Funky not frumpy!*

Cass sighed and emptied the machine. "I can dress myself, Les," she grumbled under her breath. She took the laundry basket up the stairs to her bedroom. The billows of steam in the hallway piqued her curiosity. Temporarily forgetting her visitor, she opened the door to the ice-blue guest room.

"What the…" Her jaw dropped. There in all his naked glory, totally at ease and unaware, stood Logan Malone. "Oh my God."

"Hello." He grabbed her fuchsia towel and wrapped it around his toned buns. He turned slowly, giving her a tantalizing view of his sculpted back and legs.

Her mouth watered. She willed her heart to stop thudding so loudly as she snapped her jaw shut. How did the man pull off casual in such a heavy situation? She blurted the first thing that popped into her head. "You always parade around in pink towels?"

So much for sounding suave.

He dipped his head. A wicked smile curled the corner of his mouth. Cass tried not to fan herself. Did the heat kick on?

"I prefer blue or green, but I make do with what's available." He winked. "You seem to be enjoying the view."

She nodded and licked her lips. Enjoying? Try having one of the most exciting daydreams of her life. "Well, then, Mr. Pink. I'll let you get dressed. I hate interruptions." She turned to leave.

"Cass?"

She froze. The sound of rustling came from the room. "My manly blue towels are in the wash." Forcing her feet to move, she stepped down the hallway and took a deep breath. At least she had a centerfold image to fantasize about later. She closed her eyes. When she opened them again, there stood Logan in nothing but unsnapped blue jeans. The hunter-green elastic of his boxers showed above the open zipper. A trail of fine hairs led down into the V of his faded denim.

Desperately reigning in her desire to marvel at his body, she redirected her attention to his face. "What do you want?"

Logan licked his lips. His eyes burned with flecks of amber and sage. She couldn't look away from his intensity. Her cheeks flushed. He said only one word. "You."

Cass couldn't tamp down the surge of lust pooling between her thighs. She swallowed hard, trying to think of something intelligent to say. "Don't ask for what you can't handle," she said firmly and shoved against the solid wall of his body. He stuck his arm out to block, but she darted under too quickly.

"Cass, wait."

Her brain screamed go even as her pace slowed. "No."

Logan caught up with her at the bottom of the stairs. His strong arm pinned her into the corner. "Let me explain."

She smiled to mask her irritation. "Fine. Explain as you walk out my door." She ducked under his arm once again and escaped to the relative safety of the living room.

Five minutes later Logan caught up with her once more. She looked up from the couch. He still didn't have a shirt or socks on, but at least he'd buttoned his pants. "Listen, I came early and put you in an odd position. I'm sorry I tried to come on to you, but come on. I like you." He retreated a step. "Since you're not interested, let me finish getting dressed and I'll go."

Cass dropped the remote control for the television and nodded to the mudroom. Her gaze instantly, but innocently, shifted to his abdomen. A warm rush overtook her body. She wanted to check him out with more than just her eyes. He liked her? He'd tried to come on to her?

"I'll leave you alone." She sauntered past him, intentionally brushing against that yummy body of his. His gasp as they touched sent an extra shimmer of delight through her veins. Why the hell was she pushing him aside?

"You can't go. You live here."

She laughed out loud. He still had some sense. "I needed to retrieve the kids."

"Kids?" Logan asked and choked out the word.

The dogs bounded into the room with Cass on their heels. "The brown one is Paula and the white and black one is Elliott. I prefer the name kids to the label pets."

The animals sniffed Logan's pant legs and jumped up

on him. He knelt down to their level. "I suppose you want love, isn't that right?" With double the puppy exuberance, they nearly knocked him down. He laughed and plopped down on her gleaming hardwood floor. "Chill out and I'll give you both attention."

Cass folded her arms and watched. Maybe there was more to Logan Malone than she expected. "They like you." She chuckled. "Since I brought them home yesterday, they haven't taken to anyone but me. Maybe it's a sign."

Elliott flopped over onto his back, apparently expecting a rub. Logan reached out. A low rumble vibrated from the dog's belly. Elliott's tongue lolled down from the side of his mouth, leaving a small puddle of drool. Paula simply sat and accepted Logan's attention. Her tail swept softly across the floor in appreciation.

Logan laughed too, until a crack of thunder split the air. Paula yelped and skittered under the table, knocking down a display of cream-colored candles. Cass knelt down next to the frightened animal. "I guess she's not keen on storms." To the dog, she said, "Come here, baby. I won't let it hurt you." A sudden gust of wind shook the house.

Logan stood up and peered out the front window. Cass glanced at his darkened form. He looked like he belonged in her house, like he should have a cup of coffee steaming in his hand as he watched the wind kick leaves around the front yard. "It's getting bad," he said and turned around. "I'll get out of your hair."

Cass joined him by the window. The sky reminded her of the color of worn denim — a cross between pale blue and slate gray. A branch from her oak tree skittered across the grass. "No." She watched the heavens even though she felt Logan's gaze slide over her body.

"Say again?"

Cass blew out a ragged breath. "Your stuff is already in the bedroom. Put the truck in the barn." She folded her arms. "The keys are on the counter."

"Cass."

She braced herself and stood silent. The way he said her name shouldn't have annoyed her.

Logan shifted slightly and nudged her shoulder. "Can I share your room?"

"I'm sure you'd like that," she shot back. She'd like it, too, but damn it. She had to keep her heart protected.

His breath tickled her ear. "I would."

Before she could answer, he disappeared up the stairs. Cass sat on the sofa and folded the laundry waiting in the basket. "I've gotta be out of my ever-loving mind, letting that man stay over. He's unbelievable!"

"Ah, but that's why you like me."

Cass jumped and jerked around. Logan grinned proudly. He stood a mere foot away from couch with his arms folded and had donned a form-fitting T-shirt and sneakers. He could've stepped right out of an ad on television. She, on the other hand, felt like a frump. Deciding to hedge his interest, she batted her eyelashes and asked dryly, "Do I?"

He rounded the coffee table and sat next to her. "I sure hope so."

She kicked the basket away from his prying eyes, hoping he didn't see the ultra-sensible underwear. Cotton bikini briefs definitely made her seem dorky, didn't they?

"Do you?"

A pregnant pause hung heavy in the air. The blood pumped furiously in her ears. What could she say? *I want to climb all over your body?* No. *You make me wet with just a glance?* Hardly. He didn't need the ego trip. "You're quite handsome. Any woman would be foolish to ignore your advances." She fumbled with the T-shirt bunched in her hands. "What's not to like?" Bile rose in her throat. Combine that statement with the granny panties and she really was a dork.

He took the wrinkled garment from her hands. "Let me help."

Cass stared as he neatly folded her shirt. At least he had the laundry portion of taking care of himself down pat.

He took a pair of ankle socks from the basket and curled them together in ball. This wasn't the answer or action she expected. If he'd have said, *'I'm almost done and we've got the rest of the day. Why not tuck me in tonight?'* or, *'These are some sexy duds,'* she might not have lost her gumption.

He reached past her and grabbed a pair of her ultraconservative underwear. "Cass, you haven't folded anything but the shirt. I can help." A smile tugged at the corners of his mouth. "I want to."

Cass tried unsuccessfully to rip the underwear from his hands. "What are you grinning at?"

He smoothed the cotton between his fingers. "The thought of you wearing these. I'll bet you look dynamite."

She shook her head. He'd never see her in plain cotton panties or a silk thong for that matter. He'd never see her naked. Period. "You really need someone to write your material. Without a script, you stink."

Logan laughed and handed over the folded garment. "Are you applying for the job?"

Cass picked up the laundry basket. "Let's go upstairs."

He bolted from his seat. "My thoughts exactly."

"To our separate rooms," she added, heading up the flight of steps.

He followed hot at her heels and sighed a little too loudly. "Oh."

The lights flickered as a streak of lightning lit up the sky. Cass stopped at the top of the staircase. Paula crowded around her ankles. She glanced through the circular window over the front door. "That didn't look good."

Logan's warm breath tickled against the nape of her neck. "I agree, so let's huddle together to conserve heat."

She took a fortifying breath and pointed to his room. "You stay here. As you can see, this is my book room. I couldn't decide which room should be the library, so they all are."

Logan glanced over her shoulder. "It's very nice." He picked up a copy of her latest book, *Tailspin in Texas*. "I haven't read this one, but I've heard good things."

Cass giggled. "I didn't peg you as a romance reader. I'm pleasantly surprised."

"There's a lot you don't know about me," he replied and sat on the edge of the bed.

Wary, she took a step back. "Ah. You're only staying one night. We don't need to get intimate."

He cocked his head. "You know you want to."

"Don't go there. I'll get you an extra pillow and blanket."

"For you?"

She wrinkled her brows. "Nope. I'm a loner."

"I want to tell you something."

Cass stiffened and narrowed her eyes. She could see the wheels turning in his mind. Knowing Logan as little as she did, she had no idea what he thought. The dogs whined behind her. Something felt off.

"It's not bad, I promise."

"Oh, sure."

He jumped up from his spot on the bed and crossed the room to where she stood. "When I'm around you, I'm tongue-tied because I want you to like me."

She knotted her fingers together, mostly because she didn't know what else to do with them rather than reach for him. She turned away. When did the air in the room get so blasted thin and warm? "I see."

"Do you?"

His words washed over her like a waterfall. She wanted to give in, but if she touched him, she'd never be able to pull away. She turned back around. "Logan, this can't—"

He stood inches from her. His eyes flashed just as he lowered his lips to hers. A warm rush flowed from her brain all the way to her toes. She felt sparks radiate from his fingertips as he twined them with hers. A moan escaped her throat. Oh, he tasted too good to walk away from. But in that instant, he pulled back.

"That's just a sampling," he murmured. "We could continue all night long, if you desire."

Cass swallowed hard. His erection jabbed into her

stomach. Maybe she could turn a man on after all. More thunder crashed, spooking the dogs.

"I'd better go," she whispered.

Logan nodded. "I'll be here if you need me."

Chapter Five

Cass settled down for the night in her bedroom. Removing the dirty ball cap, she shook her hair out and ran her fingers through to loosen the tangles. How did her life go from ordered to spiraling out of control so quickly? She had agreed to write that blasted screenplay, that's how.

She replayed Logan's words. *'When I'm around you, I'm tongue-tied because I want you to like me.'* That didn't seem possible. *Oh man.* The warm rush came back in full force. She touched her lips and replayed his kiss in her mind. His lips were smooth and firm like a man's should be.

In the shower, she ran the soapy washcloth over her aching breasts. Logan Malone wanted her affection. She imagined his hands in place of the soggy fabric. *I want you to like me.* She leaned against the cool wall tiles and imagined him in the stall with her. The scene from his movie, *Splinter*, came to mind. Water sluiced over her body, reminding her of a lover's caress. She balled the washcloth in her hands and imagined Logan's dick between her ass cheeks.

"Oh my God," she murmured and dropped the washcloth. She eased one hand over her breast and the other hand between her thighs. She could almost hear his voice in her ear.

"Been thinking about you all day."

"Yeah," she murmured. She closed her eyes and rubbed her clit. In her mind, she saw him palming her breasts. He rolled her nipple in his fingers, pulling just a little. Soap slid down chest, making her body slippery. She pinched her nipple.

A whimper came from deep in her throat. Her temperature

rose and the water prickled her skin. The desire to jump out of the stall and run down to his room overwhelmed her, but she held on to her restraint.

Cass slid her middle finger into her cunt and stroked.

"Shit, you're wet for me," she heard him say in her mind.

Damn. She pumped her finger in and out, then rubbed her juices over her clit.

"Want you," she murmured. She pressed and pinched her clit. The breath wrenched from her chest. Every nerve ending in her body shifted into high alert. She panted and dipped her head.

Cass pinched her nipple harder and stuffed two fingers into her pussy.

"Fuck," she bit out. She stroked faster and pressed her shoulders against the shower wall. She needed to finish. Her chest ached from panting so hard. Her restraint shattered as she embraced the orgasm. She pressed her knees together as she came.

Shivers overcame her and she slid to the floor of the shower stall. The water wasn't any colder, but the temperature in the room seemed to have dropped at least ten degrees. She brushed the wet hair from her eyes and a laugh bubbled in her throat. Logan's breath still rasped in her ear. He didn't need to coax. She already liked the man, even if she could never have him.

Cass managed to stand and finished the shower. She stepped onto the mat and wrapped the towel around her sensitized body. She could almost feel him beside her. Damn. The night would be a long one.

Once dried off, she pulled on a baggy T-shirt and clean cotton panties before crawling between the cool sheets. The temperature change refreshed her feverish body. She wondered what he wore to bed and thought about the reverent way he'd held her intimate wear. She giggled. He probably slept in the nude.

Paula huddled next her and began to shiver with fear. Cass stroked the frightened animal's soft coat. "I know, baby. I'm not fond of the storms either, but I think we're safe. The bogeyman won't get us here."

He's still in California.

Although the storm raged outside, they fell asleep rather quickly. Cass succumbed to her dreams.

Cass, come here.

Logan stretched next to her on a fluffy blanket the color of honey. It felt like down against her skin. A kaleidoscope of color flickered in the sky above them—the Northern Lights or something like that. She couldn't be sure, but it looked like the stars formed a heart-shaped constellation. The crisp scent of wildflowers swirled around them on the warm night air.

She turned to him. He cupped her cheek. His hands were blessedly warm and inviting as he kissed her. He felt like velvet and silk all at the same time. She sighed as he wound his fingers in her hair, making her scalp tingle. A sparse sprinkling of hair on his chest accentuated the taut muscles. As her gaze moved lower, she realized they were both naked. Heat stirred between her legs.

Do you know how beautiful you are?

Cass gasped and covered her breasts. Even in a dream, she didn't want him to see her in such an exposed and defenseless fashion. Logan would see her flaws and change his mind. She tried to speak, but words wouldn't form.

Babe, don't cower from me. You're beautiful, especially when you're bare. I want to kiss you everywhere. Your body is perfect and made just for me.

She blushed from her hairline to her toes. Was he serious? When she lowered her hands, Logan nodded. A wickedly sexy smile curled his lips. His hands cupped her breasts with a gentle touch. Her nipples puckered and ached for his caress. Logan's eyes rolled back in his head. A sound, a cross between a groan and a growl escaped his lips. She shivered.

A little work and these could be knockouts.

Her eyes widened. Logan's voice wasn't the same and his

features weren't his own. They were harsher, darker. The planes of his face rounded out and grew hairy. His brows knotted together and his nose looked blunt and broken. He morphed into her worst enemy — Dexter Rose.

If you lost a few pounds, then they wouldn't have to photograph you from the shoulders up. People would see you, not your cellulite.

The blanket became a bed of rusty nails, piercing her skin. Nothing could be this horrifying, but it was. The beautiful colors in the sky faded into deathly black. The air became cold. She smelled sulfur and fire. Oh God. She wanted to puke. She screamed, but no sound came out of her mouth. The gentle touches turned violent. Pinching, grabbing and tearing at her flesh.

Honey, you won't be anyone if you don't drop the weight. Follow a diet and get into shape. The way you look now isn't flattering. The public prefers skinny chicks, not a girl in desperate need of a tummy-tuck.

A clap of thunder broke over her head. Dex's dark eyes glowed with hatred and venom. Stinging rain pelted her naked skin and chilled her to the bone.

Give up on him, Cass. He'll follow the system and marry a slew of slender starlets. Come home to me. I've always loved you.

Another roar of thunder forced her to move.

She tried to run, but he grabbed her arms with bony fingers. Bruises and welts darkened her skin.

You can't run from me. Ever. I'll follow you. Remember? You belong to me.

She shook her head.

Cass?

She screamed as his fingers squeezed the circulation from her arms.

"Cass?"

She sat up in bed and tried to regain her bearings. Muscular arms enfolded her so she shoved with all her might. "Get off of me, Dex! Leave me the hell alone."

As her eyes focused, she saw Logan perched next to her

on the bed. He turned on the terracotta table lamp next to the bed. Paula sat next to him on guard. Elliott lolled on the floor. At least one of them wasn't afraid, because she felt thoroughly foolish. Fear and concern colored Logan's face. Cass closed her eyes slowly and hugged her knees. The first night they spent together and she had a nightmare. Damn. Cass forced her eyes to meet Logan's searching gaze. She ran her fingers through her tangled hair. "Logan."

"Hey, you had a nightmare. You're safe now. Come here." He opened his arms. "I tried to wake you. Are you okay?"

Cass began to shake uncontrollably. Fatigue took over, leaving her tapped out. Logan's natural male scent mixed with her soap had a calming effect. He stroked her hair and held her close. "You're safe now, babe. I won't let him hurt you."

She rubbed her chilled arms. He had to think she was crazy. She'd divorced Dex over five years earlier and he still invaded her life. The jerk had her on the run, even in her dreams. Another man held her in his arms and Dex tried to take that away.

"Logan?" She swallowed hard. Tears fell hot and fast. So much for a show of strength. "Will you stay with me tonight? I'm scared and I don't like being scared."

"I won't go anywhere. Lie down and I'll hold you for as long as you want," he murmured. No hesitation in his voice at all.

Cass fell back against the mattress. As long as she wanted. That sounded heavenly. He cuddled against her and wrapped his arms across her midsection. Her breasts ached for his touch. She yearned for him and the desire scared her more than the dream. She wasn't the type of woman who brought men to bed on a regular basis. She never instigated sex. But with Logan, she felt the primal urge to take him and brand him as her own. That couldn't be normal. Was it?

Logan kissed her temple. "Do you want to talk about your dream?"

Cass trembled. His breath warmed her skin to fever. Maybe she wasn't normal. She chewed her bottom lip to think and focus. The notion of having her way with him sent a fresh heat wave through her body. "You and I were about to make love, when you turned into Dex and told me I wasn't good enough for you. Even though I knew it couldn't work, I wanted you anyway."

Logan kissed her temple again and brushed away a tear. "No, babe. I'm not good enough for you, but I'll try like hell to make you happy. I want you too. Told you I liked you."

The rush of heat radiated over her body once more. "Then make love to me tonight."

He smoothed his thumb along her chin. Their gazes met. Passion smoldered between them like a raging wildfire. "Been dreaming about this."

She gasped. He sounded just like he had when she'd fantasized about being with him.

He smoothed his palm down her chest to her belly, but paused to toy with her belly button. He rested his forehead against hers. "You have a navel ring?"

She nodded and placed her hand over his.

"I got it because it seemed like a good idea at the time," she confessed, but cringed. Logan probably saw navel piercings all the time, but not on a woman like her. She came with definite imperfections.

He rolled the steel ball between his finger and thumb. "It's sexy and daring." He crawled on top of her and knelt between her legs. He kissed her stomach and dipped his tongue into her navel around the barbell. "I like you."

She held on to the sheets tight. The gravity of the moment swept over her. Her fantasy was coming to life. Oh yeah... Logan eased her sleep shirt over her chest, exposing her nipples to the cool air. She puffed out a ragged breath and reached for him. The rapid beat of his heart thumped against her palm. She made his pulse race? Wow.

"Damn, babe." His eyes flashed as he slid along her body and stretched over her. "How long since you had earth-shattering sex?"

She winced and stared over his shoulder. Did she have to admit the truth? "It's been a while. Kind of hard to have sex when you're single."

He dipped his head and rasped his tongue around her nipple. "I'd better remedy the situation," he said against her skin.

Cass whimpered. His husky growl combined with his smoldering touch made her shiver with anticipation. His tongue felt like velvet against her skin. She writhed and wound her fingers in his hair. "Touch me everywhere."

He took her nipple between his teeth, teasing it until she thought she'd burst. "Gladly, babe," he murmured. His warm breath tickled her other breast as he pleasured both. "Tell me you want it."

Ripples of desire ricocheted through her body. Now she understood why women enjoyed sex and love. She ached for him and he hadn't reached below her waist. She wriggled and groaned with pleasure. There was no thinking, only feeling and living. He was incredible.

She closed her eyes and took a deep breath as he eased his palm beneath the waistband of her panties. Logan cupped her pussy. His voice dropped an octave. "My naughty girl shaves."

His naughty girl? She kind of liked hearing that.

He massaged her clit with his index finger across her pussy lips, smearing her juices. "So wet and ready. I wanted to make this last, but you make it hard to wait."

She rolled them both over, taking the lead and pinning him beneath her body. "So do you, Logan." She yanked her sleep shirt the rest of the way up and eased it over her head. Her hair tumbled over her shoulders. No stopping now. "So why wait? Get naked."

"Yes, ma'am." He sat up long enough to whip his shirt up over his head. "At your command."

She wriggled out of her panties and stretched out beside him as he shoved his pants and boxers to his ankles. He kicked out of the wadded-up clothing. Her gaze roved over his body and she licked her lips. The man was mouth-wateringly hot. All muscle and perfectness.

She climbed onto his lap, rubbing her clit against his thigh. She met his mouth in a kiss and her tongue twined with his. He tasted like mint gum and beer. Her entire being tingled with delicious abandon. She stroked the sensitive skin between her legs and covered her hand in her own liquid excitement. She licked her finger before offering it to him. "Do you want some?"

He greedily sucked her fingers into his mouth. "Yum. You taste like fine wine." He flipped her onto her back and spread her legs. He slid his finger into her cunt and pumped his hand. "Scream my name, Cass. Tell me you want me."

The bedsprings creaked and groaned under their combined weight. She shivered and shook her head. A ripple of doubt surfaced in her mind. "Logan, I'm too..." The word fat floated just out of verbalization. God, if she could only turn her brain off again.

He cupped her ass and his fingers bit into her flesh. "You're too cute, sexy, curvy, perfect... I can't get enough of you."

Cass smoothed her palms over his chest, then twined her arms around his neck. He didn't care! She was enough to entice him. She whimpered. Yes, a ride sounded wonderful, with protection.

"We need a condom," she puffed. "In the drawer."

"In my wallet," he said between searing kisses.

She slid to the edge of the bed to retrieve the contraceptive. "You're too confident."

He winked, then rummaged through the drawer. When he crawled back between her legs, he held up the rubber. "God, I want you. Have since I met you."

Cass paused. A fresh wave of awareness crashed within her. He dreamed of making love to her? Blood pumped in her veins. Logan desired her. Why not make him work for her affection? She pinched her nipples, plucking them to taut peaks. "How bad do you want me?"

He ripped open the shiny foil packet and slid the latex down his thick shaft. "This bad. Come here." He grasped her hips.

Cass clutched his shoulders as he eased his dick into her cunt. Pleasure-filled pain gripped her. "Logan, you won't fit." She'd been out of the game for so long. She blew out a breath to relax and focused on Logan.

"I'm just a little ahead of you, babe." He eased himself deep into her body and paused. "But God, we fit perfectly." With slow but sure strokes, he moved his hips. In and out, building the pace of his thrusts.

She groaned. "Yeah." She basked in the feeling of fullness and completion. "You feel so good." She met him thrust for thrust. Everything within her tensed. "Logan."

He grasped her hips once more, increasing his upward thrusts. "Fuck, Cass. I'm on the edge!" He tensed and filled her to the brim. He wriggled his torso, adding a few more strokes into her body before he groaned and stilled.

"Oh, God!" she screamed and rode the wave of pleasure crashing within her body. Cass shivered and tugged Logan into her arms. Aftershocks tingled along her nerve endings. She closed her eyes and basked in the post-orgasm glow.

"Whoa, indeed." He nibbled on her neck. "Like that?"

She sucked in a ragged breath and opened her eyes. "I can't describe how I feel. It's like riding a roller coaster or standing next to the track when the cars race past."

"Better. I'm with you." Logan pulled out and crawled off the bed. "It only gets better."

When he returned to the bed, he eased in beside her and gathered her against his chest. A wave of exhaustion washed over her as she rolled onto her other side and ground her ass against his soft cock. He draped his arm across her belly and held her tight. His warmth and concern shrouded her body better than the blankets. He'd worn her out in a delicious way and she couldn't wait for round two.

Logan stared at the ceiling. He rubbed his cheek against her soft hair, giving his brain time to memorize her scent and silkiness. Goal number one achieved — Cass in his arms once again. Okay, so it happened semi-willingly. Goal number two achieved — sex with her and it blew his mind. He'd gone against his self-imposed rule not to mix work and his personal life, but she was worth the trouble. Now he needed to prove he could be a gentleman. He pinched the bridge of his nose with his free hand. Crap. His thought processes needed a severe overhaul to resemble decency. She wasn't a giggly starlet. Cass was a lady. Making love to her brought out his primal instincts to protect and cherish her. Logan could be smooth in a club, slick in the backseat of a Camaro and sinful on the screen, but with Cass his foot was permanently wedged in his mouth. She didn't need him or his reputation. Maybe that was the reason she intrigued him.

She shifted and curled her body against his, tangling their bare legs together. He prayed his traitorous cock would behave. He stole a glance at her angelic face. The hauntingly sad smile tugged at his heart. She didn't adhere to his thin standards for arm candy. Cass made her own rules without care. He liked that. He respected her. Something he couldn't quite pinpoint as simple lust simmered in his belly. They fit together like a matched set.

She sighed, which kicked the spark into a raging fire again. Once the evening's storms passed, he'd work everything out. He'd make the wrongs right, even if it got him fired or broke his heart.

* * * *

In the morning, Logan shifted under the covers seeking a warm body. His hand caressed the soft sheet.

What the…?

"Cass?" He sat up. Navy walls with Art Deco prints and

gleaming white trim shrouded him. Photos of people he didn't know lined the dark cherry shelf. *Aw crap.* This was her bedroom—without her in it. He scratched his chest. *Maybe she's downstairs.* He took a deep breath. His stomach growled. The scent of breakfast food wasn't wafting in the air.

He climbed out of bed to make a pit stop in the bathroom. As he passed the dresser, he noticed a snapshot in a silver frame. Logan picked up the photo. Cass and Dex with the lights shining on Niagara Falls behind them. He put the frame back in its spot and scratched his forehead. She'd kept a memento of their good times. Maybe Dex wasn't out of the picture...

The roar of engines, extreme cursing and bleating back-up lights demanded Logan's attention. At the window, he saw the parade of trailers snaking up her gravel driveway. He noticed Nikita standing next to the large white barn, growling at into a cell phone.

Logan ambled downstairs to hunt for Cass. When he reached the kitchen, a pale blue piece of paper on the black granite countertop caught his eye. A smile curled his lips as he read the elegant script.

Logan,
I don't know what to say after a night like that, but thank you. I have a book signing at the Hawthorne at noon and won't be back until late. Good luck on the production. You are Jonathan.
Cass
PS. You are as hot in bed as you are on the screen.

Logan glanced at the clock on her oven. 10:23. He raked his fingers through his hair, knowing he needed to be on set at noon. And he still needed to shower and move his rental truck.

Logan sighed. "Give me something to work with, Cass. Don't want us to be a one-fuck relationship." He thought about her cryptic note. *You are Jonathan.* That made no sense. Sure, he played the role, but to be the real man? If she could portray Sophie, he would be thrilled. He jogged up the stairs. A photo in the stairwell of Cass holding a baby stopped him in his tracks. She glowed. He scratched his chin. The baby looked just like Cass. Did she have siblings? He couldn't remember her mentioning family. The baby couldn't be hers, could it?

The generic ring of his cell phone diverted his attention and alerted him to an incoming call. He sprinted the rest of the way up the stairs, but the image of Cass and the infant stayed in his mind as he answered the phone. "Malone." He smoothed down his disheveled hair. Uneasiness slipped over his brain. "Hello?"

A garbled voice spoke from the other end of the line. "Don't instigate a fight you won't win."

Logan held the phone away from his ear, looked at it and frowned. He brought the device back to his ear long enough to reply, "I think you have the wrong number."

"This is the right number, Logan Malone. You have the wrong idea."

His brows bunched together. "Wait. Are you referring to Cass?" He no more than finished the sentence when the caller clicked off the line. Logan puffed out a ragged breath. This made no sense. 'A fight you won't win.' What fight? For the role? He'd earned the role fair and square. For Jade? He didn't want the irritating socialite. He swallowed hard. For Cass? She was worth far more than a fight, but who wanted them apart, especially when they weren't even together? He shoved the thoughts aside and focused on getting dressed.

* * * *

Ten minutes later, he crossed the makeshift gravel drive leading to the set. He nodded to the raven-haired waif holding the clipboard. "Hi, Ania. Do you have the keys or is Nikita guarding them with her life?"

The assistant rolled her eyes. "She would if I didn't grab

them first." She held out a hard plastic card on a key ring with two keys clinking together. "Yours is the second one on the left. Tiffany insisted on the largest trailer and Nikita swore she needed the one on the other side of yours. Honey, you're surrounded by estrogen on this picture."

Logan dipped his head and took the keys. "Go figure." *Surrounded by women, except the one I want.*

Ania crossed her arms and cocked her head. She narrowed her eyes. "So who's the lucky partner for this one?"

He placed his hand over his heart. Oh boy, did he need to commence damage control and lasso his sex drive. The rumors needed to stop, pronto. "Me?"

She raised one brow. "Yeah, you. I want to know who I'm covering for this time."

He winked and inwardly winced. Ania had covered for the blunder with Katrina by lying through her teeth at the press conference. *They're just really good friends. Oh, brother.* "Ania, I won't need an alibi for this picture. I'm going to try the straight and narrow for a change." Straight to Cass' bed for another round and another chance to get her to fall in love with him.

She covered her mouth with her hand to hold back the rush of giggles. "Right, Romeo. Hey, Maggie!" She waved at the co-director, who crossed to their position. "Get a load of this — Logan's keeping it in his pants for this production."

"I see. Ania, I think Nikita needs the schedule for tomorrow's shoot. Can you get her a copy ASAP? She's really on a tear," Maggie said quietly.

Ania strolled away, still in stitches. "Sure."

He felt foolish. He definitely needed to halt the gossip. "Did you find her?"

He turned. "I'm sorry, Ms. Bowles. Say again?"

Her lips formed a cherry-red line and her eyes burned. He suspected hatred. "Keep your roaming eyes in check," she bit out. "I asked if you found Cass."

He nodded. "I did, on both accounts." She glared at him. "Do you know your lines?" He shook his head. Ah, straight to the point. "Not yet." That hadn't been his priority, but learning them was his only focus now.

She jerked her chin upward. "You have two days to figure it out. I'd suggest holing up in your trailer."

"Fine," he snapped and saluted. Logan shoved the duffle bag higher onto his shoulder and forced himself to walk to the trailer. "Two days to focus and no Cass. Yeah, I can do that. All I need to do is bring her words to life. Words of love and sacrifice, knowing she's only across the lawn. Yeah right."

Chapter Six

Monday morning, Cass dropped the felt marker and slumped, then leaned back in her chair. "Not a bad showing, Les. What's next?" The signing had turned out to be a better time than she'd expected. Plenty of readers had shown up and the venue had ended up being a quaint bookstore.

Les placed a bottle of soda on the table. "I know you wanted water, but I thought a cola for the after-party was more apropos. We get to mingle and schmooze. Leah wanted to get people into Hawthorne Books and Gifts. You are the big draw and it's working."

Cass took the beverage and followed her friend into the conversation room adjacent to the bookstore. Knickknacks lined the cherry wood paneled walls. Antique floor lamps with brightly colored stained glass shades illuminated the cozy space. The biting scent of coffee and tempting sweetness of teacakes floated through the air. She sat down on one of the many nude overstuffed couches with knobby fabrics that dotted the layout.

A middle-aged woman with streaks of silver in her flowing auburn hair touched her arm and joined her. "Ms. Jensen, I'm such a big fan. When does the next installment of the *Shivers* series come out? I can't wait to see what happens to Kyle."

Cass smiled. She loved her fans. "Thanks for asking. I haven't finished the outline, but Kyle's telling me he wants to settle down. To do that, he's gotta earn the love of the good woman."

"Exactly."

A petite woman with long honey-blond curls stood next in line. She produced a worn copy of *August Rain*. Cass forced her gaze away from the bronzed male model on the cover. He reminded her of Logan, whose image, naked and clothed, wandered through her mind. "To whom do I make this out?" she asked, trying to blurt out the memory.

"Rhea." The woman giggled and covered her mouth with her hands. "I just had to meet you."

Cass scrawled her name and brief message to Rhea, who disappeared immediately. "I guess she didn't want to meet me that badly," she muttered.

Les nudged her arm. "Why don't you stay put? Cora Monroe from the *Gazette* has a slew of questions for you concerning the production. She won't let us go without a short interview."

As Cass turned, Cora pushed in to sit on the overstuffed hunter green armchair. "I hear Tiffany Dufraine plays Sophie. Can she stretch her talents to make the character believable? Her work in the remake of Wonderwall lacked dimension."

Cass tucked a lock of hair behind her ear. "I think so. We selected the actors together. I didn't decide anything on my own. Tiffany has a captivating presence so I'm sure she's fine." She forced down the lump in her throat. That answer sounded too roundabout for her taste.

Cora scrunched her bulbous nose. Her thick glasses magnified her overly made-up mousy brown eyes. "I see. Rumor has it that Logan Malone stalked your personal residence in order to land the audition. Is that true?"

Cass shook her head. "You mentioned a personal home. Should I live in a public residence, like a hotel?"

The crowd laughed and Cora fumed. "So he did hunt you down?" she asked through clenched teeth. "Your readers want to know."

Cass took a casual sip of her soda. "No. He went through the audition process same as the other actors up for the part. His charisma best matched the qualities of Jonathan."

"Is he your boy toy?" Cora asked. Cass choked, spitting soda on a disgruntled Cora who shrieked, "This blouse is one-of-a-kind silk!"

"I'm not seeing anyone." Cass offered Cora a bunched-up napkin. Although she did want another roll in the sheets with Logan, she wasn't about to announce that to Cora. "I'm not in the market for love, I only write about it."

Les swooped in. "Time to go. Sorry, Cora. I'll send you some Tide and a better write-up." She shoved Cass past the awkward stares of the customers in Hawthorne. "Come on."

Leah Banks, the owner of the Hawthorne, met them in the parking lot. Her hands fluttered as she spoke. "I'm so sorry about Cora. I forgot about her lack of tact."

Cass shrugged and reached up to dislodge the clip from her hair. "It's fine, really. I just didn't expect the ambush — which is why it's called an ambush, I suppose." She laughed and shook out her tangled locks. "See, I'm good."

Leah's dark chocolate-colored eyes watered and widened like a frightened child. "You will come back?"

Cass gave the worried proprietor a hug. "Absolutely. Pencil me in sometime around the end of November."

The smile returned to her coral lips. She nodded and blew out a long breath. Her flowing auburn hair danced in the breeze. "Will do. Thanks, Cass."

Her gaze swept over the full parking lot. A man huddled next a baby-blue sedan seemed to stare at her. She shivered. Suddenly she didn't feel quite secure. Why, she wasn't exactly sure. Fans showed up at the house occasionally and many followed her from speaking engagement to speaking engagement. Maybe it was the fact that he was a man and not the handsome actor staying in her guest room that freaked her out. She forced her attention to Les. "Are you ready to head out?"

Les shook the keys. "I'm ready, but you look white as a ghost. Is Logan here?"

Cass laughed, but felt no humor. "That guy over there is giving me the creeps. Let's go before he decides to come over."

Les saluted. "Say no more. We're outta here!"

Five minutes later on the freeway back to Crawford, Cass slipped out of the black blazer she'd worn to the appearance. The cool air whipped over her skin. "I'm glad you suggested the tank top. I roasted in there. As usual, you we're right."

Les snorted. "I'm not always right."

Cass fiddled with the satellite station, changing the music and the subject. "What do you mean? You turned me on to Ezra and now they're my favorite metal band. Plus, I know Levi thinks you're something special."

"What about Logan?"

Cass froze. Talk about out of left field. She stared at Les for a moment before turning to the open window and the ordered rows of spiky bottle-green cornstalks dancing in the breeze on either side of the freeway. "What about him? I'll hook you up if you want." Not really. She wanted to keep him for herself, but she knew better. He'd probably already moved on.

"You need a boy toy!" Les shouted.

Cass felt her cheeks burn and knew it wasn't from the wind or late day sun. "What?"

Les shrugged and wound a lock of hair around her finger. Today the strands were a bright fuchsia. Tomorrow she might have green or electric blue streaks in her hair. "You spend too much time alone or with the boys in the band. You need a real man to simmer your blood and give you the red-hot sex you deserve."

She'd already had red-hot sex with Logan and wanted more. Cass rolled her eyes and studied a passing semi-truck. "Right."

"I'm serious. You need involvement with someone who isn't a safe bet."

"When did you come to that conclusion?"

"When Logan showed up, so did my best friend. Cass, you got your zing back. He didn't know what to think because you put him in his place. I missed that from you."

Cass waved her hand to dismiss the rationale. "He's really an ass." *But I like him and loved making love to him.*

Les held up her index finger. "True, but that ass has a fine ass. Don't tell me you didn't notice."

Cass knotted her fingers together. Notice? Yeah, she'd noticed. His ass looked even better right out of the shower and felt wonderful under her hands when she and Logan fucked. Her nipples puckered beneath her tank top. Dammit. "I did."

Les smacked her hands on the knobby steering wheel in time with the song on the stereo. "So it's settled. You'll make a play for Romeo, have oodles of monkey sex, write the steamiest novel of your life based on your experiences and live happily ever after. It's gonna work. I can feel it."

Cass folded her arms. This silliness had to stop. He'd get bored with her long before she realized the relationship was over. "What if I refuse?"

Les swerved around a slower car. "Don't push that challenge."

Cass shifted in her seat and resumed watching the passing landscape, which evolved into an array of sage-green soybean fields. Ensnare Logan Malone? Sure. What's the worst that could happen? He could run away laughing or fall madly in love with her too. She shook off the excitement. Their pairing wouldn't happen. "Well, Corbin and Ray want to practice tomorrow evening. I'll get to work on your plan once I get more done on *The Little Things*, like three weeks from next Sunday."

"Procrastinator."

Cass grinned. "You know it."

* * * *

Logan grabbed a bottle of water and tugged the earphones

from his ears. He slumped over to catch his breath and dump the refreshing liquid over his head. The run felt good, but the water did nothing to soothe his mood. Three nights since he'd been with her, including one night of unsuccessful sleep as he'd tossed and turned while fantasizing about making love to Cass again made the morning read-through a disaster. It was beyond time to get his head in the game.

Strains of Vinnie Joel met his ears. Through the large windows on the back of her house, Logan saw Cass and two men dancing. She collapsed in a fit of giggles against the larger, bald man. The lankier blond haired man laughed and held out his hand. Cass spun into his arms. They swayed to the song, apparently singing along.

He wanted to scream. Anger and jealousy burned through his system. She wasn't his to claim, but the urge struck nonetheless. A dance track followed the rollicking song. Cass ground her butt into the bald man's ass. He spun and yanked her arm out, like she was a guitar. She looked up and kissed his chin.

Logan saw red. He wanted to be the man receiving her kisses again. The man who danced and laughed with her. All he had was one magical night of passion, a handful of searing kisses and a note thanking him for being a friend. He meant nothing to her. At least not as much as the clowns she cavorted with. He slapped at a mosquito biting his neck.

"Don't itch that or I'll have to have her write it into the script."

Logan jumped and jerked around. Maggie stood before him with a quiet smirk curling her blood-red lips. She clicked the buttons on her silver MP3 player and adjusted her black jogging shorts. "You really have a thing for her, don't you? Did you two sleep together?"

He turned back to see Cass smothered in the embrace of both men. His heart bled. He felt raw. "It doesn't matter now."

She chuckled. "You quit too easily." Logan opened his mouth to snap at her, but she cut him off. "We're doing a publicity jaunt into town tomorrow. The Crawford Public Library's *Broken Wheels* Event starts at five. You and Tiffany will be there to answer questions, sign autographs and pose for pictures. Nikita insists she needs to go to represent the directorial staff. Translation—she wants the spotlight. I'm going along to support Cass."

Logan's deflated spirit soared. "She'll be there too?"

She rolled her eyes and replaced her earphones. "It's her book."

"I'll be there and on my best behavior. It's an excuse to see her without looking like a stalker." He mopped his brow and raked his fingers through his hair. "Awesome."

Maggie clapped him on the shoulder. "Good choice."

He jogged back to his trailer. The grass crunched under his sneakers, but it felt like he ran on a cloud. *I can see her and appreciate her work. Then maybe I can also explain and beg for a second chance to make the right impression.*

* * * *

The next evening, Logan drove through the quaint little town of Crawford in search of the library. Dozens of cars filled the adjacent lot, spilling over into the church one across the street. 4:36. Wow. Apparently Crawford really liked their writer. He found a parking spot along the sidewalk and stopped the rental truck. He checked his teeth and hair in the rearview mirror and sprayed on a bit of cologne. He winked at his reflection. "Knock her panties off, stud."

A moment later, he entered the back of the library auditorium. He zeroed in on Cass, clad in curve-hugging denim and a flowing coral peasant blouse. She wore her dark hair up in ringlets cascading from a clip. His heart rate surged. He could almost taste her sweetness and feel her in his arms again.

"Why so many chairs?" Cass asked and put her hands on her hips. He fought the urge to slip up behind her and wrap his arms around her waist.

"It's a panel discussion," Les replied plainly.

"Since when?"

"Since we showed up," Maggie interjected.

Cass turned to hug her friend. "Oh!" She locked gazes with him instead. Her eyes widened for a split second with a combination of shock and a spark he wanted to foster into another scorching blaze. Her voice dropped to a purr that singed him to his very core. "Oh." Crimson tinged her cheeks. He thought she looked adorable.

Les clapped her hands. Teal ringlets bounced as she moved. "Okay, kids. Let's sit. I want Logan in the middle with Cass on his left and Tiffany on his right."

"What about me?" Nikita snapped and shoved in next to him. "Chunks doesn't deserve all the attention."

"You will fill the audience," Les replied sweetly.

Logan stepped toward Cass. "Sounds good to me."

She gasped, making him want to press his lips against hers. He'd ask about that ridiculous nickname later.

Nikita grabbed a folding chair and plunked it on the stage next to Logan's prescribed seat. "I'll sit here."

"You did like the center of attention," Cass muttered and looked away.

Logan laughed. "Nice."

Nikita tangled her fingers around Logan's. "I am the center of attention."

"Only in your mind," Cass snorted.

He peeked around Nikita's spiky hair to smirk at Cass, who shook her head. Ah, he loved her fire. People filled the audience, making it impossible for a private conversation.

Les grabbed the microphone and waved at the crowd. "Introducing our panel—the people you've been waiting for…a portion of the cast of *Broken Wheels* and our very own Cass Jensen."

Logan whistled and cheered. Nikita dug her elbow into his ribs. "Stop it," she hissed. "Act dignified."

"I am. I'm dignified as I show my interest in the author's

body—of work." He chuckled at his statement.

Les directed the questions from the audience, aimed mainly at Cass. He watched her come into her own as she spoke about her work. She glowed and he soaked up her every word.

"Now, Logan, we hear that your Jonathan has more of a temper than the original character. Can you explain?"

He winked at the blonde who posed the question. "I believe in staying true to the script. But remember, I also read the original novel. The Jonathan concocted in my imagination had dual incentive to succeed, first to his team and second to Sophie. The fire in his soul drove him and I wanted to capture that sensation in my portrayal. I know Crawford has sparked a fire in me." Through his peripheral vision, he noticed Cass blush from her hairline to the collar of her blouse.

"Is it hard to write with such a sexy man on the property, Cass?"

She smiled and tucked a lock of hair behind her ear. He noticed her hand shook. "I need my concentration, so I just treat him like one of the boys."

Logan stifled a growl. *The boys get a few more benefits, though.*

After ten more minutes of questions, Les opened the floor to pictures and autographs. A particularly busty bottle blonde sidled up next to Logan. She pointed to her ample breast spilling out of the teal tank top. "I want your autograph right here."

He grinned and filled her request. "There you go, doll."

Cass covered her mouth with her hand and coughed loudly. She regained her smile and autographed another book. "Doll, my…" she muttered under her breath.

He chuckled to himself. *Cass didn't like the standard actor lines? Good.* He wanted her to know the real Logan Malone anyway. The actor was him doing his job.

Les leaned over Nikita's shoulder. "I believe that's your phone ringing. The rule states that no patron or guest may use cell phones in the library, so beat it."

Nikita glared and complied. "It's probably Bobby Reynolds. He owes me a favor."

With her chair vacated, Logan took the invitation and inched closer to Cass. "Hi, beautiful."

A blue-eyed brunette held a book out for an autograph, effectively interrupting his chance at flirting. "Can I get a photo with you two?"

Cass nodded. "Sure. Squeeze between and Les will take the shot."

"Thank you." She hugged Cass and sat down. "I've read all your books." The girl then turned to Logan. "She's awesome. You should snap her up."

He grinned at Cass. "I agree."

Once the girl left, Cass' eyes widened and the color drained from her face. Logan struggled to follow her gaze. He saw nothing other than a group of middle-aged women standing in a circle. Cass muttered something, but when he turned to calm her, she was gone.

"Where's she going?" Tiffany asked. "I want out. I need a smoke."

Les shot Logan a dirty look. "Where is she?"

He shrugged, feigning disinterest. Cass's fearful expression stayed in his mind. "She disappeared." *And I need to find her.*

"Hurry up, Ms. Dufraine," Les said. "Logan, see if you can find Cass. Mrs. Pembroke brought every Cass Jensen novel she owns. She expects personalization on each and every one."

He nodded and set out to case the parking lot. Horns honked amid the rumble of semi trucks through town. He chuckled at the action of the night in the small burg. Behind the sandstone library sat an intimate reading garden surrounded by a wrought iron fence in the shape of open books. In the middle, a soothing reflecting pool welcomed visitors to rest. White daisies, crimson roses and bunches of tall zebra grass decorated the meditation areas. He found

Cass curled up on one of the benches shaped like a stack of hardbound leather books. "Hi."

She didn't look up. "Hi yourself."

"Is this seat free?"

She hugged her knees. "The garden's here for everyone."

He sat close enough to feel the heat of her body, but still not touching. Even the sound of the night seemed to filter away. "Good idea, bringing me out here for some private time. Wish I came up with it myself."

"You're right—you do wish."

He took a deep breath, relishing in the sweet perfume of the flowers and the intoxicating scent of Cass. Car doors slammed in the distance, signaling the end of the event and the departure of the crowds. "You're right, as always." He wanted to ask her why she fled, but chose to skirt the issue—for now. "Do you like daisies?"

Cass looked at the white flowers, running her fingers over the delicate petals. "Mr. McCorkle tends them well."

He shifted and took her hand. To hell with restraint. "So why are you out here alone?"

She held perfectly still and stared at the toe of her navy ballet flat. "The room got stuffy."

"Cass." Her name came out more condescending than he intended. "That's a load of bull. What did you see? I know you freaked on me."

She studied her hands. "I didn't freak on you."

Logan grumbled. "You took off like you saw a ghost." She shrugged, which both irritated and excited him. "Babe, let me show you how I appreciate your work."

She offered a thin smile that made the hair on the back of his neck stand on end. "I'm not your babe, Logan. I probably never will be—not like I was the other night. I don't see why you try so hard."

Logan caressed his fingers along the nape of her neck, smoothing a lock of her hair. "I can't stop thinking about the way your touch sent fire through my body and being with you lit up my soul."

She pinched her nose between her thumb and forefinger and laughed. "You really do need that script consultant."

He wrapped his arms around her, feeling her stiffen for only a moment. "She won't accept my terms of agreement."

Cass offered a faint, almost nonexistent smile. "She's smart, but unsure."

Logan cupped her jaw in one hand. He kept the other arm secure around her waist. "Let me give her reasons to be sure."

She shook her head, but her gaze never left his. She licked her bottom lip. "Really?"

The nervous gesture sent him into another galaxy. "You have my full attention. Always did."

She wriggled from his embrace. "I doubt that."

He tugged her back into his arms. His heart thumped loudly. "Bullshit," he replied and pressed his lips to hers.

Cass whimpered and tried to shove him away. But in the same instant, she softened and opened to him, finessing her tongue against the seam of his lips. He felt the walls surrounding her defenses wobble and a fire raged low in his belly. "It can be like this all the time, babe," he murmured.

"Logan." She gasped and opened for him.

He nodded and kissed her again, relishing the satiny texture of her skin. "That's me, sweets."

"I don't want—"

He smoothed feathery kisses along her neck and jaw. "Yes, you want me just like I need you again."

She sighed and arched into him. "I want—"

A shriek split the tender mood and blurred out the rest of Cass's words. Flashbulbs popped. "Logan! Logan!" More squeals accompanied a throng of excited fans. "We love you, Logan!"

Cass looked with wide eyes over at the mob. She slid out from under his arm and hid behind him. "What are they doing here? Les said nothing about the media."

Logan forced down a growl. The real reason for the mob emerged in a pink tube dress and matching stiletto sandals.

"Logan, honey, I missed you!" Jade shouted. Her bleach blonde hair fell in flirty waves around her shoulders.

"Ignore her, Cass," he muttered over his shoulder. "This isn't what you think."

"I doubt that."

Logan turned to see Cass walk away with her head held high and her stride strong. She hadn't believed a word he'd uttered and she never told him what sent her out of the auditorium.

Jade snaked around him, mugging for the gaggle of cameras. Logan kept his arms tight as his sides and gritted his teeth. The noise of the street raged in his head. "Jade, darling, this isn't the time."

Her hand meandered to his ass. "It's always the time," she whispered.

He pretended to nuzzle her neck. "Sweetheart," he purred, "your time ran out. Don't do this to me."

She slapped his butt as a reprimand. "Never."

He inched away from her and waved to the noisy crowd. More camera bulbs flashed. One woman threw a black thong in his direction. Inwardly, he winced. "Sorry, folks. I have an early call tomorrow. I need my beauty sleep, but I'm sure Jade will entertain you in my place."

"Logan!" she snapped, although her smile never wavered. She stomped her high-heeled sandal on the sidewalk in an annoying set of clicks. "Come here."

He simply waggled his fingers to the media and strolled along the crooked gray concrete path beyond the garden and out to his truck. The smell of a wood-fire grill wafted through the air. His stomach growled. As the breeze shifted, he caught the scent of warm bread or pizza dough. He looked across the street to see a small pizzeria with orange neon in the fogged window. Pizza sounded good too. Maybe he could invite Cass for a late-night snack.

He jerked around when Maggie snagged him in the parking lot. "Time to go, Romeo. I can't postpone the production so you can log more face time."

Tiffany stuck her bottom lip out. "You didn't tell me the media stopped by."

Maggie narrowed her eyes. "Malone."

Nikita threw her head back and laughed, making Logan want to throw up. "He brought the cameras to Hicksville, USA! I told you he couldn't keep it in his pants."

"Nikita, Tiffany, get in the van. I need to speak to Malone," Maggie bit out. Once the others were out of earshot, she cornered him. "What did you do?"

Logan leaned against the fender and dipped his head to acknowledge a passing car loaded down with screaming teenage girls. He redirected his attention to Maggie and replied, "I got rid of the paparazzi. End of story."

"So why is Cass in tears?"

He lost some of his attitude. "Tears?" Shit. He didn't want to make her cry over a miscommunication. "Les sent me out to speak to her. Something in the auditorium freaked her out, but she wouldn't say what. I made progress until the circus showed up."

Maggie glared and stepped within inches of his face. "Leave her alone."

Logan fiddled with his truck keys. The glare of the street lamps seemed brighter and hotter all the sudden, like an interrogation. The smoky scent of the grill churned his stomach. A piece of paper fluttering on his windshield caught his attention. He grabbed it and crumpled it up without bothering to read it.

"Did you hear me?"

Logan grimaced. He knew darn well, but asked anyway. "Who should I stay away from?"

"Try everyone who isn't one of the actors on set."

Logan shifted and opened the note. With crap like Jade's drama and Nikita's insistent interference, no wonder Cass took off. She'd rather be alone than be caught up in his drama. He read the turquoise printing. A menu from an ice cream shop. Someone had circled a few words. He rolled his eyes and ignored the tension headache building behind his eyes. He didn't care about ice cream or the daily specials. "Fine. But it won't be easy."

"What's that?" Maggie asked and peeked over his shoulder.

"A flyer from one of the local businesses." He tossed the paper on the front seat. "Someone probably blanketed the area with them."

Maggie spun on her heel. "Oh, and about the woman issues in your life, make it easy and keep your hands to yourself."

Chapter Seven

By Saturday evening, Cass wanted out. She'd locked the doors and holed up in her office to work. She kept to herself, preventing any contact with Logan in the hopes that she could get him out of her system. The line of reasoning didn't work. She only desired him more and thought about him constantly.

She peered through the kitchen window to the set a few hundred yards away. She knew the scene well. The heroine was supposed to fake her love for Jonathan by acting hurt to force him to care for her. Logan, as Jonathan, chopped the stack of wood for a fire. The orange glow of the setting sun gave his skin a flawless look. Cass's mouth watered and she sighed. Damn, Logan was sexy. The scent of his cologne permeated the guest room like an omen. He'd always be a part of her. She could still taste his kiss on her lips. The man personified raw sex appeal.

"Are you coming to the races tonight?"

Cass closed her eyes and clutched her chest when she heard Les' question. "Were you trying to give me a heart attack?"

"Sorry," Les said with no venom or remorse. "It's Saturday—race night. I hear Levi's got a fast ride this week," Les said, ignoring the death look from Cass.

"I didn't realize you were right behind me." Cass took a deep breath. "Don't do that unless you want payback. I will pay you back."

Outside the window, Logan turned and stared at the

house as if he could see her. She sucked in a long breath and gripped the countertop. Too late to ignore him. "I don't know," she said way too slowly.

Just one more kiss, one more time in her bed...

Les rested her chin on Cass's shoulder, grabbing her arms for leverage. "What are you watching?" she asked in a singsong manner.

Cass tugged the thin fabric closed and wriggled away from her friend. "Les, look at the dirt on this window! I should wash it, tomorrow."

Les dug her elbow into Cass's rib cage and winked. "He's a good reason to ignore me." She chuckled. "He's a sexy sweater."

Cass nodded sadly. A damned sexy sweater, as Les put it, and oh, so out of bounds. How could she push him away after she'd already slept with him once? Oh, yeah. The interruption by his public and the barely-legal blonde. Her shoulders sagged. Why did he have to look so freaking cute, especially half-naked? It wasn't fair.

Les pulled Cass away from the glass. "Come on. We got lawn seats waiting for us at the track. I'll drive and we can talk on the way."

Cass retrieved her jacket. Racing wouldn't clear her mind, but it would be a fun way to spend the evening. Minutes later, they sped along Highway 30 en route to the High Banks Motorsports Complex.

"Levi says the motor you purchased is a good one," Les chirped.

"It's what they needed," Cass replied. She admired her friend's determination. "I'm happy to help. Do you want my assistance to collar Levi? I know it's been six years since your only official date, but I know he's interested in you."

Les turned on to Old Fort Dixon Road. "He's wrapped around my little finger. He just doesn't realize it yet."

Cass laughed at Les' nonchalant attitude. Good for her. "He will."

"Levi, Ray, me... you're helping so many people. Is Logan

on that list?"

Cass felt the color drain from her face. "What?"

"I talked to Maggie about the scene in the library parking lot."

Cass drummed her fingers on the window frame. The image of the guy from the Hawthorne parking lot flickered through her mind. "I'm not helping Logan. He's perfectly fine on his own."

"Are you sure?"

Cass shrugged. She saw no use in getting everyone fired up over a figment of her imagination. "I hate the media glare."

"Or Dex's glare?"

Cass studied the cornfield. "I like being out of sight, which means out of mind."

Les pressed the gas pedal hard, careening along the winding road. "You got it bad for Logan and you're going to punish yourself so Dex won't magically show up. Give Logan the chance he deserves — or did you?"

Cass furrowed her brows. Les wasn't supposed to know about the animal attraction simmering with Logan or that she'd already had sex with him.

"Stop hiding and stir things up. Maybe you'll even give Ray incentive to act."

Cass sighed. Ray was another problem altogether. "He'll have a fit." Not that she wanted to be with Ray. She liked him, but he wasn't the one who made her body sizzle.

Les seemed to ignore the matter. "Have you two slept together besides that first night and or spent time together besides at the library event?"

Cass folded her arms. "What do you mean?"

"Oh...my...God," Les said, drawing out the phrase. She shrieked. "You go girl!"

Cass sunk low in her seat. "For heaven's sake."

Les screamed. "You slept with a movie star! I am so jealous. He's gotta be hung like a freakin' horse! Down to his knees, isn't he?"

Cass covered her eyes and laughed nervously. Dear Lord. "Les, that's not ladylike!"

"Ask Levi. He'll tell you I'm no lady. That night at The Ricochet...I rocked it. But enough about me. What was it like?" Les continued to push the envelope. "Six, eight or ten?"

"Les!" The conversation officially reached the sewer and continued to sink with lead weights. Embarrassment welled within Cass' body.

"Inquiring minds want to know." Les laughed. "Give."

Cass rolled her eyes and tsk-tsked. She didn't like to kiss and tell, especially when the details didn't exist. "I can't."

Getting suddenly solemn, Les asked, "What happened once I left?"

"Let's just say we reached a plateau." Cass shivered. They'd made love, he'd held her and she almost believed there was a chance maybe they could be happy together.

Les screeched around a curve in the road a little faster than need be. After a few more moments, she broke the heavy silence. "Spill it."

Cass shifted. Trust Les to use a blunt command to coax a simple explanation. She wanted no witnesses and Les off the road before she said anything more. "I will once we park."

Les jerked the car to a stop in the field next to the track. "Okay, now spill it."

Cass knotted her fingers together. Her tongue felt fifteen sizes too big. "He stayed and we talked."

"So?"

Cass studied Les' facial expression and learned nothing. No clues whatsoever. "He stayed the night. In the guest bedroom."

Les stopped the car and nodded her head. "And?"

Cass could see the wheels turning in Les' mind. Good or bad, she didn't want to know the contents. "Really."

Les held her palms up and wiggled her fingers. "Tell me the rest."

Cass squeezed her eyes shut. "I had a nightmare concerning Dex and Logan held me. We slept together and in the morning, I bolted." She waited for the backlash, expecting Les to tell her she was weak, stupid, naïve. Crazy. Being with Logan had been unreal and so damned wonderful. It had to be neurotic.

"I'm glad you slept with him. You deserve to be happy." Les stared blankly out the window. "That said, you have to crawl out from under Dex's rock one of these days. He was a bastard, no doubt about it, but you can't let that keep you from being with someone long-term. If Logan makes you happy, then rein him in and go for the ride of your life."

Cass chewed on her bottom lip. "With Logan, it's a game. I'm only a pawn."

Les waved her hand. "Men aren't all like Dex. Take Ray, for instance. He'd cut off his right arm to be with you."

"I know," Cass replied. She heard the roar of the engines as the cars started the practice session. Already, dirt and dust flew through the air, making it hard to see.

"I think Herb had better water the track one more time," Les said and laughed. "If not, we'll end up covered in a couple extra inches of filth!"

Cass chuckled, happy to change the subject. Anything was a wanted distraction from Logan.

"Ray said something to Levi about wanting to work up some new tunes in the pits after the race," Les continued. She and Cass fought their way to the gate and paid the entrance fee. "You'll need to practice. Levi's got a whole slew of songs he wants to resurrect. I hope you join in because they need someone to do the harmonies."

Cass sighed again. Singing was another outlet for feelings she didn't know how to deal with. "We'll see."

* * * *

Once filming shut down at nine-thirty, Logan worked up the nerve to talk to Cass. After the library incident and the malicious phone call, well, the odds were stacked heavily against him. He needed to get to the bottom of it. As he strolled to the house, mulling over what he wanted to say, his phone buzzed in his pocket.

"Malone."

"Where are you?" his agent, Carmine, asked.

"In Ohio, working on *Broken Wheels*. You got me the audition," Logan snapped. He brushed his foot over the freshly cut grass in her backyard. He missed the luxury of having a yard, having a place that wasn't part of an apartment building.

The smell swirled around in his brain, reminding him of Cass. Sweet Cass. "Why?"

"Have you seen the *Tribune*?" Carmine growled.

"No, why?" Logan rolled his eyes and plopped down onto a wicker chair on the back patio. Since he'd touched down in the Buckeye State, he hadn't bothered to look at a paper. Why would he peruse a California newspaper? He drummed his fingers on the woven white armrest and studied the flowerbed of petunias under her living room window. A section of flowers about a foot wide were mashed. He strode off the deck to investigate and found a set of footprints clearly imprinted in the dirt. Five or six cigarette butts littered the ground around the prints. Who needed to spy on Cass? He remembered when she'd bolted from the library. Was this the person who freaked her out? It didn't matter.

He wouldn't let anyone threaten her life.

"Logan!"

He returned his attention to Carmine. "What?"

"There are pictures of you and Jade Weir clubbing. Not that that's a surprise, but she's gone to Eliza Calais with an interview stating that you two are an item. When were you going to tell me you're getting married?"

Logan stopped cold. He didn't remember any cameras or anything about marriage. Hell, they'd never even slept together. A thought crossed his mind — what about

Cass? If she had any doubts or second thoughts about his sincerity, the blitz solidified them. Shit. He sprang into action. "Ignore it. Jade's snippy because I gave up on her. She finally decided she wanted a relationship and I walked away, plain and simple. It's her means to get back at me. I'm not about to lose out because of Jade's warped pride."

Carmine let out a string of indecipherable curses. "Well, no shit. So what are you doing about it?"

"I'm here in Crawford chasing the woman of my dreams," Logan said proudly. He made a mental note to take a picture of the footprints with the camera on his phone once he disconnected with his agent.

"Who is it this week? Tiffany, or are you back to Nikita?"

"Ha-ha," Logan snapped and strolled across the deck to the driveway. Time to shake the bad rep and move on with his life. "Tiffany is married and Nikita is old news. I'm with Cass Jensen." It was a little white lie, since they'd only slept together once, but soon he'd make it a reality.

There was no sound on the other end of the line. Logan kicked at a rock in the driveway. No more foolishness. "Carmine? Are you there?"

"Yeah," Carmine said finally. "I had to check the speaker on my phone. It must be broken. I thought you said Cass Jensen. She's Dex Rose's ex...and not your type."

Logan spoke through gnashed teeth. "She's gorgeous and perfect the way she is. That bastard didn't deserve her."

"Right," Carmine said and drew the word out.

"Jesus."

Carmine laughed. "Are we going to get defensive, now? Please. I'll count it as a phase."

Logan jostled the locked doorknob on the main door and ignored Carmine's jab. Maybe Cass was home. The knob never budged. Drat. A piece of paper with his name on it flapped in the breeze. He frowned. Another stupid note? What the hell? He ripped the paper from the door and read the contents. At least it wasn't another menu.

Logan,

Take these directions and go to The Ricochet. A surprise waits there, but don't show up before midnight and don't ask questions. Tell Tex you're with Hillbilly Boots. I'll explain later.

Les

Logan scratched his head and continued to ignore the verbal barrage from Carmine. An invitation from Cass' best friend? Something seemed off, he just wasn't sure what. Did Les want them together? Or to showcase his bad reputation?

"Are you listening to me?"

Logan glanced around. By the time he cleaned up and got dressed, it would easily be eleven. What could he do for another hour? Rehearse his lines, mentally map out his actions for Monday's shoot, watch a baseball game. Or fantasize about Cass. He closed his eyes.

Definitely think about Cass.

"Logan!"

Logan looked at the phone in his hand like a foreign object. "Are you still there, Carmine? I figured you gave up on me. I gave up listening to you."

"Not yet, but I should," Carmine grouched. "This phase has got to—"

"Look, man. I gotta go. Whatever Jade says, just ignore it. I'm not in a phase and I'm not with Jade. I'm in love with Cass."

"You just killed your career. Your fans want you because you're attainable. If you're with someone like Cass, that won't be possible."

"Why? Because she's gorgeous." Logan kicked a clump of grass, scattering it in the late August breeze. That monster had treated her like dirt, and now Carmine felt the need to add his own abuse. No more.

"You can do your own damage control," Carmine snarled. With that, he disconnected the call.

Logan fumed and strode to the flowerbed. He

photographed the footprints, tucked the phone in his pocket and started back toward his trailer. The note said no questions. Not good enough. He had a ton of questions, starting with the obvious. Was this a trap? What did Les really know? And what about Cass? Was she angry, hurt, or did she hate his guts? He groaned. Midnight would never come if he continued to worry.

Back in his cramped living space, he logged onto the Internet in search of answers. Why did Nikita, and now Carmine, insist on insulting Cass? Logan clicked on the *Delish* magazine website to view his supposed indiscretions. The headline "Romeo courts his Juliet. Or should we say Jade?" popped up immediately. *No. No. No.*

Logan accessed the accompanying gallery—three telephoto images of Jade Weir in the parking lot chasing Logan. In each, she smiled at the back of his head. The last shot had Logan opening the driver's door of the neon-green '75 Camaro he'd sold in May. The viewer was to assume they left together.

He groaned. The next six shots were from inside the club, all during their thirty-second dance a week ago. Logan frowned. Image one—Logan groping Jade. Image two—Jade rubbing on Logan. Image three—Jade in close proximity to his ear and flashing an ostentatious diamond ring.

Enough! He closed the page and rubbed his eyes. Cass deserved nothing less than the unabridged truth. Those pictures were far from honest. No more. When he'd chosen to become an actor, he'd trained relentlessly. Now that he had a taste of Cass, he'd pursue her with the same dogged determination.

Logan typed Dex Rose in the search engine. What did he have to do with her absurd nickname? He clicked on Dex's personal page. A myriad of images of Dex littered the screen followed by a crawler of his personal bests. "Lots of bluster concerning Dex's careers, but no mention of Cass." In the column titled Personal, he found the only scant reference—

married for four years during his early time in Hollywood. Divorced and happily single, Dex now lives in Catalina. Logan rubbed the back of his neck with his hand. "Happily single? Yeah, right. He's happy Cass lives across the country. She's far enough away that he can cheat, but still within reach when he wants a reconciliation." He ruffled his fingers through his hair. Something didn't add up. Unconvinced by the description, he added Cass's name to the search. The results included a smattering of articles from magazines concerning Dex. The last link on the page garnered his attention — Dex&Cass4Ever.com.

Logan clicked on the link. Fabricated photos of Cass and Dex floated in a slideshow across the screen. The handful of actual pictures of the couple looked strained and posed. The only heading read — Dex and Cass Rose, married May 22. Love conquers all.

He wanted to scream, puke and beat the hell out of anything within reach. Instead, he pressed on with his investigation. He clicked on the statistics tab and found a photo of Cass. Her hair fell in teased curls around her face. Thick makeup hid her natural beauty. She appeared emaciated, but thankfully, her modesty was still intact. Her smile reminded him of a video vixen, too sexy for her own good. At the bottom of the picture were the words, *Forever my girl.* Dex's girl? Like hell. She didn't deserve to live in fear. Logan shivered. He might not be the man she needed, but he'd willingly give up his life, if that's what it took to protect her.

A soft knock at the door interrupted any further Internet exploration. He closed the information box and then the screen. "Come," he called. His heart hoped and prayed for Cass.

"Logan? I need a minute with you and you locked the door."

His bunched his brows together. He disengaged the lock and yanked the door open. *Tamp down the attitude, man.* "Sorry, Maggie."

She handed him a sheath of papers and remained on the stoop. "I have script changes and an addition to the revised shooting schedule. We have rain in the forecast and can't shoot the race footage this weekend."

Logan looked over the notes and nodded. "Okay. I wanted a free day, so this works for all of us. Please, come in. My gramma would throttle me for forgetting my manners."

Maggie grinned. "I know, but I'm here for professional reasons."

"I assumed so." Christ. Did he have that kind of aura that people thought one look and he wanted to hump them?

She laughed. "Half of the night shots are done, save for the love scene and I don't want to do that until the end. Corky agreed that should be last so you and Tiff feel comfortable together. Plus, he wanted us to film some of that on the sound stage in California to cut down on production costs. Other than that, we have a bunch of inset shots to do later. But that's no big deal."

Logan looked up. His throat went dry. "Comfortable? What are you planning?"

"She's going to be topless and you'll be totally nude. That's my plan. An ass shot will boost ratings," Maggie replied firmly. "Especially yours."

He shook his head and jumped up from his spot on the couch. "That wasn't in the contract."

Maggie's hands shot to her slender hips. "I guess you should've read the contract," she growled.

Logan fumbled and moved the laptop. "Damn it."

She frowned, knotting her brows together. "What's the problem? Last year you showed everyone your family jewels during the wrap party for *Blood Rites* when you got so drunk."

He blushed, thinking about his drunken performance. Not his best showing... He'd have to tell Cass that and hope she didn't laugh him right out of her life. "Maggie, I think I'm in love and don't want to screw it up."

Maggie cocked one manicured brow. "If it's really love,

you shouldn't have to think about it."

He nodded. "I know."

Maggie didn't look convinced, but stayed quiet.

"Don't tell me you disapprove." God. He needed to know he had someone on his side.

Maggie bit her lip. "Watch your back. That's all I'll say."

He opened his mouth to question her, but she scooted out of the trailer too quickly. He thought about the website. The photo of Cass exposed hit him right between the eyes. Cass had trusted Dex at one time and he put her through hell. Would she trust him? Even more, would Dex really try to keep them apart? A quick look to the clock set him on course to meet her. Slowly and cautiously, he would eliminate her fears and show her the love she deserved. He'd show her the love in his heart, even if it took the rest of his life.

* * * *

He drove across town to a rickety-looking wooden barn, named The Ricochet. An overabundance of bullet holes peppered the doorway for an outlaw effect. Was it a bar, honky-tonk or dance hall? He didn't know, but it looked nothing like the clubs in California. Sure, it sported neon, but he bet the shots of bourbon weren't fifteen bucks apiece. The structure itself had probably belonged to a farmer in its heyday and now served to entertain the generations of farmers coming after him. Logan appreciated the oddly refreshing atmosphere. An aura of honesty and roughness swirled outside. He bet the patrons shot from the hip, had good times on Saturday nights and spent Sunday morning firmly seated in the local church pews.

A couple clad in cowboy boots and jeans pushed past Logan and entered the establishment. He felt sorely out of place in battered sneakers, a concert tee and his favorite baseball hat. "Are you Logan?" A large man in overalls invaded his space and shoved him back. "Are you?"

Logan turned toward the voice. He adjusted his faded hat

and looked the man straight in the eye. "I was the last time I checked. Why? Are you Tex?" She'd told him to find a guy named Tex, at least he hoped that was the guy's name.

The man looked down his nose at Logan. "I could be."

Logan tipped the bill of his ball cap to get a better look at the bouncer and vice versa. He'd once believed celebrities should get in without hassle everywhere. Something told him he wasn't going to get a break here. "Les sent me to find you. I'm here with Hillbilly Boots."

The man folded his arms across his barrel chest and his expression stayed blank. "Funny," he said without laughing. "She sent me to find you, but they never mentioned a middle-aged punk trying to pass himself off as hot shit."

Logan folded his arms, mimicking the large man. He could be a blockhead when challenged and he felt seriously challenged. "Is Cass here? If not, I'm gone. I don't put up with harassment."

Tex nodded sharply. "You'll see her." He held his hand out. His thick, blunt fingers wiggled. "First, you owe me five bucks."

Logan peeled the money out of his wallet, not bothering to ask what for. "Where's she at?"

Tex grinned. He had at least three teeth missing. "I said you'll see her. Now beat it."

Logan removed his hat and ran his fingers through his hair, leaving it in disarray. He was about to enter an ambush. If Cass saw the photos, then he deserved every lashing she could dish out. He replaced his ball cap, pulling it down to obscure his identity, and entered the building. Before he passed through the foyer, strains of an oldies song met his ears. The singer had an alto voice that complimented the sadness of the lyrics. She sounded sexy, but withdrawn. For some reason, the voice seemed damned familiar. He knew plenty of divas, but few frequented dives such as The Ricochet.

He followed the music into the great hall. Colored lights in addition to the sparkling disco ball flickered around the cavernous space. The room resembled a converted hay barn, complete with a second-story loft. Enormous fans circulated the stale smoky air. A wide wood plank dance floor took up the lion's share of the area. An oak bar decorated with hundreds of liquor bottles ran the length of the building. The crowd filled the dance floor, making it hard to see the band. At least one hand swatted Logan's ass as he made his way to the bar. He vaguely heard whispering.

"Is that him? I can't be sure."

"It's gotta be him. I saw his naked ass in *Delish* magazine."

Logan pursed his lips and groaned. *I wore a cleverly placed towel and smile in that particular photo spread, thank you very much.*

"Nah, he's in Hollywood with some hot blonde."

"I heard he disappeared to the Bahamas to shoot a skin flick."

I have a name. Logan shook his head. *And I'm not interested in some hot blonde or starring in porn. I'm interested in making steamy scenes with a sultry brunette.* He ordered a beer and slowly scoped the scene. People gathered to enjoy the good music, good times and pleasant company. He scanned the crowd. Cowboy boots, huge belt buckles, cowboy hats, scores of denim and proudly bared cleavage. Plenty of women, but not the one he wanted.

The next song redirected Logan's attention to the band. His jaw dropped in shock. There on the stage stood Cass and four men. The emerald green baby-doll blouse shifted with her body as she danced, seductively hugging her curves. Like the women surrounding him, Cass sported cleavage, but hers looked flirty without being trashy. Her hair, styled in fat ringlets, bounced to the beat and framed her glowing face. Her smile lit up the room. Damn, she looked sexy. Heat stirred in his belly. He longed to pick up his old six-string guitar and join her.

The guitarist slung his axe around her midsection and played the solo while Cass wriggled in his embrace. The guy looked like a brute. Shaved head, black cowboy hat and one hell of a menacing presence. He was the guy she'd danced with back at the house. Just as the other day, she looked happy, free and tiny against his six-and-a-half-foot frame. White-hot jealousy shot through Logan's body. He couldn't deny she had talent. Was this bald behemoth the one she favored or did she want the skinny blond fellow? Damn, he hated competition. She finished the song and bowed to the crowd. Everyone cheered, including Logan. He watched in awe as she descended the stage.

"Are you upset?"

Jarred from his territorial glare, Logan turned to see Les next to him. "Hey."

"So, are you upset? She does this about once a month, if the boys can talk her into it. She's good."

"No." He stole a slow gaze over Cass's body. "She's fabulous." He took a long draw from the beer bottle and shifted to consider Les again. "Does she know I'm here?"

"Not yet. I needed to talk to you first."

"Shoot." Logan imagined what she might say. *Cass saw the photos. She's angry. Never speak to her again. How could you? You're just like Dex. No more sex, so blow that out of your ass and leave her alone.* "Go ahead."

Les looked down and then straight in his eyes. "She likes you."

Logan nearly swallowed his tongue. His heart kicked into overdrive. Like could easily blossom into love with a little hard work on his part. Blood pounded in his ears. They had a chance. "Oh really?"

"She likes you, but she's afraid. You seem to attract attention everywhere you go. She doesn't appreciate being forced into the spotlight—except when she's got the band with her." Les put her hands up to stop his intended retort. "Keep it in your pants. I know you didn't plan the mob or the creep watching by the door."

Logan frowned. Cass worked on her own terms, probably because Dex forced her into uncomfortable situations. Now he did the same just by being himself. And there was some creep keeping tabs on her. Oh, hell no.

"I assume you meant well, but remember she's fragile." Les leaned against the bar. "There probably wasn't anyone watching her, not that she'll admit I'm right. Dex abused her. Every day he says he's coming back because he can't live without her. He's relentless and I think a tiny part of her hasn't come to terms with them failing at marriage. Now do you see why she's spooked?" She put her hand on Logan's. Concern etched her face. "She's scared you'll be like him."

Everything made perfect sense, including his mysterious phone call. He pushed her way outside her comfort zone. Beyond that, someone from Dex's camp wanted them apart. But could she still love Dex? Logan removed the hat and raked his fingers through his hair again. "I would never..."

"I know." Les patted his arm. "She needs you, but she'll never say it. Damned pride."

He cocked his head. "So what do I do? I can't just walk away."

"Let her decide and go at her pace. When she wants you, go with it. If she runs away, give her time and let her come around. I know it may seem exasperating, but it builds her trust. Cass needs to know you're willing to bend."

Logan took another swig from the bottle. "You're smart. How do you know what to do?"

Les shrugged. "I was her divorce lawyer." With that she slipped away.

Logan leaned heavily against the bar. No shit. He returned his attention to Cass. She sang another three songs, teasing and tempting him. He'd watch her forever if she'd let him. He wanted to wrap his personalized guitar around her and enfold her in his protective embrace. She could fly as long as she came home to him. His heart thumped loudly. Right now, she looked too beautiful to pass up.

As the DJ switched to a dance song, Logan crossed the wooden floor only to lose her to the arms of the blond bassist. She laughed and swayed in his embrace. Her seductive movements, though with another man, stirred more than just his lust. She stirred his soul. He adjusted his hat and smoothed his shirt before reaching her position.

The blond with mischievous blue eyes noticed. "Why, Cass, you have a fan."

Cass spun around. A momentary flash of panic swept across her face, quickly replaced by a goofy smile when he lifted the bill of the ball cap. She threaded her fingers together. "Corbin, this is Logan. Logan, this is Corbin Moss."

Logan dipped his head.

Corbin kissed Cass on the cheek. "Go get him, tigress." He winked and slipped out of sight.

She shifted against the wave of dancers. "This place is a step down for you. What are you doing here?"

He grinned, yearning to devour her on the spot. "Meeting a good friend."

She looked away. Her cheeks tinged a soft shade of pink. "Oh."

Logan slipped a lock of her hair behind her ear, brushing her jaw as he moved his hand. "Hello, good friend."

Her gaze met his. Sapphire flecks burned in her eyes and a smile curled her burgundy lips. His heart swelled in time with his cock. He wanted to hold her in his arms and kiss her until they both felt the flames of desire. "You look hot tonight."

She poked him in the chest. "I'll bet you say that to all the girls."

He tipped her chin with his index finger. "Not since I met you." A shove from the crowd pushed them together. She grabbed his shirt to keep her balance. He slipped his arm around her waist as added support.

"Wait." Les elbowed her way through the throng of dancers. "I want a picture of you two for the website. It's good PR and you two make an adorable couple." She twiddled with her phone. "Smile!"

Cass snuck a glance at Logan. "Did you put her up to

this?"

He traced his nose along her cheek and closed his eyes, drawing in her essence—lilacs and warm female. "I wish I had."

"Liar," Cass shot back with a giggle.

"Turn and smile, already, Logan," Les complained.

He opened his eyes and willed his dick to behave. Cass stirred his soul and forced him to be a better man with just a smile. He wanted to sample every inch of her body and claim her as his own. "I'm smiling."

"And stabbing me in the hip," Cass whispered.

Logan laughed and rubbed her back. He pressed a kiss to her temple and whispered, "Give me a chance. I'll try not to let you down." He handed Les his phone. "Take a couple shots with mine too."

Les sighed loudly. "Fine, but smile and look at me for mine, will ya?"

Cass laughed. "I have been."

Logan shrugged and stole a sideways glance at Les. He flashed a quick grin and returned his attention to Cass.

"There. At least you look cute." Les pocketed her phone.

"Thank you."

Logan nuzzled Cass, savoring her uniquely sweetness. Damn, she tasted good. He saw Les roll her eyes through his peripheral vision. "Just take the picture, Les." Cass shot him a confused look. He met her slightly parted lips with a kiss.

"Got it!" Les shouted in triumph.

Cass dropped her head to his shoulder and giggled again.

Les snapped another picture. "You two really do look adorable," she said and handed the phone back to Logan.

"Thank you, Les." Logan shot her a wide grin then turned back to Cass and took her hand in his. "May I have this dance?"

Cass used her free hand to brush stray hairs from her face. A slow smile blossomed on her lips. "I'd love to," she said finally. "But, when did you get here?"

"I got some time off the set and worked up the courage to see you. I thought you hated me." He scooped her into an embrace. "After the fiasco at the library, I wouldn't blame you."

Cass's face reddened. "I don't hate you. I'm just not sure I like you." They swayed together while the rest of the crowd formed lines to two-step.

He licked her earlobe, memorizing every last bit of her. "Tell me what to say, Cass. Tell me what to do. I'm yours to shape and bend."

Cass rested her head on his chest. She gripped the fabric of his T-shirt. "Keep up what you're doing right now."

Logan pulled her tighter against his body and tilted his head to brush against her hair. The blouse was so soft in his fingers, but not as soft as her silky skin. "Consider it done."

Her breath tickled his ear, making his hard-on throb. "How much did you hear?"

Logan didn't catch her words. "Hmmm?"

"Did you hear me sing?"

Logan lifted her chin to stare into the blue depths of her eyes. God, he loved getting lost there. "I heard the last few songs. You sound as beautiful as you look, babe." He brushed his lips softly against hers. Her eyes drooped shut, making him crazy with need. The kiss deepened and her tongue slipped between his teeth to explore. She tasted like cola and Cass, his natural aphrodisiac. A moan rumbled in her throat. He liked the assertive Cass. "Will you sing some more? For me?"

She backed away. Her jaw momentarily clenched. Did he push too far? He swallowed hard. A thin smile crooked her mouth, but it quickly built into a full grin. "You really liked it?"

Logan nodded. *Liked? No, try loved.* He could listen to her forever. "Very much so."

Her lips brushed his ear. "Then I'll make them play my favorite song for you." Cass dropped her head back to his shoulder.

The DJ switched records, which made her look up. "I think they want me to do a couple more songs. Will you stay? I want to know you're out there," she said. She smoothed the creases in his shirt. The simple gesture felt electric sparks going to his heart. Yeah, he could give up the showbiz life to make her happy.

"I can't think of another place I'd rather be." Logan kissed her again. "Wasn't that one of the lines of your song? Or was it, 'I'll go to the ends of the earth as long as I can make the trip with you, babe?' Either way, it's all true."

Chapter Eight

Cass licked her bottom lip, relishing the taste of Logan. The colored lights strung around the bar sparkled in his dark eyes. The scent of fried food and pepperoni pizza, coupled with the conversational noise over the thumping bass line, invaded her senses, but all she really noticed was Logan...until Ray interrupted them.

"Cass entertained us earlier. Let's give a round of applause and see if she'll return and sing a few more songs."

She glanced at Ray, then back at Logan. "Do you mind?"

Logan cocked his eyebrow. A contented smile kinked the corner of his mouth. "You owe me."

She leaned in close. "I do." A ripple of excitement ran the length of her spine. He wanted to listen and liked her hobby. A fresh burst of confidence washed over her. Ends of the earth? With her? Wow. If this was what love felt like, maybe it wasn't as awful as she'd imagined. God knew the sex between them sizzled. She hurried up onto the stage and took her place beside Ray.

"Everything okay?"

Cass grinned at Ray. "Everything is just wonderful."

"I told you she was fine," Corbin snapped.

"Lay off." Ray's tensed. He glared down his nose at her. "Who is he, anyway?"

Cass arched her brows and placed her palm flat on his muscled chest. "Easy, boy. Corbin's right, so put your claws away."

Corbin strummed his bass guitar. "I told you not to worry,

Ray. Now can we play?"

Ray folded his arms. "Work on your solo, Moss." To Cass he said, "I don't like him."

Cass waved as Corbin stalked away. She rested her hands on her hips. Ray would risk bodily injury to keep her safe, but Logan wasn't a threat. "Then it's a good thing you aren't seeing him."

"Are you?"

She shook her head slowly and snorted at Ray's jealousy. He'd managed to scare off any and all potential suitors. No more. She wanted to love again with Logan, to be exact. "Maybe."

Ray restocked the picks in his shirt pocket and cradled his guitar. "I want to talk to him." He smoothed his snug black T-shirt to accentuate his solid build in a show of bravado. "I've heard of him. He's got quite a reputation. I want to make sure for myself that he's good enough for you. I can't handle seeing you hurt—again."

Cass rolled her eyes. "You act like I'm not smart enough to know his type," she said, thinking about Logan's faded blue jeans and vintage concert T-shirt. *I'd like to rub my hands all over him again.* "I'm a big girl, pardon the pun, and I can make my own decisions."

He cleared his throat and glared at her. "I never thought of you as a 'big girl'," he growled. "I thought of you as Cass, my best girl friend. After the crap with Dex, I can't help feeling a bit territorial. Look, I trust you, not him."

She huffed and matched his steely gaze. "Then talk to him. Rake him over the coals if it makes you happy. Know this, I like him and I'm ready to try again." She fought the lump in her throat and studied the board on the floor. Wow. She really said it. Out loud. She was ready.

"Why not try with me?"

She froze. "What?"

Ray strummed the guitar and hid his eyes under the brim of the cowboy hat. "You could've explored my body and experimented all you wanted without fear or rejection. I wanted you to. I've always wanted you, Cass."

She took a step back. Where did this come from? He'd told her she was like a sibling and now he desired her? Come on. She needed solid friends in her life, especially Ray. A physical relationship was a complication they wouldn't weather well, especially without smoldering attraction. "Ray, it wouldn't work. We'd wreck our friendship."

Ray opened his mouth, but the announcer cut off the argument. "One more time, let's hear it for Hillbilly Boots!"

Cass heaved a sigh of relief. Ray probably wanted to push the envelope and preach caution. Territorial to the bone, he couldn't protect her forever. Desperation burned in his eyes. "Let me talk to him. I want to make sure he's on the level."

"Fine. But you'd better play my favorite song."

She felt Ray's angry stare bearing down on her like a lead weight. She shook off the ill feeling and addressed the crowd. "This one is for all those couples out there in the first bloom of love." She stole a glance at Logan. He leaned against a support beam and lifted his hat a couple of inches. His smile gave her added confidence.

"I never thought I could feel something this strong and it scares me to think it's all real," she sang.

Ray backed into her like he always did and sang harmony. She looked at Logan. Was he upset or did he understand? His head dipped in approval. The wicked smile piqued her interest. Did he see them spending more time together again? Cass wanted to spend the entire night with no one but Logan.

"What feels right can't be wrong. We're in for a helluva deal. I'm game for the trip, if it's with you," she sang. Cass faced Ray as he pressed into her, nearly kissing her. Before Logan, she'd let him sneak in the occasional smooch. The song dictated it, but not tonight. "With you, I'm flying. My feet don't touch the ground. Can you feel this love? You reach me without a sound."

Ray pressed tightly against Cass's backside, but there

was no telltale sign of arousal. This was just a test of the boundaries. She eased away to lean on Corbin, who dropped his head to her shoulder. She giggled and floated across the stage.

Logan bobbed to the beat and winked at her. He snapped a few more photos with his phone. She sucked in her stomach. Though she danced along to the song, she still wished he'd let her strike a more flattering pose. *Damn insecurities.* A slow, sexy smile tugged at the corners of his mouth. A spark shot straight to her core. Something much deeper than animal lust ebbed within her body. Could he be the one?

"Even if it's not forever, I don't care where we go, as long as I'm with you. I don't care, as long as I'm with you." As the last notes of the song faded away, she bowed and the audience cheered.

Logan's voice rose proudly above the rest. For the first time in a long time, she felt free. Singing had started off as a hobby. Tonight, it became a passion she wanted to share with him.

"We're giving Miss Cass the rest of the night off," Ray said and strummed the next song. She knew the sarcasm in his voice. He wasn't pleased. When she sang, they made more money. And the race team needed money. They'd have another shot next week. She'd kick in for another motor to soothe the hurt feelings.

Corbin winked. "Have a nice night, Cass."

She waved to the crowd. Before she left the stage, Cass cornered Ray. "Thank you for understanding, even if you don't."

She pushed through the crowd and met Logan by the bar. He held his arms open until she cuddled against his chest. His T-shirt was a soft cushion against her skin. And boy, how it showed off his muscles! "Hi again."

A grin kinked the corners of his mouth. "I knew you couldn't resist me," he murmured.

A shimmer of excitement ran the length of her spine. She

chuckled. "You're so full of yourself."

"That's why you like me." She stepped out onto the crowded patio and Logan followed. People around them began to whisper, but she never heard it. She only saw Logan.

"Who wrote that song? It's not in the same voice as your novels, but I like it."

Cass looked away. "Ray wrote it — for me."

Logan acted unconcerned. "You should record it."

She smiled to herself, thrilled to find a man who wasn't afraid of Ray. "Yeah — we'll get right on it."

"Does he write a lot of your material?"

She snickered. Her material? "It's his band, not mine. He's Levi's crew chief on the track, but in The Ricochet, it's all about Ray. I was an afterthought that brought in patrons, or so they claim. He got me up there because he liked me."

Logan brushed his knuckles against her cheek. "Never an afterthought, babe. He sees your beauty in and out, like I do."

Cass blushed. Logan saw her inner beauty? What a pleasant surprise. Did he see her sex appeal too? "So why are you here? I never gave you a clue."

"Truth? Les left me a note and directions." Logan placed his hat backward on her head. "I think I'm starting to grow on her. She invited me."

Her mind reeled. Les? "You're kidding."

"At first, I thought she had ulterior motives. But no."

Cass arched her brows. "I got the impression that she hated you. I know I'm not impressed." *Yet.*

Logan cupped her chin. "She's quite protective. I see why, even if you're fibbing about liking me."

Cass grinned. "I refuse to stroke your ego."

He waggled his brows. "Will you stroke something else? I liked it the first time."

She thumped his arm. "You wish," she said, although the only thing she'd been able to think about for the last few days was sleeping with him.

Ray burst into one of his favorite and loudest songs, interrupting their conversation. Cass plugged her ears. Trust Ray to butt in. "He's on a roll now!" she shouted.

Logan nodded to the exit. A wide smile curled his lips. "Shall we?"

Her gaze vacillated between the band and the door. Didn't Les say go for it? She laced her fingers in his hand and tugged him from the bar. In the parking lot, Cass paused to catch her breath. He brushed wispy strands of hair from her face. She ached for his touch. Like an unspoken command, she met him for a kiss. Desire slammed through her body at warp speed.

"Tell me what you want from me and it's yours," Logan said against her lips.

She gazed into his eyes. Her entire body tingled and burned from his touch. "You can't camouflage your celebrity." Butterflies fluttered in her stomach.

He brushed a lock of hair behind her ear. "I don't want that any longer."

She shrugged and shivered, only to have Logan wrap his arms around her once more. She rubbed her cheek against his chest. He smelled like sin. "You can't change who and what you are."

"I will for you." He tangled his fingers in her hair. Pinpricks of electricity tickled her scalp. His sexy groan warmed the junction between her thighs. He looked around. "I want to kiss every inch of you until you scream my name. Can we go somewhere a little more private?"

Cass chewed the inside of her cheek. "We can go to the pond on the far end of my property. It's quiet and secluded. Plus, I can leave you there if you misbehave."

"I like how you think." Logan gave her a quick succession of kisses on her lips, cheeks, nose and temple. "I'll follow you."

She shook her head and fought to catch her breath. "You can't."

He furrowed his brows. The skin around his eyes crinkled.

"Why not?"

"I came with Les. You'll have to take personal directions."

He nodded. "Perfect."

She rode tucked into Logan's arm, listening to the rock station blaring from the radio. She sang along softly with the current song and watched the world streak by.

"You know Death Charge Twenty-Six by Ezra?"

Cass shifted in her seat to smile up at him. Silly man. "You'd be surprised how many songs I know in a variety of genres. Just because I write romance and sing harmony in a country band doesn't mean I'm limited to sappy, romantic music. I like to rock and dirty guitar licks too."

He laughed. "I suppose I underestimated you. I'll bet hanging around with Ray and the boys probably increased your musical vocabulary."

She tucked back into his arm. "You catch on quick."

Logan caressed her shoulder with the pads of his fingers. His contact, even through the cotton, sent superheated sparks to her core. This was where she belonged. He kissed her temple, making it tingle. She rested her hand on his thigh as they crossed the railroad tracks on Hilliard Road. He bounced the truck over the tracks and her hand slid to his groin. His breath caught but he didn't ask her to move.

She grinned. Men like Logan surely wanted wanton, willing women, not cute and cuddly wifey types. She tucked one foot under her butt to whisper in his ear. "Metal is one of my muses, especially when I'm writing sex."

"Sex?" he asked in a husky voice that gave her added confidence.

She unfastened the button on his jeans and stuffed her hand beneath the waistband of his boxer shorts. "Uh-huh." She stole a glance at his face as she wrapped her fingers around his cock. Logan's jaw went slack and his eyelids drooped.

Skittish excitement coursed through her veins. His groan encouraged her exploration. The desire to please him overwhelmed her. She stroked him, learning the nuances of his dick.

Logan gasped. "Honey, if you keep that up, I'll put us in the ditch."

Cass pointed to a dark drive surrounded by towering trees. "Then turn here. The gravel path winds back to the pond. No one will see and you can't run anything over." The idea of loving him this way out in the middle of nowhere seemed crazy and sexy. Her ragged, bruised heart felt light, but full. All because of Logan.

He stopped the truck and switched off the engine. He groaned and shifted as she continued caressing his dick. "I need to..." He lifted his hips long enough to shove his jeans and underwear around his knees.

He grasped the door handle and sucked in his breath.

She blew across the crown of his penis. A drop of fluid glistened on the tip. She licked her lips and kissed the thick head.

Logan brushed her hair away from her face. "Cass, you don't have to..." He trailed off.

She took him to the back of her throat. He felt like satin encasing steel, but tasted like no other. She felt the primal urge to mark him as her own, even if only for the night. He bucked hard against her mouth, signaling the onslaught of his orgasm. She stole a glance to his face. His head was back with his eyes closed. His fingers raked through her hair. Logan's breath became harsh and labored. "Cass! Cass, oh, babe!"

Cass scratched her nails against his nipple through the fabric of his shirt and it pebbled at her touch. A ripple of power radiated from her fingertips. Was she truly capable of giving a man oral satisfaction? The notion sent heat and moisture pooling between her legs.

"Babe, that's right. Fuck, you feel good." He groaned. "Let me be inside you. I need to feel your body around me."

"Yeah." She sat up and unbuttoned her jeans. She needed fast and hard. Needed to know he wanted her.

Logan fumbled in the back pocket of his jeans. "I'm

prepared." He withdrew a condom from his wallet. "Come here."

She kicked out of the tight jeans, panties and her boots, leaving the clothing in a heap on the floor. Cass ran her fingers between her legs. Her pussy juice slicked on her cunt.

"Holy fuck, that's hot." Logan ripped open the condom packet and sheathed himself. He reached for her. "This is where you belong—with me." He grasped her hips and helped her onto his lap.

Cass eased down onto his cock, stretching and filling her pussy with him. Everything within her tensed. She shivered and groaned. With him, sex would never be slow and tender. Fast and frantic fit so much better.

"Fuck yeah." Logan nodded. "So good." He wound his arms around her and held her tight to his chest. The position didn't give her much room to move, but made her feel protected. He sucked on her tongue, mimicking sex.

She rocked on his thighs. Having him inside her soothed the holes in her soul. She draped her arms around his neck and wrenched her mouth from his.

"Yeah." He took control and bounced her on his lap. He lifted her until his cock was just barely within her before plunging her down onto him again. His head lolled on his shoulders and he gasped. "Fuck. Won't last long."

She wanted to answer him, but words escaped her. Her thoughts fuzzed as she fought to catch her breath. Her nipples ached. The orgasm knotted in her belly and fire licked her from within. She rested her forehead against his and moaned.

"Cass," he bit out. His eyebrows knotted and he closed his eyes. "Jesus, I gotta come." He surged into her and tensed. His cock throbbed.

Cass continued to ride him, nudging herself toward climax. She reached between her legs and plucked at her clit. The combination of her fingers on her pussy and him inside her tore through her restraint. She bit down hard on her bottom lip as she gave into the orgasm. From head to toe, she shivered.

For what seemed like an eternity, neither of them spoke. She cuddled in his arms and fought to keep warm. The night wasn't chilly, but with little on, she noticed the temperature change.

"Damn, babe." He petted her hair. "Blew my mind."

"That was the idea," Cass said. When the world around her stopped spinning, she brushed her hair from her eyes.

"Beautiful," Logan said and rubbed her cheek with his thumb. He gulped air. "If I had a question, would you answer it?"

"Sure." She stilled. Something didn't feel right. She ignored her uneasiness and sat up on his lap. "Fire away."

"I wanted to ask you about Dex."

Cass swallowed hard. What a beautiful night…shot to hell by the mention of her bastard ex-husband.

Chapter Nine

Logan didn't try to grab her as she slid off his lap. She scooted back to the passenger side of the truck cab and fumbled into her underwear and jeans.

Fuck. He should've known asking her about Dex would get touchy. Still, he needed to know where she stood with her ex. He removed the used condom and tucked it into the ashtray, then shoved his deflating erection back into his pants.

Cass slid out of the truck and circled to the driver's side. "Okay, let's talk. You wanted to know about Dex?"

Logan rubbed the back of his neck. "Maybe we'd better slow down."

Where did that come from? That wasn't his feeling at all. He hated the tongue-tied feeling he got every time Cass neared. He wanted to be the only man for her and he'd be damned if he left her alone if there was a monster lurking around her house.

She withdrew from the door and folded her arms. "Well, if that's how you feel, then fine. You got what you wanted — again." He felt like she'd kicked him in the balls. He deserved it.

She held up her hands and he noticed the devastation in her eyes. "I'll see you around." She turned and headed away from the pond. Frogs croaked and splashed into the water.

Logan pushed the truck door open and rounded the hood quickly. He captured her in his arms, ready to make up for his stupid comments.

"Cass..."

She wriggled out of his grasp. "No."

He couldn't let her slip through his fingers. "That's not what I meant." He gripped her hand. "I thought..."

Cass shook her head. "I know what you thought. You thought you'd just stroll into my life and destroy the defenses I worked so hard to build. You wanted to prove to the world that you could conquer me. A little hanky-panky on location to satisfy your overall tally before moving on, I suppose? Well, I've been a fool for one man. I won't be a fool for another."

Her words ripped right through him. He deserved every cut and barb. The notion of pulverizing Dex ran rampant in his mind. He didn't want to be the other devil in her life. He didn't want her to walk away. "Our relationship has changed, meaning you need to tell me what I've got to do to make you comfortable. Tell me how far I have to crawl to build you up. I'll do whatever you ask me to do," he pleaded to her back. "I need you and I'm willing to walk away if that's what you want."

She froze. "What did you say?"

"I'll do whatever you want me to. Please look at me."

Cass turned, but didn't meet his gaze. Logan continued to beg. "Ignore my stupidity. I spoke before I thought about what I wanted to say. Please give me – give us – a chance."

Cass sat down on the nearby stone bench. She curled her legs under her body and folded her arms. "I'm not happy, but I'll listen."

Logan exhaled. *Pacing, I need pacing.* "Cass, tell me what you saw the night of the library event."

She flinched. "No."

He sat down next to her. "Fine, then tell me about Dex. I can't forget the scene in the studio lot. Did he hit you often?"

She stared out at the calm water. A tired sigh escaped her lips. "Yes." Her shoulders sagged, ripping his heart out.

Logan inched closer. "He abused you?"

She nodded, but didn't say anything.

He scooted another inch, until he could feel the heat radiating from her body. "So that's why Les and Maggie wanted to slice off my nads."

Cass furrowed her brows and turned. "Excuse me? Did you just say — ?"

He nodded and wrapped her in his embrace. "With a dull blade. I plan to heed their warnings."

She rested her head against his chest and a tear stained his sleeve. From laughing or crying? He didn't know.

"They knew, Logan. They saw what no one knew about. Les orchestrated my exit."

He kissed her temple. "I'm sorry."

She disengaged from his hold and stood. "I'm sure you'll find my story on some fan page, but I'll tell you the God's honest truth. I'm tired of everyone getting it wrong." She stared at him. "I had a relatively long awkward period and believe it or not, I was shy."

Logan drummed his fingers on the back of the bench. "I can see that." He formed a mental picture of Cass at eighteen. Quiet, with an assertive streak ready to bloom and a killer smile. Any man who looked the other way missed out on a gem with gorgeous blue eyes and a heart of gold.

"I met Dex in college at some stupid dorm party during my sophomore year. Even then, he was a master manipulator. Girls flocked to him and I wasn't any different, but unlike the other girls, he developed a fascination with me. I didn't see it. I mean, I only dated two other guys before him and neither was serious. He made it so easy to believe what he said. One night this guy Jonathan, from my photography class, asked me to a movie."

Logan sat up straight. "Jonathan, as in my character?"

She offered a tiny, rueful smile. A slight breeze kicked up, wrapping them in the sweet scent of wildflowers. A goose squawked over their heads. Cass brushed a lock of hair from her eyes. "I liked the name and he was sweet."

He stood up and crossed the small gap to her. "I read

somewhere that you wrote the part with me in mind. Is that true?" Oh, he sounded full of himself now. "I mean—"

"I did." She shrugged. "Jonathan's shoot from the hip style and way with women came directly from me watching way too many of your movies. I didn't know what your personality would be like, but I knew what you looked like. The rest just sort of fell into place."

He took her hand in his, rubbing small circles with his thumb. "What did Dex do when Jonathan asked you out? Did he threaten you?"

She nodded. "Dex said no one understood me like he did. He claimed Jonathan only wanted to see me so we could cram for an exam. I doubt it. He studied aerodynamics and I focused on journalism. We took the photography class for fun."

"So what happened?"

"That night, he waited outside my dorm with my dad and grandmother in tow. When Jonathan showed up, he met the war party—and retreated. He never spoke to me again and I wanted to die from embarrassment. Dex, you see, he saved the situation because it was all his idea to be that way in the first place. He presented me with a diamond and proposed on the spot. He said we were soul mates and fated to be together. Totally outnumbered and dumbfounded, I accepted. The day after I graduated from college, we married in the county courthouse. I didn't even wear a wedding dress because he didn't want to wait. He decided that our next move would be to California." Her chin quivered. She averted her gaze. "A year later my father died of a heart attack, but I didn't find out until days afterward because Dex refused to let me use the phone. He withheld a lot from me."

A tear slipped down her cheek. Logan brushed it away with his thumb and drew her close. "Sweetheart, I'm so sorry."

"No need." She wiped the rest of her tears away and cleared her throat. "I came home in time for the funeral, but my grandmother never forgave me for leaving. She died before I could make peace. I found out later that Dex knew all along, but kept quiet so he could audition for *RollaHead*. He got the part, broke out as an actor and I lost my family."

Her voice came out in a husky whisper that stirred deep feelings in his soul. "So why not leave the no-good bastard right then?"

She ran her fingers though her hair and settled on the edge of the bench. She twined her fingers together. "He was my reality at the time. I didn't know better. But we did have some good times, like our vacation to Niagara Falls. It was like one long date." She chuckled. "Silly, huh? A grown woman not knowing the man she married was a monster. I was, and still am, afraid of him. It didn't matter where, as long as he could strike, he would. But he got smart. Now he doesn't leave visible marks."

Logan sat down next to her and closed his eyes tight. Dex wasn't smart and didn't deserve her pardons, but he was connected to some of her pleasant memories. "The experience made you stronger and forced you to write, didn't it?"

She licked her lips and sighed. "I had to survive." She turned to consider him. "I don't feel sorry for me, though."

He wrapped an arm around her. "I would've kicked his ass."

She snuggled against him. "I'm sure. I'll admit the broken jaw hurt the worst. I'm not laughing about it by any means, but I look at it this way, I survived. I'm stronger than his abuse."

He stiffened and turned. Anger burned in his brain. "He broke your jaw?"

She looked at him with enormous indigo eyes. A crooked frown twisted her lips. "When I didn't smile enough at the *RollaHead* premiere, he punched me during the limo ride home. You can't tell where my jaw bone didn't heal properly."

Logan caressed her cheek where she pointed. She looked

perfect to him. "What else did he make you do? I heard rumors of an eating disorder."

She nodded. "He had an affair with Shanae Mickelson on the set of *Hard Candy* and decided that waifs looked better beside him on the red carpet. He realized that my" — she hooked her fingers in the air — "bulky curves weren't sexy anymore, so I starved myself."

Logan reeled. He remembered the five-foot-nine bottle-blonde twig with fake DD breasts. Hell, he might have dated her once or twice, but he couldn't recall. That didn't matter now.

"I dieted myself to death and didn't eat anything I liked, including chocolate and pasta. Mind you, I'm a sucker for chocolate. When I got down to one-fifteen, Dex said I needed implants because my boobs weren't big enough. I looked awful and he didn't spend any extra time at home. Actually, he went out more, so I drew the line. I could get by on the street better than I did with him. So, I got out."

He stroked her back, more to calm his anger than reassure her. "If he couldn't love you for you, then he never deserved you."

She gazed up at him. The blue hue turned a brilliant shade of sapphire. "Does that include you?"

"Most definitely."

A tiny smile curled the corner of her mouth. "Maybe I don't actually hate you."

He laughed and kissed her again. "I kinda like you too."

"Will you stay with me again tonight?"

He held out his hand. "Let's stop by my trailer first and I'll stay with you as long as you let me."

You have me forever.

She wrapped her arms around his chest. "Don't make me hate you for real."

Logan kissed her temple. He blinked back tears of joy as they walked hand in hand to his temporary home. "Thank you, babe. I'll do everything in my power to show you the love you deserve."

Chapter Ten

Cass stepped into Logan's trailer and bit back a gasp. Except for clothing on the floor, it was bland. Beige carpet lined the floor while cream-colored furniture simply took up space. She detected absolutely no personality in the living area, save for his sloppy piles. An overstuffed cream-colored faux leather couch lumbered against one wall of the cramped space. A rickety-looking desk made of blond wood struggled under the weight of fifteen or so curled scripts.

Logan rummaged through a heap of clothing on the couch. He reminded her of a squirrel seeking nuts. She couldn't help but laugh. "Did you find it?"

He glanced over his shoulder and continued searching. "What?"

"Whatever you were looking for. I don't think it's in there." She shoved a load of paperback novels out of the way. She scanned the titles—a couple of books were about World War II, one about racing and three were her personal works. She pressed her lips together to hide the grin. He really did have her work. The empty space revealed a grainy color photograph with red lettering smeared on the surface. Cass picked it up and immediately dropped it. Her breath caught in her throat. It was Logan with Jade Weir in a tight embrace. Jade had no top on. Someone's handwriting expressed their 'fucking awesome time'. Her stomach clenched. This was too close to home. All the photos and videos of Dex cheating came to mind. Was Logan really any different? She knew he had prior girlfriends. His dating life was daily fodder for the media, but the image, combined with the awful label, tore her apart inside.

Logan turned around and froze.

"You're white as a ghost. What's wrong?"

"Did you forget to toss this?"

Logan bent to pick up the photograph. Deep creases formed on his forehead. "Where did you find this?"

Cass bit the inside of her cheek, forcing her tears away. "The table."

"This picture is over three months old. Look at my hair — that's the spiky style I wore for the last season of *Mending Fences*." He tugged a shaggy lock. "The last time I got it cut was sometime in June. This was probably someone's idea of a sick joke. Tiff likes to play practical jokes, so I wouldn't worry about it."

She glanced at his rumpled hairstyle and swallowed her irritation. Filming took up most of his time and Jonathan was supposed to have shaggy hair.

Still, how did she compare to the pencil-thin woman? Cass shrugged to hide her upset. "You're right. Did you like her? The tabloids made it sound like an obsession." Okay, so that didn't sound as humorous as she intended.

Logan sighed. His shoulders slumped. "Yes, I did at one time. She claimed to be having a relationship with me, but it's not true. You're the only one I want."

Cass exhaled, realizing she'd held her breath. As much as she hated it, she couldn't look away from the offending image. "Right," she said, drawing the word out.

"I can say I wouldn't worry about it, but I understand. It's hard to get that image out of your brain." Logan tucked his laptop into his bag, then grabbed her hand and strolled out of the trailer. "I'm sorry. I don't know who left that picture in my trailer."

As they made their way to the house, Cass noticed a light in the living room. Not like the lamps. "Do you see that?" She stopped and pointed to the tall windows on the back of the house. "There."

Logan stepped in front of her. "Are the dogs loose in the house? Maybe they walked in front of a night light?"

"They're in the kennels in the garage," she whispered. "There's a baseball bat on the wall next to the door in the garage. Get it."

Logan gave her a shaky grin. "Good thinking." He retrieved it. "Stay here and wait until I tell you it's clear," he warned and tucked her behind his arm.

A gunshot split the thick silence in the air. It could be a hunter or it could also be a gun-wielding psycho murderer.

Cass covered her mouth to hide the shrieks and dug her body into Logan's. Across the garage, Paula and Elliott waited patiently for attention in their respective crates.

He cupped her chin. "Will you stay with the dogs until I make sure no one's out there?" She nodded. "I mean it, Cass, stay here. And call nine-one-one on your cell."

"I will." She shook with uncontrolled fear. Who wanted to do her or the dogs harm? Or was the person gunning for Logan? "Please be careful. I can't dislike you if you're dead."

He cocked his brow and chuckled. "I'll be right back, I promise." With that he crept from the garage.

Cass closed the door and released the dogs from their crates. Every possible scary scenario ran through her mind. Logan could get shot, stabbed or end up bleeding and mutely calling her name. She raked her fingers over Paula's coat. Elliott growled. He sensed the danger too. She felt every nerve in her body snap to attention. According to the clock, only ten minutes had passed since Logan had left. She swiped the main screen on her phone and dialed emergency.

The door to the garage opened a crack. Elliott growled and Paula quaked. Cass' blood ran cold. How could such a wonderful night turn so ugly? She forced herself to speak. "Logan?"

The door opened and Logan carefully eased into view.

"It's safe, but you have a broken window." He still held the bat. "Whoever it was, they wanted to send a message." He held up another copy of the picture.

Cass crept away from the dog to read the note. *A coward dies a thousand times, a hero only once. Don't be a hero.*

Who considered her a hero? Or was the message meant for Logan? He'd give his life for Cass. "What does it mean?"

Logan rubbed his forehead with the back of his hand. "I wish I knew."

Flashing blue and red lights flooded the garage. Cass slumped against Logan and sobbed. "I want my peaceful life back."

Sheriff Mackenzie met them at the front door. "Hi, Cass. We don't come out here to check on you enough. I should've guessed there would be an issue because of Dex. Where's the problem?"

Cass watched in amazement as Logan took charge. He directed the normally intimidating officer to the window. "Someone broke the glass with this rock." He pointed to the far wall of the living room. "The bullet hole is over there, but earlier today I came to the house to speak to Cass and I noticed a set of footprints under her living room window. I took a picture with my phone."

Who wanted to wreck the flowers? And why did Logan sneak around her house? The living room flowerbed was on the north end, away from the deck. Nothing made sense besides the headache thrumming behind her eyes.

The sheriff flipped open his pocket notebook and proceeded to take notes. He shook his head as he wrote. "Marlon, get in here and extract that bullet. Good thing you did that guest spot on that crime show, Mr. Malone, you've helped. I'll have one of my men check out the flowerbeds for those prints. Mind if I ask who's in charge of security for the film set?" Logan rubbed Cass's arm. "Wasn't it the Stockard Company?"

She chewed the corner of her mouth and wiped her cheeks dry. "Correct, but their parameters don't include the house, only the cabin and adjacent fields. The production company wouldn't pay the bill to secure the entire area."

The sheriff nodded again. "I see. Seems like waste to hire a property and not protect all of it."

Deputy Marlon Cross strode into the room. Only three years older than Cass, he looked far younger with his bright emerald eyes and copper-colored sideburns tapering around his baby face. "I'll check for casings outside when I'm done." He elbowed past the sheriff and turned to Logan. "Good eyes, but a lousy show."

Logan scrunched his nose as the deputy walked away. Cass laughed despite her fear. "Romeo isn't jealous, is he?"

He cupped her chin and backed her into the kitchen. He stroked her cheek with the pad of his thumb. "I'm territorial," he murmured.

Sheriff Mackenzie spoke into his radio, then he taped off the living room. "So you plan to stay here tonight or are you making other arrangements?" he asked, interrupting her private moment. "I'm sure Ray wouldn't mind the visitor."

Logan frowned. "Why would she stay with Ray?"

She gripped Logan's hand and spoke to the sheriff. "I want to be with the dogs. This is our home. I'm tired of living in fear."

Logan wrapped his arms around her and stroked her hair. "I don't want to compromise anything, but you're right. You shouldn't have to live in fear. I'll tell the guards to increase their presence up here, if the sheriff allows it."

The sheriff smoothed his thick salt and pepper moustache with his thumb and index finger. "Well, it isn't wise. The perpetrator may come back." He switched his weight from his left foot to his right and scratched his chin. "I'll dispatch Ronan Levine to keep an eye on the place. He's off tonight, but I'm sure he could use the overtime to pay his alimony."

Cass gave her preliminary statement then headed back to the garage to take care of the dogs. When she glanced out the window, another police vehicle followed a rusty red pickup up the lane. Once Mackenzie assured her Ronan was in place and she'd be fine, Cass locked the front door. Her strength dissipated and she sank to the floor. The dogs crawled onto her lap. She wanted to cry, but the tears weren't there. Hell, nothing was there.

"Are you going to be okay?" Logan knelt in front of her. "I'm sorry, babe."

She sighed. "Lock the doors. We'll crash upstairs."

Cass made her way to the second floor. She switched on the lights and hefted Paula and Elliott onto the bed. She sank onto the mattress and buried her face in the pillow. She wanted the world to go away except for the dogs and Logan.

Logan brought his laptop into the room. He sat down beside her and clicked on the Internet. "I want to show you something."

Cass held her breath. A cloud of panic settled around her heart. The Internet wasn't scary on its own. Heck, it was one of her favorite resources to connect with her fans and fellow writers. But something about the concerned way he spoke made her blood turn to ice.

He pointed to the screen. "What's this about? Let me understand."

She buried her face in her hands to prevent the oncoming nausea as she looked at the webpage. God, there was no explanation for what she saw and now anyone with a computer would know how low she'd sunk to keep her ex-husband at home. Yeah, she'd lost the weight, but she didn't look like herself. She wanted to melt into the floor to hide.

Logan placed the machine on the nightstand. He cupped her jaw to meet his gaze. The creases around his eyes deepened. "This wasn't your idea, was it?"

Cass shook her head. "I knew about the picture, but I didn't know he posted it."

"How many times has he tried to re-enter your life?"

"More than I can count. He hates to lose. He probably posted that image to remind me of what we had. He forgets it's over."

Logan curled his fingers into a fist. "The ass."

She inadvertently cringed and scooted away from him. She trusted him, but the old feelings of worry, dread and fear came back in waves. She'd probably never be able to see a fist without wincing.

"Fuck." Logan dipped his head. "You shouldn't have to live in fear of anyone — even me."

She stole a glance at the laptop. She knew nothing of the site. How many other people had seen that image? "I'm afraid to find out how you came across that webpage."

He closed the computer. "I researched you."

Cass paused. "You what?"

"I looked you up on the Internet. It seemed like a good thing to do at the time."

"God." She buried her face in her hands. "I should've known. Nikita probably egged him on and I wouldn't be surprised if she planted those pictures. "

"Why?"

"She's Dex's sister. That makes her a prime suspect."

The color bled from Logan's face. "His sister? That sister? Her last name is Cline, not Rose."

Cass snorted. Logan didn't know? He'd screwed around with Nikita and never met Dex? "Who else? She's the one he told you to go play with instead of me," she said. "They have different fathers."

Logan shoved his hands into his hair, making it stand on end. "That explains a lot. But…"

Cass smoothed the invisible wrinkles on the bedspread. Nothing made sense. "What do you mean?"

"A year and a half ago, I chased Jade to Jamaica trying to get a date with her. We used to club on the weekends and I thought she was into me. The only thing that woman is into is endless supplies of money. Jade's a one-woman hurricane."

Cass scrunched her brows. "What's that got to do with Nikita and Dex?"

"Nikita didn't like being the other woman in my life. I broke things off with her for Jade." He offered a thin smile. "I had fucked-up priorities back then. My recent financial issues sorted them out for me."

Her brain ached. The media claimed Logan made over three million per picture last year alone. "You make movies. Don't you get paid handsomely?"

"No." He frowned. "Once everyone gets their cut, I'm left with very little. What I did make, I drank away at the clubs and blew trying to keep up with Jade. My ego was the size of Europe."

She pursed her lips, teasing him. "Oh."

He cupped her chin and winked. "I had a reality check that helped deflate it a bit."

She laughed nervously, but didn't pull away. "So why do my movie? We have a miniscule budget."

Logan shrugged. "It's a stupid reason."

"Let me get something." He rummaged through his bag, then handed her a worn copy of *Broken Wheels*. Her heart soared and she momentarily forgot her fear. Had she touched him with her writing? "My book?"

"Your writing is fine, but no." He flipped to the back. "I saw your picture in the back of the book and was intrigued. Your eyes and that smile captivated me. It's like you knew a secret you wouldn't tell. I fantasized about you."

Cass looked at Logan with wide eyes. He'd masturbated to her picture? The tips of her ears burned. "Oh." That pose came from a series of pictures Maggie had suggested she use for promotions. Maggie had tousled her hair to make it ooze sex. Cass remembered wearing a favorite blue sweater. She had trusted the photographer to airbrush the evidence of Dex's abuse that morning. Apparently the sexy look Maggie had intended worked for Logan. A sizzle burned low in her belly. She liked being the object of his fantasies.

"I did read this one and not just to research the part. Honest."

She fingered the well-creased binding. "I can tell."

Logan pointed to the image. "Besides the horniness, I wanted to meet the woman who wrote such intense love scenes. I figured she must have the hottest sex life. The jerk in me wanted to get tips." He caressed her back, like she was a treasure. "The heroine served as my image of you and I wanted to meet that hot babe."

Her temperature spiked. He'd wanted to meet her. No warning about her past, no signs disclosing her issues... Logan wanted her. "Your script writer showed up today."

Logan shrugged. "Yeah. I'm slowly becoming the king of smooth."

Cass studied his chiseled profile. "I agree."

"I begged Carmine to get me an audition." He wrapped his arm around her. "He said you settled on Speed, but I wanted the role more than my next breath. I figured I wouldn't get it, but I might get to meet the woman of my dreams."

"And that corny line about getting flustered wasn't just a line? You told the truth, didn't you?" Plain old Cass with hips, a bigger-than-average backside and an average rack flustered a sexy, hard-bodied actor, known as one of 'America's Hunkiest Men'. Maybe she was sexier than Dex claimed. She couldn't argue with Logan's logic or withhold her growing smile. He lusted for her. *No freakin' way!*

"Cass... I'm sorry if I —"

Cass placed the pad of her index finger on his lips to quell his apology. "Shh. I'm honored. Stunned, but honored." It wasn't every day she managed to bring a desirable man to awed silence. "So where does that leave us?"

He grasped her hand and kissed her knuckles. The amber and green flecks smoldered in his eyes. "I'll be honest. I like you, Cass. I wanted to get to know you. From the moment I saw you at the audition, I fell for you and hoped maybe you'd like me too."

What was she supposed to say to that?

"I want to make love to you every night and wake up to your gorgeous face every morning. I want to know that

I'm the man fulfilling your wildest fantasies and I want to know you're safe. Is it too early to feel that way? Probably, but I'm an all-in kind of guy."

She crawled into his lap and slid her palms along his chest. "Make love to me."

"Hell yes." Logan gasped and eased his hands under her shirt. "After the dogs move onto the floor. Come on, guys. Down." Once the dogs had scrambled onto their dog bed, Logan caressed her back then eased the garment over her breasts. He feasted on her mouth and swallowed her ragged breaths. He broke the connection long enough to tug the shirt up over her head, then resumed kissing her.

She rocked on his lap, rubbing her denim-covered pussy on the bulge in his pants. Fire licked her from within and she leaned back in his arms to catch her breath. A whimper escaped her throat as he palmed her ass.

"So beautiful." Logan buried his face in her cleavage. He nipped and kissed the upper swell of her chest. With the flick of his fingers, he unhooked her bra and bared her breasts. "Better." He sucked one nipple into his mouth and palmed the other.

Her head lolled on her shoulder. Her nerve endings sizzled and she threaded her fingers into his hair. "Logan."

"Right here," he said against her boob.

"Feels good." She tugged on his hair. "So good."

"Stretch out." He draped her on the bed on her back, then scooted off the mattress. He stood long enough to pop the button on her jeans and tug the denim down her legs, leaving her in nothing but her panties.

She sucked in her stomach and held her breath. She couldn't look him in the eye. She trusted him, but he had so much power.

"Don't hide from me." Logan settled between her thighs and planted his knees. He crouched over her. "You're gorgeous." He left a trail of heat in his wake as he kissed his way down her throat to her chest. He nipped the top of her breast and pinched her nipple before licking around her belly button.

Logan caressed her pussy through the fabric of her panties, pressing on her clit every so often. Electricity shot through her body. How did he know right where to touch to send her senses reeling?

Cass squirmed as he dragged her panties down her legs. He blew warm air across her pussy lips, then parted her thighs. He knelt on the floor and buried his face in her cunt. He peppered the sensitive skin with licks, nips and soft bites. He slid one finger into her channel and she squirmed.

Excitement shot through her veins. He had her flustered and focused on his attention to her pussy. She tingled and her blood warmed to fever. Her legs trembled as he pumped his finger in and out of her cunt.

She gripped the sheets and shivered. "Logan." Her thoughts fuzzed.

"Right here." He added another finger to her pussy and continued to pump. "Ready to come apart?" He smoothed his free hand over her belly and up to her breast. He pinched her nipple.

The combination of pleasure-filled pain on her breast and the fullness in her pussy sent her into orbit—not that she'd hold back. She welcomed the climax.

"Logan," she said, her voice breathy. "Oh wow." She could've sworn she was floating. She closed her eyes and basked in the light, airy sensation.

"I'm just getting warmed up," Logan said. "Can't get enough of you."

When she opened her eyes, Logan stood over her. He'd already peeled his clothes off. He tore the corner of the condom packet and sheathed himself.

She wanted to reach for him and tell him she'd put the rubber on him, but her body refused to cooperate. Instead, she allowed him to drape her right leg on his shoulder. He eased his dick into her cunt with slow strokes. His brow furrowed and he drew in a ragged breath.

"Christ, you're so wet." Logan filled her to the hilt and

136

paused. "I'll never get over the way you feel around me. So tight and perfect."

With the different angle, he managed to touch a new place inside her. The instant thrill and bliss overwhelmed her. She covered her breasts with her hands and met his gaze. Passion burned in his eyes and a bead of sweat slid down his temple.

"Fuck," Logan bit out. He slid in and out of her with deliberate thrusts. He filled her, then pulled most of the way out before starting again. "You make me want to come apart on contact."

"Uh-huh." She couldn't breathe or think and was rather proud of her more-or-less coherent answer. She rode the wave of excitement and trembled again. She arched her back, allowing him deeper access.

"Babe." Logan's thrusts increased. The springs on the bed creaked and the headboard connected with the wall again. "Fuck," he growled and closed his eyes. He tensed and shoved deep into her cunt. The sound of him grunting split the relative silence in the room. "Holy shit." Logan opened his eyes and added a few slower thrusts. He rested his forehead on hers and stilled within her body.

She couldn't move—not that she wanted to. She liked simply existing with him and sharing the perfect moment. She never thought she'd find someone who both consumed her and set her free the way he did.

Logan broke the silence first and kissed her. "I bet none of your fans ever did that." He chuckled. "I hope they haven't anyway."

"You're an original." She kissed him back and draped her arms around his neck. "I'm glad you showed up at that audition."

Elliot trotted over to the side of the bed, snorted, then strolled back to the dog bed and plopped down.

Cass chuckled. "Guess he wanted attention."

Logan nuzzled her cheek. "They want to protect you and might like me, but they're not sure about me."

She twined her legs with his and curled her arm around his waist. "Don't give them reason to change their minds," she murmured.

"Sweetheart, I'll do my best to never hurt you."

Cass barely nodded. Her body felt weightless and ultimately satisfied. She trailed her tongue along the prickly growth of beard dusting his neck, tasting salty sheen of perspiration covering his skin. "I'm easy, aren't I?" she asked in a whisper.

"You just needed to meet the right man to bring out your inner wild woman." Logan tucked her hair behind her ear. His nails scratched the row of silver hoops decorating her lobe. "Babe, we have a lot of catching up to do. I'll show you what a sexy, sensual woman you really are, but it's late and I'm tapped out."

"Me too."

"I want to stay here with you, but I should go to the trailer."

She frowned. "Have you lost your mind?"

Logan kissed her knuckles. "I'm afraid whoever wants to hurt you is doing it because of me. I'm worried that me being here will put you in danger."

Cass crawled on top of him and planted her knees firmly on either side of his waist. "I'm scared, tired and in desperate need of comfort from a male. I want one who is about thirty-one years old, with shaggy dark hair, hazel eyes, and a killer smile. He has to know how to use his hands and make a woman scream his name. He must love pushy dogs and must be willing to provide protection against potential burglars, assassins or nosy directors. Know anyone like that?"

Logan cupped her face in his hands. "Would you settle for a thirty-two-year-old?" He brushed his lips in a caress over her mouth. Her tongue twined with his, teasing him.

Cass shivered and inhaled his earthy scent. How could one man affect her so completely? She slid her knees down to align their bodies. His erection rubbed against her pussy lips, making her groan. "I feel much safer. Stay so I can snuggle against you for the rest of the night."

His eyes lit up and he wriggled out of his boxer shorts. "All you had to do was say so."

Chapter Eleven

Hours later, Logan surfaced from sleep. When he palmed the sheet, Cass wasn't beside him. A streak of fear shot through him. Where was she? He sat up and scrubbed both hands over his face to help him wake up. He sniffed the air. A hint of something frying lingered around him. Bacon? Potatoes? He wasn't sure, but he wanted to find out.

He stepped into his boxer shorts and wandered downstairs. When he rounded the corner, he located the source of the enticing smells. Cass padded around the kitchen in an oversized T-shirt and a pair of boxer shorts emblazoned with garish red and yellow race cars. For a man who normally liked curve-hugging clothes on women, her disheveled look drove him bananas. He scratched himself, running his hand over his morning wood. Damn, he wanted to fuck her right there on the kitchen counter.

"That smells wonderful." Logan eased up behind her and snagged her in his arms. Bacon sizzled in a large skillet. A concoction of eggs and potatoes crackled in another pan. His heart warmed. This was a first in his life. No woman had cooked for him except his mother and grandmother.

She snuggled into him. "Thank you."

Enticed by her soft flesh, he nipped her neck. "You smell wonderful, like a satisfied woman."

Cass clicked off the stovetop and spun around in his arms. He nudged her down the counter to ensure her back wasn't against the heat and wedged himself in his new favorite place — between her thighs.

"I slipped away to make this and to let you sleep. You have a big day today. Why don't you rest and I'll bring this up when I'm done?" Cass asked.

Logan kissed the tip of her nose, cheeks, her temples and finally her lips. He couldn't get enough of her. "No, I'm up. Plus, you don't need to serve me breakfast in bed. I should serve you."

"Good Lord, don't start a fight over food." She crinkled her nose, but her eyes glittered. "We do need to go back upstairs so I can show you something."

Logan raised a brow and followed hot on her heels. She yanked him back into her bedroom. They collapsed in a tangle of arms and legs on her bed. He took pride in being an alpha male, but the sinful look in her eyes and sly smile on her lips suggested relinquishing control would benefit them both. "Oh, babe." His heart raced and his mouth went dry. "Cass, you're trouble and I live for trouble."

She grinned and slid down to her knees. With tentative strokes, she explored him. He groaned. The more she touched, the more he wanted to be with her forever. She eased his cock free of his boxer shorts and ran her finger along the thick shaft.

Logan rose up on his elbows. "You don't have to do this. I... Oh, honey. Fuck." He sank onto the bed and moaned. Too late. She had him right where she probably wanted him and he didn't care. Cass licked her lips and kissed the crown of his erection. "You taste like wine too," she rasped and ran her tongue along the underside of his cock. "Do you like this?"

Logan fell back against the mattress. Like? This was way more than liking... This was on the verge of love. Hell yes, he loved her. He nodded sharply, followed by another groan. He needed her more than his next breath.

She continued to lick his penis then took his cock between her lips all the way to the back of her throat. She explored his sac and caressed the sensitive flesh. She alternately caressed and lapped him, savoring him. She was hot, wet pleasure meant only for him.

Logan lost himself in the feeling. She made him feel

special. "Oh, God, Cass... Cass!" He threaded his fingers into her hair, gently guiding her but still allowing her to set the pace. She increased her attention to his dick and her hair tickled his thighs. "Baby, I'm on the ragged edge."

She didn't let go, but rather held on tighter and bobbed her head. Each lick and suck pushed him closer to climax.

Logan shuddered. "I'm coming." He let go of her hair and gripped her comforter. He rode the tidal wave of emotion — love, lust, devotion and passion. No more denying. Logan was in love with Cass. She gave him freedom in her arms. Without missing a beat, Cass took him to the back of her throat once more. She swallowed his seed and moaned. He closed his eyes. He couldn't see her cleaning him up, but he felt the extra licks on his cock before she released him.

He wanted to hold her, but needed a few moments for his world to stop spinning. He kept his eyes closed and gulped for air. Damn, she pleased him.

After a few moments, Logan reached for Cass. "Babe, that was extraordinary."

She sidled up next to him on the bed. He wrapped her in his embrace and gasped for breath. Cass kissed his neck. "Yeah, it was pretty awesome for me too."

Her gravelly voice turned him inside out, sending blood rushing to his erection. "I want to make love to you, right now." He smoothed his hands over her breasts. Her breathing hitched and he came completely unglued. He needed her at that very moment, more than his next breath. "Tell me you love me."

Cass nodded. "Yes."

Logan needed to hear the words out loud. "Yes, what?" *Please let her feel the same.*

Cass rose up on her elbows. "Yes, Logan, I love you. It's crazy. I haven't loved anyone in a long time," she puffed. "I fell for you back in California. I needed you to say it first, because I was afraid you didn't feel the same."

That was all the persuasion he needed. Logan pulled the T-shirt over her head in one fluid movement. He caressed the soft curves of her hip and belly, then smoothed the shorts down her legs. "Babe, you're beautiful."

"You are too, Logan."

He fumbled for a moment. No one ever told him he was beautiful and meant it. Women told him he was handsome and sexy, which amounted to nothing more than empty Hollywood flattery. Most of his ex-girlfriends said he was a bastard and a narcissist and he agreed. Then again, there was no one in his life like Cass. She saw him for who he was, plain old Logan Malone. A man trying to squeeze into a mold that had no perfect fit. He palmed her cunt and speared his index finger between her pussy lips. Already wet and primed, God, she knew how to please him. "Spread your legs for me. Show me your world," he said and filled her with two fingers. She wouldn't need much more prepping.

"Love when you do that." She hooked her arms around her knees, allowing him total access.

Logan removed his fingers and stood long enough to undress. In seconds, he eased between her legs and lined up the blunt head of his dick with her cunt. She squeezed him, but accepted him into her body. He pumped his hips. Damn. When he looked into her eyes, he couldn't hold back. She owned him — heart and soul. He wanted this woman in his arms for the rest of his life.

"Logan." Her lips parted and her eyelids drooped. Her warm breath skittered over his cheeks.

"You're so tight. You fit me like a glove." Logan slid all the way into her and he leaned over her for a kiss. He wasn't going to be able to keep himself in check. Not like this. He fixed his gaze on hers and pumped in and out of her body. He'd never get enough of the look on her face, the passion and desire burning in her eyes. She met him thrust for thrust and her cunt clamped tight around him. Didn't she want the moment to end? He sure as hell didn't, either. He punctuated his thrusts with kisses all over her face. She loved him. How the hell had he become so lucky that he could not only be with her, but have her affections too? He didn't know and refused to question his good fortune.

Cass tensed around him and whimpered. She closed her eyes. Her forehead shimmered with perspiration. "Logan. I can't—oh my God." She trembled and dug her fingernails into his shoulders.

His head swam. God, he loved her.

Yes. Loved. Her.

He groaned. "Fuck, yes." He fed off the energy of her orgasm and gave into the tingles in his belly. He shuddered. His restraint tore as he slammed his dick into her cunt.

Mine for always.

Cass squealed and collapsed in release. He could only imagine what went on in her head. Did she run on pure sensation or was this an experience to file away for later? Would she want to repeat it? He wanted to make love to her every night, every day forever.

"Fuck." He emptied his seed in her pussy and closed his eyes. She'd wrung him out. From head to toe, his body screamed for rest. But he'd loved every second of sex with her. She brought out his primal side and his passionate one too.

Logan collapsed on top of her and braced himself with his elbows and knees. He needed to feel her, to share her warmth and light. "So good. I don't know how I ever enjoyed sex before you."

She cupped his face in both hands. "Me neither."

Time to take charge and gamble with his heart. "I love you, Cass." He buried his face in her neck, kissing and tasting her salty skin. Yeah, this was right where he needed to be—in her arms and in her life as her man.

The shrill ring of the phone interrupted their comfortable mood. Cass shook her head. "Oh, no. Not now."

The answering machine picked up after five rings. "Cass! This is Nikita. I know you're home, so pick up the phone, Chunks. Look, I can't find Malone. We have only a handful of shots left—the ass shots. I assume he's with you because he seems to like you, but I don't know why. Have you seen him? Call me on my cell once you find the phone. This is ridiculous."

Logan frowned. No wonder Maggie warned him. Cass deserved so much more. His voice came out in an unintentional growl. "Chunks? Tell me she's not referring to you."

Cass averted her eyes. Color rose in her cheeks. "She thinks it's cute," she admitted softly.

Logan growled. No one called the love of his life Chunks. Hell no. Nikita had issues of her own, including her atrocious sense of style and foul mouth. He erased the message. Without leaving her embrace, he grabbed the handset and dialed Nikita's number. He set the receiver to the speaker setting. "I've had enough of this."

After two rings, Nikita answered. "Cass? Where were you? We need—"

"She's busy, with me," Logan replied gruffly and pressed the button to disconnect the call. He kissed the tip of Cass' nose and grinned. She deserved the world and he'd try his damnedest to make it happen.

She exhaled and her breath fanned over his chest. "I suppose this means you're late for filming?"

Logan shrugged. "I don't care. They've made it this far without me. What's another hour or two?"

She shook her head and chuckled. "You're in her gun sights."

"She wants more than that, but I'm not taking the bait." Logan laughed. "Besides, we're filming the love scene today. After that, we have a bunch of close-ups and second-unit stuff that they'll want to do before we head back to California. Soon we can have all afternoon and night without interruptions." He nibbled on her neck, needing a few more moments with her.

"Oh, Logan..."

He palmed her breast and her nipples pebbled under his touch. "Yes, babe," he murmured against her neck. "Say

145

my name. Scream it at the top of your lungs. Tell me you want me."

Cass moaned. "You know I do."

He smoothed his fingers down to her thighs. As if on silent command, she opened to him. "Yes," he murmured. "Beautiful." He caressed her searing cunt lips. As he pinched her clit between his thumb and index finger, the phone rang.

"What the hell?" he asked and plopped backward onto the bed.

"I'll bet that's an angry call," Cass said. "You weren't ready and willing to go back to work this morning."

Logan picked up the receiver and contemplated flinging it out onto the backyard. He switched the setting to speaker again. "Malone. Talk to me."

Cass groaned. "They might be calling for me, you know."

After the nasty call from Nikita, he didn't give a shit who was on the phone.

"Logan, this is Maggie. You remember, the associate director? Yes, I'm sure you and Cass do. I seem to be running interference between you and Nikita."

Logan palmed Cass' bare butt. "Yes, Mags. We got a call a little bit ago. Why isn't Ania dealing with Nikita?"

Maggie groaned. "Because she's spitting fire. Ania was smart enough to hide. She claimed a doughnut run as an excuse. And, Cass, I'll get you for telling him my nickname."

"Oh, well." Cass giggled. "Add it to the already long list of things I did wrong."

"Logan, I need you here in an hour, ready to do the scene."

Logan bit back a groan. That blasted scene again. "I'll be there. I know my lines. Mind if I bring Cass, or at least invite her to watch?" Knowing Cass was there to see his performance would make the scene so much easier. Then again, the hard part would be keeping his hands off her.

"Sure," Maggie said. "I could use the added friend support myself. Ania's a sweet woman, but I don't trust her not to blab to Nikita. I'll look forward to showing you our set, Cass."

"Perfect. I'll see you in an hour-ish," Logan replied. Why not see how long he could postpone the inevitable?

"Less than!" Maggie shouted.

Logan disconnected the call. So she didn't buy his stall tactic. Oh well. "As you heard, that's my day. Nude with the wrong woman and missing the right one the entire time." He began nibbling on her neck. His leg swung over hers, as if to pin her down. "I need you there for moral support and incentive to finish as soon as possible so we can get back to bed."

Cass sat up and yanked the blankets over her chest. "The nude scene."

"You wrote the scene. Don't you remember?"

Talk me out of it, Cass. Please. Tell me to stay.

She shrugged. "I write a lot of nude scenes, it's just hard to picture your man involved in one of them when it's not with you. Make sense?"

"I hear you." Logan caressed her stomach through the bedding. "But for now it's part of the job. I'm not real keen on the idea myself. I'd rather you were Sophie."

The phone rang once more, except this time it was Logan's.

"I'll bet that's Nikita." Cass sat up. She dragged the sheet with her as she left the bed. "She's ready and you're not able."

"I don't care. I'm good right where I am."

"Logan." Cass rolled her eyes. "You can't hide from her forever. I should know because I've tried."

"Would help if she wasn't so fucking Nikita." He swiped his finger across the screen to answer the call. "Malone." He rubbed his cheek against her pillow, as if to mark himself with her sweet scent.

"Honey, I need you. I miss that tight little ass of yours," Nikita purred on her end of the line.

Logan gritted his teeth. "I'm busy. I told Mags I'd be down there in half an hour. I'll see you then." With that parting comment, he disconnected the call. Screw her fixation with his ass.

"Half an hour? You told Mags an hour," Cass called from the other room.

Logan forced himself out of bed and into the bathroom. He eased up behind Cass, as she brushed her teeth. "I always tell Nikita the wrong time. It confuses her. Hey, I'm too busy getting wrapped up in you."

Cass spit out the foam. "Well, it's probably better this way."

He cringed. "What do you mean?"

Cass spun around in his embrace and wrapped her arms around his neck. "I got a call from my editor, Naya Jones. She wants my short story by the end of the week. She's pressing for me to finish the novel by the end of September."

He pouted. "It's only August twenty-second."

She toyed with the fringe of hair at the nape of his neck. "Yes, but I'm generally early with my work. Being late must mean I'm distracted. Naya doesn't know about us and she wouldn't appreciate it being left out of the loop."

Logan dropped his hands. His shoulders sagged with defeat. "You're ashamed of me?"

Cass pecked him on the lips. "No, but my work coming in late drives her nuts. Late equals lack of conviction in her book. I gotta get back in the game and finish, that's all."

Logan puffed out a long breath and nibbled her bottom lip. He caressed her hip in lazy circles. "So I'm a happy distraction?"

Cass beamed. "The best."

He liked being the best.

Chapter Twelve

Cass clapped her hands together and cheered. She'd been in front of the computer for almost five straight hours, but she'd finished the short story. She spun the office chair around. The sound of canine nails on hardwood preceded the dogs as they bounded into her office.

"I think we deserve time in the sunshine! What do you think?" Just as she spoke, the phone rang. She saved the document and picked up the receiver. "Hello?"

"Cass."

She gritted her teeth and a shiver ran the length of her spine. This wasn't the man she wanted to talk to. "What do you want, Dex?"

"Now, Cass. I hear you have a boy toy," he said, his voice smooth.

"Yes, I have a new man in my life. Is that a problem?" She was courting the devil's wrath by irritating him, but she couldn't hide from him forever.

"Don't try to walk away from me. I'll let him know about your—*our* past. He won't like knowing you're damaged and used up. But me, I still love you and can cherish you the way you deserve."

Cass blinked and blindly slapped at the papers on her desk. Her heart lodged in her throat. "Dex—"

Instead of letting her answer, he hung up. She slumped in her seat. She closed her eyes and tried to process his vague threat. Great. One more skeleton thrown in her face by the devil. What was next? A tax audit? Did she have a root canal scheduled that she'd forgotten about?

She patted the dogs and turned back to the blank computer screen. "Let's make a treat and visit the set. Want to see Logan?"

Both dogs wriggled around her ankles. She'd take that as a yes. Cass saved the document once more, but this time onto a reusable disc and headed downstairs with her laptop under her arm and the two dogs hot at her heels.

For the next two hours, she mixed cookie dough, baked and worked from her laptop on the novel. She kept herself busy, but sometimes Dex's threats and the break-in came to mind. Some of the stress went away as she snuck a few bites of raw cookie dough. Words flowed more freely from her fingers, giving more meat to the skeletal novel. Right now her priority was to finish so she could spend unhindered time with Logan.

When the buzzer sounded, she switched off the timer and the oven, then removed the pan of cookies from the heat. "Last batch is done," she called to the dogs. "Should I take some to the workers?"

Elliott barked and knocked over a plant with his tail.

Puppies... She shook her head. "Okay, I'll take some to the crew and give a couple to Logan. But first, I need to clean up the mess you made." She cleaned up after the dog and made a mental note to move the plants from the floor.

Once she'd put the broom and dustpan away, Cass packed the cookies in four airtight containers. She patted her pocket, making sure the key was still there. She hoped Logan would appreciate the surprise.

She put the dogs on the dog run and walked to the set. A bead of sweat trickled between her shoulder blades. The idea of bringing a wagon occurred to her halfway along the journey. No matter. Soon she'd get to see Logan and distribute the fruits of her afternoon labor.

She spotted Ronan, her plainclothes cop, pretending to sleep in the cab of his truck. His cowboy boot-clad feet sat propped up on the dash and his hat covered most of his face. He almost reminded her of Ray — minus about thirty pounds of lean muscle. She snuck over to his position and left a baggie of cookies on the dashboard.

As she crept away, she heard Ronan's quiet reply. "Thanks, Cass."

She shifted the boxes higher in her arms and continued on her way. Before she could enter her own cabin, she signed the visitor's log. The security guards nodded and took a baggie of cookies each. The blond guard who looked like a body double for Logan stopped her. "We'll keep an eye on the house. Logan told us the score. We got your back."

He told them? Part of her was annoyed and embarrassed that he'd mentioned the break-in to anyone. The rest of her appreciated his protective nature. She winked. "Thank you."

"Do you know a black-haired guy, about thirtyish? I noticed him looking in your windows. I thought he was a crew member, but I haven't seen him since I spooked him."

She scrunched her nose. "He doesn't sound familiar, but I'll make sure to lock my doors and close the curtains from now on. Thanks."

Two crew members rested on the front porch. Cass called to the man sitting on the railing. "Closing down time, or are you on a union break?"

"Funny," the bald one called in return. "Comin' to see us?"

She grinned. "I thought I'd bring a sugary treat because I know you all work hard without enjoying the financial benefits the others get." She handed them each a cookie. "You deserve a something nice every once in a while and you know I have a soft spot for the folks behind the scenes."

The dark-haired grip returned her grin. "You thought you could buy us off with sweets?"

Cass nodded. "Is it working?"

"I heard you donated the rent money to increase our wages," the bald one said. "No rent at all?"

"Nope. You're not bothering me and the movie puts some of my land to use, so why not donate and help others?"

"Wish there were more out there like you," the other one said. "You treat us like human beings."

"You should be treated that way because you are and you're welcome." The grunts were the ones who deserved the most thanks and the highest wages. Hearing their thanks was payment enough. "Here's the box for you all. Share," Cass instructed in her most motherly tone. "I'm taking some inside for the others. See ya!"

Once inside the cabin, she did a double take. She hardly recognized the space. All her rustic furniture, what she pictured would be in Jonathan's home, was gone and replaced with modern-style furnishings. The log planks were hidden behind a layer of gold paperboard. If this was what the powers that be thought of her location, then how had they butchered her storyline?

"Cass?"

She spun around. The queasiness subsided a bit. "Hey, Mags!" She held up the remaining containers and grinned. "I brought refreshments."

"Perfect. I could use the calories. Nikita's making filming difficult today." She snatched a cookie from the bin. "Yum! You always did make the best chocolate chip cookies."

Cass eased the lid onto the remaining box. "Thank you. What's Nikita's problem? As if I don't know."

"She wants to practice each scene with Logan before they shoot," Maggie said through a mouthful. "It's not pretty because he flatly refuses. Nikita thinks he needs a choice of women. Neither one will back down, so we're gonna be here all night."

"I see. It's sad what a girl will do for a man and unfortunately, I should know. Can I watch or will Nikita get pissed?"

Maggie laughed. "She's pissed, but it's my movie too, so snoop away. I want to make sure we're doing the story justice. We had to cut some race scenes and pare down the sex scenes, but otherwise I think you'll be pleased. It's more like what you wrote—except with Nikita's fucking modern furniture. Now fork over the cookies. I need the sugar high."

Cass shrugged. She should've known there was more going on than met the eye.

Maggie waved her hand. "Did I mention Nikita's trying to write herself a part on screen?"

Cass's jaw fell. "How so?"

"Nikita's rewritten some of the dialogue so Logan has to do more with his shirt off. You know, a lot of hunched over the engine sweating type of stuff."

She patted her friend on the shoulder and tamped down her frustration. "I trust you, Mags. I'm sure whatever you shot is fine."

A knock at the door interrupted their conversation. "I'll be right back in a minute," Maggie said. "Go snoop."

Cass crept back to the bedroom, where she assumed the filming took place. The tangle of cords actually gave the location away. She peeked around the door to see a very naked Logan kissing Tiffany. No body stocking, just a flesh-covered dick sock. Close enough to naked. He brushed her hair back from her face.

Cass choked down bile. Seeing such a private act in a public fashion bugged her.

"I have nothing but my heart to give you," Logan said.

Cass knew that line.

"Oh, Jonathan." Tiffany cupped his cheek but instead of looking deeply in love, she looked sick to death. Of what? Logan oozed sex. There was his fine ass, his caring heart and his smile that could disarm anyone. What was the problem?

"Cut!" Nikita shrieked. "This is bullshit. I'm not feeling the love here. Do it again. Try to use your acting skills!"

While Nikita spoke, Logan's gaze locked with Cass's, sending fever through her body. He raised an eyebrow and ever so slightly raised a shoulder. He seemed to ask,

Are you okay with this? Cass dipped her head. She couldn't exactly tell him to stop. Acting, even nearly naked acting, was his job. Logan's shoulders sagged as he took a lingering breath. He nodded in return. He signaled to Cass in slight movements. He pointed to himself and then over to her and then wiggled his brows.

She nodded and her cheeks burned.

"Let's do it again, but try to do it right," Nikita snapped, interrupting their private moment. "Action."

Logan closed his eyes in what Cass assumed to be his focus technique. He cupped Tiffany's breast once again. "Honey, this can't last. I have nothing but my heart to give you."

Tiffany smoothed her palm over his cheek. "That's all I want. All I've ever wanted." She slid her fingertips down the length of his body to his ass and grabbed. "But this will do until you truly love me. I want you and I want you hard."

From her position in the shadows, Cass nearly choked. She didn't remember writing that line. Sophie was a gentle character, not sex-starved. What were they doing to her sweet romance novel?

Ania eased up beside Cass. "Yeah, this is sick. I can't control her either. I agree with Maggie. You wrote it much better."

Cass glanced at the assistant before locking gazes with Logan.

"Oh, babe I..." He shook his head and backed away from Tiffany. "I can't do this because that wasn't the line. I know this scene and Cass didn't write 'I want you hard'. He grabbed a towel to cover his nudity and stomped off the set. "Screw your ridiculous rewrites."

"I told you," Ania whispered and disappeared.

"Fucking balls!" Nikita screamed. "Logan, come here, now!"

Logan stood at his full height, put his hands on his hips and strolled to her position. "What?" It sounded more like a challenge than a question.

"That twit wrote stupid, sappy dialogue. Mine's much rougher, which translates better on film. Either do it or walk. But keep this in mind—we'll sue you for your paycheck and then some."

"Take it. I never cashed the check," he bit out, never blinking or backing down. "I don't want it if I'm reduced to doing your perverted translation of her work."

Cass snorted. Seeing Logan in nothing more than a towel, arguing perversion and finance with a fully clothed Nikita while Tiffany lounged in a thong in the background amused her.

"Then kiss me and I'll show you what I want you to do," Nikita coaxed, smoothing her hands along his rippled chest.

"I will not kiss you! It's not in the scene and you aren't Sophie." Logan backed out of her reach. "I'm tired of skirting you."

"Can we just get on with it?" Tiffany complained. "I'm getting tired and cold."

"You need the practice!" Nikita screamed, ignoring Tiffany. "If I let you go it alone, you'd screw it up. I know what Chunks wanted—boring, watered-down shit!" She cupped Logan's cock through the towel. Her voice dropped to a husky whisper. "This is what I wanted. Cass can't see us, so she can't get pissed. I'll bet she's back at the house pining over Dex right now."

Cass nearly fell over. Blood thumped loudly in her ears. *Nikita still wanted Logan? No change from the audition.* But come on—*Cass won't know?* She tamped down the growing anger. She'd never pined for Dex.

"I don't care what you want, sweetheart. I'm spoken for. And stop calling her Chunks. Her name is Cass!"

Nikita shrieked. "You're too good for the likes of her!"

"Hey." Tiffany waved her arm. "Stop arguing so we can finish. I want to see my hubby before we get too old to reproduce again."

Logan and Nikita looked at Tiffany in tandem and

155

shouted, "Shut up!"

Cass stepped from her shadowy hiding spot and cleared her throat. Logan started to cross the room, only to have Nikita grasp his arm and yank him back.

"Not now, Nikita," he said.

Cass summoned her courage and bitchy attitude. "Is the twit interrupting anything?"

"Never." He gave her a peck on the cheek. He wriggled his brows. "Besides, you aren't a twit. Quite the opposite."

"Get out!" Nikita shouted. "Jesus. This is a fucking closed set."

"I came with cookies." Cass proudly produced the boxes and ignored Nikita. "Anyone want any?"

With Nikita still draped on his left arm, Logan took Cass's hand with his right. "Sounds great. I'm famished."

She offered him the box and whipped around to share with the others. "I brought plenty. Enjoy!"

Nikita slapped Logan's rump. "Cass, this is a closed set. You must leave until filming has completed for the day. You know the rules."

Rules? Nikita never abided by rules. Why start now? Venom boiled deep in Cass's body. She'd never liked Nikita and the constant insults only cemented her feelings.

"Oh, grow up, Nikita." Maggie came from behind Cass. "I invited her, so lay off."

Cass backed up as Nikita stormed across the room. "That's it!" Nikita cornered Maggie. "I'm not having her interrupt our work every five minutes. She's got to go!"

"What you want is for her not to take Logan away," Maggie snapped.

Logan clapped his hands. "Cass made us a treat? Awesome." He turned his attention to her. "How's the book coming?"

"Progress is slow, I'm afraid." She traced his areola with her fingers, making his nipple taut. Hers reacted in kind, painfully so. "I got into the short story. All finished and submitted, in fact, but the novel has me stumped. I can't get the characters to behave. All they want to do is have sex. Must be what I've got on the brain."

Logan groaned and tugged her close. "Speaking of sex, why don't we go to the other bedroom? I need air. And you."

Cass left the boxes on the table and followed Logan into the second bedroom, which currently doubled as a messy dressing room. She wondered if there was still a floor under the heaps of clothing.

Logan pinned her against the wall. He nearly smothered her with kisses, not that she minded. What a way to go.

"I missed you, babe. You have no idea how hard it is to pretend to be in love with someone I can't stand. Nikita's on my last frayed nerve," he breathed against her throat. "Make me remember why I fell in love with you."

Cass wanted to melt. His heart, his love, really belonged to her alone. She closed her eyes and let the sensations wash her away. A tiny cry escaped her throat. "I think it had to do with being the exact opposite of any other date you've had." Oh, that sounded intelligent.

He bunched her shirt above her breasts and moved to kiss her cleavage. "No, that has nothing to do with it. It goes a little deeper." He worked open the button on her jeans and slipped a hand into her panties. "Oohh, the cotton ones. My favorites."

She couldn't think straight. Not when he sent delicious sparks of desire through her body. Acting this way was risky and out of her comfort zone. Anyone could walk in at any time. Why didn't she care? He made her care about him in a very exciting way she'd never felt before. The hint of sarcasm pricked her conscience. He couldn't be serious. She tried to answer his earlier question.

"Maybe it had to do with my sparkling personality?"

With a light swish, her jeans and panties pooled at her feet. Logan lifted her right foot out of her ballet flats and helped her out of the constricting fabric. He knelt before her. "Nope." He trailed his fingers over her sensitive flesh before slowly entering her.

Cass trembled. "Oh, Logan…" She gripped his head and stroked his hair.

Holy shit.

"Ummm," he hummed. "Honey and the finest wine."

She bucked into him, grinding down on his finger. "Oh. My. God!"

Logan repaid her swirling desire by kissing her inner thighs, teasing her. He thumbed her nipple through her bra. "Yes." He drew the word out in a hiss. "Yes, your ability to take my breath away—that's what made me fall for you. I want you all the time. I can't keep my hands off you." He stood and smoothed his fingers across her lips, allowing Cass to taste herself. "I spent all that time out there flaccid. One second with you and I'm steel." When he stood, he shucked the towel.

Cass groaned as his erection rubbed her clit. "Logan." Definitely steel and so good. Her heart filled to the brim.

He nibbled on her neck and slowly thrust into her, letting her feel every inch of him. "I love you, Cass."

He nodded, kissed her and began to thrust again. "Damn." Something clunked against the wall.

Cass arched into him. A moan escaped her throat. "Logan!"

He groaned and pressed tighter into her, stretching her. "Scream my name."

She tightened her arms around his shoulders. "It wasn't me. I think they caught us."

Logan froze once more. His face drained of color. "Well, shit."

"Logan! Stop fucking the help and get out here!" Nikita screamed. "I—*we* have better things for you to do."

"Go away, damn it!" he shouted. "Babe, I'm sorry. I thought—"

Cass quieted him with a kiss. "I got caught up too." She laughed nervously against his mouth. "It's okay."

Logan pressed his forehead to hers. "I hate having to stop

midway through. I'll make it up to you. Promise."

She slid her leg down Logan's as she retreated. The anguish in his eyes stayed with her. She wished she didn't have to leave. She licked his Adam's apple. Even through the stage makeup and slight scent of Tiffany on his skin, she still found his masculine essence—home and soap. She even liked his day-old beard. It felt scratchy and sexy against her throat. "You need to get done in there so we can continue what we started."

"Even if I want you now?"

Cass cupped his face in both hands. "How does it feel to miss what you want?"

"Sucks, but I'll manage."

Cass slid her panties and jeans back up past her hips. Logan grabbed a towel to dry off, muttering something about ripping Nikita a new asshole.

"Instead of causing bodily harm, take this." Cass retrieved a key and keychain from her pocket. "This way you can come and go as you please. It'll make life easier. My house is your house."

Logan held the key. A silver C dangled from the ring. "We'll be at this all night tonight. You don't mind?"

She drew him in for a kiss. "I trust you. The dogs like you. Les thinks you're pretty okay. Even Maggie finally came around. That's enough for me. I know that your being naked with another woman will happen. I'm dealing with it as long as it's only on film."

Logan nipped her bottom lip. "I have no one in my heart but you, babe."

Cass rested her head against the door. She sighed. Apparently this was what happened when dating a celebrity with a lunatic director hassling him and another celebrity couldn't get over her. "Then we'd better stop so you can get done quicker. Don't take *all* night. I want private time with you too."

Logan grabbed the towel and wrapped back it around his hips. "I love you, babe."

"I love you too, Logan." She meant it. Cass opened the door, only to see Nikita waiting on the other side, tapping her boot.

"About time. Logan, I need to see you a moment. And, Cass? Take those awful cookies. The crew keeps getting crumbs on my sets."

Cass rolled her eyes and scooped up the empty boxes. As she did, she heard more arguing. She shouldn't have turned. Nikita trapped Logan in a kiss. One more game Nikita played as a test. Logan pushed away from her.

"Enough!" Cass shouted and dropped the boxes. She took a deep breath and cocked her brow. "I'm not sure what's going on here, but I'm not standing for this." She put her hands on her hips and flipped her hair over her shoulder. "I warned you, Logan. I can't handle the cheating. Nikita, stop before your brother gets involved any further. I'm done with the both of you."

Logan's heart sank as Cass turned on her heel and left. *What the hell just happened?* She gave him a key and then claimed she was done with him? Yes, she'd overacted, but was she serious?

Nikita cackled beside him. "Now you see why she can't forget Dex and Josh! They're in her soul!"

Logan whipped around to look Nikita in the eyes. His blood boiled. "Josh? Who's that?" Another man? Another lover? He prayed Cass didn't have many more secrets.

Nikita folded her arms and a mischievous smile curled on her lips. "Oh, she didn't tell you about her son? Yeah, she and Dex had a son, named Joshua Dexter. She's no angel, just a tramp in saint's garb."

Logan swallowed hard and tried to process Nikita's words. Had? The child was gone? He remembered Dex's website. There was absolutely no mention of a child. No reference at all. Why didn't Cass mention him? Was that the little boy in all of the pictures? He rubbed his forehead. Someone needed to give him answers.

He folded his arms to match Nikita's stance. "What happened to Josh? Tell me, right now."

She curled her lip in a snarl. "He died of SIDS when he was three months old. She didn't take proper care of him and so she lost him. Now do you see why she can't leave Dex? He's the only man who can give her children, she's just too naïve to believe the truth. She claimed she never slept with anyone else. Yeah, right."

Logan narrowed his eyes and clutched the key, digging the metal into his skin. "You're wrong!" Cass was too smart to believe this garbage. Sudden Infant Death Syndrome was no one's fault. No wonder she didn't talk about Josh. He was a wound she couldn't deal with. His heart went out to her. Leave it to Nikita to use the past against Cass.

Nikita grinned and shoved the glasses back up her turned-up nose. "Cass couldn't do what he expected."

Logan braced himself. "Why did she divorce Dex then?"

Nikita stepped nose to nose with him. "He divorced her."

Logan glared at her. He knew she lied. "Cass told me otherwise."

The sly, narrow-eyed grin returned to Nikita's face. "You'll see it's all a façade, the cuteness, the sweetness. She's not what she makes herself out to be."

"She's the strongest woman I know," he said and stopped in the extra bedroom. He grabbed the first pair of boxer shorts he could find, then stomped out to the front porch. Engrossed in conversation, Maggie sat with the grips.

"Maggie, I'll be right back," Logan said. He'd wasted enough time.

"Where do you think you're going? We need to finish!" Nikita shouted and started after him. "I'll call the producers!"

"No, you won't," Maggie said and grabbed her co-director. "Let them work this out."

"Thanks, Mags," he said and broke into a sprint.

"You're welcome, but next time put on some pants, not boxers," Maggie called.

Logan laughed off Maggie's suggestion and breezed past the security guards. Ahead, a cloud of dust swirled down the driveway. He filed the information away for later use. He'd call Ronan once he spoke to Cass.

He bounded into the house through the back door. Cass sat at the kitchen counter with her laptop. She had her hair hastily wrapped around a pencil with messy chunks of hair framing her face.

"Cass?" Logan stopped at the end of the counter. His stomach tightened. "Can we talk?"

She turned when he called her name. She'd worn wire-rimmed glasses—now add some stilettos, a black teddy and those glasses, and he could have one helluva fantasy come to life. Oh yeah. He was a lucky man with a one-track mind.

"What are you doing? Are you done for the day?" She took off her glasses and dropped her hands into her lap. "Why are you so pale and wearing your boxer shorts inside out?"

Logan bent over to catch his breath and think through what he needed to say. He remembered his choice of clothing. Damn. He should've listened to Mags. Too late.

"Who is the little boy?" Nice delivery. "I mean, can you tell me about Josh?"

Cass's eyes grew wide and all color drained from her face. "What brought this on?"

Logan sat down next to her at the counter. He drummed his fingers on the dark granite surface. "Nikita blabbed. She thought she needed to fight fire with fire."

Cass left her stool and crossed the room. She plucked a photograph from the bookshelf and caressed the edge of the frame.

Logan eased up behind her. He rubbed his hand along her back. His gaze switched between the image of a baby boy in a blue teddy bear sleep suit and her falling expression. Tears wet her dark lashes. He wished he'd never pressed the issue. "Cass, you don't have to tell me. It's not my business," he soothed. "I'm sorry."

Cass took a deep breath. "Since she opened the conversation and left me no other option, this is Josh. I should've told you, but I wasn't sure how. I don't like to talk about my past." Her chin quivered. "God, this isn't easy." She sighed. "Dex and I were intimate before we married, but always with protection. The wedding night, he insisted we have sex without it, because we needed children to be complete. Until that point, he sheltered me into believing everything he said—even if I didn't agree. He was my husband, so why not? I didn't know a whole lot about sex. I spent more time working on my schoolwork and being a good girl than learning about the birds and the bees. Guys only paid attention to me because they counted me as one of them. Dex acted like I was someone special."

Cass gripped the frame tighter, her knuckles turning white. "On our wedding night, I got pregnant. Once I confirmed the pregnancy with a test a month later, I told Dex. I was ecstatic. He went ballistic. I was confused. He'd made such a big deal about having children. All of the sudden he claimed fathers in Hollywood weren't as popular as single men. He'd been playing on my naiveté and hoping the pregnancy wouldn't happen right away or something." She turned away and rubbed her forehead with the pads of her fingers, her shame hung thick in the room. "That night, he yanked me out of the bathroom and nearly broke my arm."

Logan gasped and fought the wave of nausea crashing through him. How could any man be that evil? He wanted to rip Dex's balls off with his bare hands. "And your family didn't stand up for you?"

Cass shook her head quickly. "I didn't have access to them anymore."

Logan raked a hand through his hair. "Babe, I'm sorry."

"Dex insisted I get an abortion, but I held my ground." She began to sob. "I had Josh a month early and he was so small. His heart wasn't strong enough to leave the hospital.

Dex forced the issue and instigated the release process earlier than the doctors wanted. Josh never made it to three months and there was nothing I could do." Her words came out in a jumble, but Logan caught every awful detail. Dex had robbed Cass of her family, her child and her life.

Logan rested his forehead against hers. "The abuse was not your mistake."

"I told myself that so many times, but I never understood why he did it." Her voice cracked. "Why?"

He stroked her hair and tried to find an answer. "Because he's a monster. You and Josh were the innocent victims. Don't blame yourself."

She shook her head. "It's not that simple. I didn't leave Dex fast enough for Josh to grow up — if that was even possible."

How could Dex be such a coward? How could he not love the mother of his child and his child? Logan clenched his jaw, grinding his teeth together. A dull ache started behind his eyes. He'd lose everything — all the trappings of fame to make it up to her.

"I tried to be whatever he wanted me to be so he would stop hurting me. I thought that if I was his ideal wife, then the abuse would stop. Stupid, stupid, stupid." Cass buried her face in her hands and sobbed.

Logan's heart shattered. She had fire, vitality and a glow that Dex had all but burned out. No more. He vowed to bring it all back, permanently. He wiped the tears from her cheeks. "Cassie, you're safe now. Josh knew you loved him. He's keeping an eye on you and protecting you from Dex, just like me. Nikita wants to cause trouble, but I'm glad she started this. I see the strong woman you really are and love you all the more for it."

Cass turned to stare at him. "You do?" she whispered.

"Yeah, with all my heart. I do have one other question, though."

She brushed her hair off her face. "What?"

"Did you really mean we were through?"

"No." She sagged in his embrace. "I said it to get a reaction out of Nikita. If I told her how I really felt, she'd go right to Dex—if she hasn't already."

A cold shiver ran the length of Logan's spine and it wasn't from chilly air. "What do you mean?"

"I got another call from Dex this afternoon. He said he'd tell everyone about our past." Cass paused. "He's going to try to ruin everything. I know him."

"Damn it." Logan shook his head to make sense of everything. She was right. Dex had a trusted spy in his sister. He used his power of intimidation to win because he thought he still had Cass under his thumb. That notion brought Logan's simmering anger to a boiling rage.

"Logan?" Her voice cracked. "What are you thinking?"

"I'm ready to mutilate that coward, that's what I'm thinking."

"Why?"

"Cass, he's trying to bully you to keep you in line. I'm not going to stand for it. You're all I've ever wanted and I'm not about to let that ass have the upper hand."

She kissed him and smoothed his disheveled hair down. "That's the sweetest, yet most destructive thing anyone's ever said to me."

"I meant every word."

"You'd better get back to the set before Nikita has a coronary and fires you."

He cupped her chin, brushing his lips against hers. "Let her. I could use the vacation."

Chapter Thirteen

At four in the morning, Logan trudged along the backyard in loose jeans, flip-flops — which he secretly detested because he hated to look at bare feet, especially his own — and another rumpled concert T-shirt. Okay, so he wasn't rolling in high fashion. Who cared? Cass loved him, warts and all. Being with her made him look and feel sexy. He rummaged through his pockets and located the key to her home. She wanted him in her home. No fucking way.

He had the condo in Santa Monica, but it was more like a furnished storage container. He slept there, ate there, had had enough sex for three lifetimes there, but never called it his home. It was disposable, like the women in his life had been. Females were merely rungs on his ladder to fame and fortune.

For thirty-one years, that line of reasoning had worked fine. Then he'd met Cass. She was more than he ever deserved and everything he wanted. His life. His love. He still couldn't believe she returned his affections.

Logan locked the door and crept upstairs. Along the way, he recognized the images of Josh. The baby in the cradle, in Cass's arms in the hospital, propped up for his first photography session. Even without makeup, Cass glowed when she held her child. He wanted to make her feel that way once again. If she wanted, he'd give her another child.

At the top of the stairs, he noticed her light was still on. Both dogs turned to the sound of his footsteps, but Cass never moved. With one arm stretched out, she faced the wrong direction. She looked so peaceful, clad in nothing more than his dress shirt, wispy-thin panties, and socks.

His heated gaze swept along her smooth legs. A shiver of desire ran the length of his spine. He assumed she'd fallen asleep working at her computer, while trying to stay awake to greet him.

His heart momentarily stopped. He couldn't see her chest move or tell if she was still breathing. Was she dead? The balcony doors were wide open. With enough determination, any skilled intruder could easily scale the wooden posts. But the screens weren't broken. He bounded to the bed and checked for her pulse. Instead, Cass shifted slightly and fell back to sleep. The shirt slipped open to reveal the tops of her creamy breasts. Logan puffed out a long breath and ran his fingers through his hair. Thank God for the false alarm. The idea of losing Cass scared him shitless. Now that he found his missing half, he wouldn't let her go.

Still, she looked appetizing in his clothes.

Without disturbing her, he moved the laptop. Color flooded the black screen. Logan grinned with pride. She used the picture Les took that night at The Ricochet as her wallpaper. Good old Les. And damn, didn't Cass look sexy too? He liked her flushed and primed. Careful to not to disturb her open documents, he closed the lid and plugged in the machine. Better to be safe than sorry. He turned around to scope out the room. On the entertainment system, he saw a stack of DVDs. Curiosity drove him to read the titles. Somehow he didn't think he'd find porn, but hey, whatever floated her boat.

Driven
Allen Martin – PI for Hire
Blood Rites
Mending Fences

He swallowed a chuckle. The discs were selections from his résumé. The open case suggested that she'd fallen asleep watching the Generation X comedy *Shakermaker*. Probably not an insult, as the movie earned poor reviews from the critics and went straight to DVD. If she could stomach his lousy body of work, then maybe she really did care. Or she saw the diamond in the rough. Who knew?

He ventured into the bathroom to brush his teeth and scrub the taste of Tiffany from his mouth. He had no idea what Tad Stevens, Tiffany's actor husband, saw in her aside from her body. She had a selfish streak a mile wide.

Logan pushed that thought out of his mind. He longed to taste Cass, but didn't want to wake her up. He glanced out at her prone body. Her hair fell in straight wisps around her shoulders. He wanted to run his fingers through the dark strands and kiss her until they both ran out of energy.

After he'd stripped to his birthday suit, Logan hurried through a shower. He dried off and shifted Cass's position on the bed so she could enjoy her pillow. Before succumbing to sleep, he wrote a quick note for her and placed it on top of the laptop. Once he replaced the towel, he climbed into bed with her, stark naked. He smoothed the satiny locks from her face. She looked angelic and he felt damned lucky to have her. She was the one. His one.

Instinctively she curled into him. "I missed you," she whispered.

He wrapped an arm around her. "I missed you too, babe." Knowing she cared enough to attempt to stay awake for him made his heart swell to overflowing once again. He liked having a woman genuinely care for him.

* * * *

The next morning, Cass woke to a hairy leg twined with hers and a thick erection pressing into her backside. Logan's warm, masculine essence toyed with her senses. How could one woman with a rough relationship track record end up with such a wonderful, caring and sexy man? She didn't know and wouldn't tempt fate. She rolled over slightly to kiss his forehead. Logan barely stirred. He felt like dead weight pressing down on her. A purplish cast under his closed eyes led her to believe filming lasted too long into the night. The poor man. Maybe she could rectify the situation. She slipped from under his arm and shifted to her knees to stare at his glorious, naked body. Instantly her nipples tightened, begging for his touch. Heat pooled between her legs. Staring wouldn't be enough. She needed to experience him.

As if on cue, Logan flopped onto his back, giving her the ultimate access. Her mouth watered. She loved tasting him. His eyes remained closed. Would he wake? She didn't care and shucked her panties. She cupped his heavy sac and dragged her tongue along his shaft. How could she not satisfy him and herself? Somehow, she doubted there would be a time they *weren't* satisfied in bed.

He groaned. "Yeah."

Emboldened, she wrapped her fingers around his cock and flicked her tongue along the blunt head. When he didn't move, she took him to the back of her throat and relished his musky taste. She stole a glance to his heavy-lidded eyes. Her gaze locked with his as she took him to the hilt once more.

A sleepy smile curled on his lips. "Oh, babe..."

He wanted her to do this? Duh. She wanted to continue? Hell yes.

Cass continued to kiss and caress him with her tongue. She reached up and plucked one of his nipples. The freedom in her actions and the thrill of sucking him off filled her brain. She'd never felt so strong or powerful in her life—she could make him happy with just the brush of her lips over his cock.

Logan tugged on her hand. "Come here," he said in a thick, sexy voice that turned her senses inside out. "I want you on top of me."

Not yet. She stroked him and licked the head of his dick once more. "I felt this prodding my backside and needed to take care of it," she teased. "Or was that your subtle hint for me to give you oral sex?" She swallowed him down and hummed.

Logan shivered and bucked against her mouth. "Come here."

Cass sat up and raked her fingers down her body. She cupped her breasts, then unbuttoned her shirt and let the garment pool around her hips. Her nipples beaded in the chilly air.

He licked his lips and smiled. "Yeah, babe." He grasped her wrist, tugging her along his body.

"Hi," she said and kissed his earlobe. Heat from his feverish body seared hers. No wonder naked skin to naked skin contact was his favorite.

"I like your wake-up call and you can do this any morning or every morning, but I need to make love to you more." He situated her legs across his hips. His cock throbbed against her clit and sent shivers through her body.

She grinned and ran her tongue along his scratchy, unshaven jaw. Damn, she loved feeding his need.

He closed his eyes and sighed. "Ride me, Cass. I need to be inside you. A part of you. Make me whole."

She nipped his bottom lip. "We need a condom."

He ran his fingers down her back. "I want to feel you with no boundaries." He nipped and licked her throat. "All of you."

She reached into the nightstand and retrieved a foil packet. "Use this. You don't need that kind of complication."

He scrunched his brows. "Complication? Nothing we've done has been or will be a complication."

Unable to believe him, Cass stifled a shudder. He knew how to say the right things. For once in her life, she wanted to buy into his lines, but trusting him completely wasn't coming that easily. For now, she'd focus on sex with him. She slipped the condom onto his cock and straddled him. "Fill me, Logan."

Logan nodded. He grasped her hips, easing her body down onto his cock.

As he stretched her, she groaned and shifted. She traced her fingers up and down his arms while rocking back and forth.

"Oh, Logan." Her hair slipped in front of her eyes. She moaned and dug her nails into his skin. Feelings she couldn't describe welled to the surface. This was all too much and everything she desired at the same time.

He quaked with orgasm. He tugged her hard against his body. "Yes, babe. Let go. Let go and love me."

She collapsed on his chest and buried her face against his neck. She struggled to catch her breath.

Logan wrapped his arms around her and smoothed his fingers along her skin. "I love you, Cass."

She rubbed her nose against his jaw, simply enjoying the feel of him still hard inside her. "I love you, too."

"What's your plan for this afternoon?"

Perplexed, she raised her head. Mind-blowing sex and he wanted to know her afternoon calendar? She could hardly think straight. After a long pause, she forced her mouth to move. "What?"

He ran his thumb along her cheek. "I have a surprise planned for this evening, but have some things to do this afternoon." He twirled a lock of her hair in his fingers. "I wasn't about to wake you up last night, but you looked beautiful."

She pressed a kiss to his hand. Man, he changed subjects quick. She pushed aside the idea that he might be hiding something. No. Logan wasn't a liar like—well, he wasn't. She knew it deep in her heart. Soon she'd allow herself to trust him completely.

"I need to work on my novel. I'm getting way behind, but I have to help with the wrap party on Friday. I promised Mags that the boys would play for entertainment. Les and I are in charge of food. We'll go shopping this afternoon." She rested her head on his chest. "By the way, thanks for noticing. I wanted to look hot when you came in, but couldn't last that long."

"Honey, it was like three or four in the morning. No one should've been up at that hour." Logan kissed her knuckles. "Did you have company last night?"

She cocked her head. "Besides the dogs, no. Why?"

"I saw someone race down the driveway and thought maybe you had a visitor."

She shrugged. "You probably saw Ray. Their race shop is my barn and he likes to work odd hours of the night. I know I'm the one who normally freaks over weirdoes around my house, but Ray wants to be sure the championship car is up to his standards." Of all the odd things happening to her lately, the one person she didn't worry about was her best guy friend. Ray might keep strange hours, but he didn't pull punches.

"Are you sure?"

"I wouldn't worry about it." Something about his question threw her for a loop. She didn't feel nearly as sure as she did a few minutes ago.

"Then about tonight, meet me here at four."

Her eyes widened as she shoved aside her apprehension. "An afternoon of lovemaking? That's romance."

Logan patted her ass and kissed her. "I meant meet me here at four, dress comfortable but sexy, and plan on having fun, not in our bed, smart-aleck. Well, not right away."

She tipped her head in thought. *Our bed?* She liked the ring of that. "Deal. I'll work on the novel this morning while you sleep and shop right after lunch."

He flipped her over onto her back, pinning her under his muscular body. "Perfect."

Chapter Fourteen

Saturday afternoon, Logan settled down in his trailer with his phone and laptop to make a few calls. Once he found the information he needed, he closed the computer. Everything he desired or wanted to do could be accomplished in town. Sweet. He'd forgotten the pleasantness of a small town— everything close by and quaint.

Logan left his trailer and started out on his errand run. First stop, Maggie. He looked on the set and around the cabin with the crew, but couldn't find her. He asked a couple of the prop guys if they'd see her, but no. He shoved his hands into his jeans pockets and headed in the direction of the raised voices in the barn. Would she be there? Who knew, but if there was something going on that wasn't supposed to, he'd take care of the problem. He grabbed the barn door, but before he could open it, the door swung open.

Maggie stomped out onto the gravel and turned. "I don't care. This is what I do!" she shouted.

Logan stepped out of range of the door, then eased into Maggie's path. "Who are you talking to, Mags?"

She puffed out a breath and glanced over her shoulder. "No one in particular. Why? What did you hear?"

He folded his arms. "I heard a bunch of shouting that wasn't any of my business. Are you okay?"

She shoved him across the gravel drive to a pine bench by the shed. She narrowed her eyes. "I'm fine, just don't worry about it." She frowned. "What are you doing here? I thought you were either holed up with Cass or working on your lines—which you're doing a good job with. Those lines are shit, but you're doing better than I thought."

"Why thank you." Maybe he wasn't such a slouch in the acting department after all. He stuck his hands in his pockets. "Are you free for an hour? I want you to go shopping with me. No monkey business, I promise." God knew he needed her on his side if he was going to go through with his plan.

Maggie shook her head. "Sure, but why me?"

Logan grinned. "It's classified."

Maggie rolled her eyes. "I suppose if you tell me, you'll have to kill me? Something like that?"

"Nah. I'll explain along the way — if you're game."

"Let's go."

* * * *

Logan stood outside of the bathroom and leaned against the doorframe. "Are you about done in there?" He widened his stance and listened for Cass. "I want to get moving. It's ten after five." He'd orchestrated a surprise and didn't want to be late.

"Ouch!" she called. "Just a minute."

He frowned. "What are you doing?"

Cass opened the door and blew out a long breath. "I was curling my hair to look sexy," she said with a sigh. "It didn't work. It just went flat and I may have burned my forehead. I'm not sure, but the skin is pink."

He brushed a hank of her hair off her face and examined the slight pink spot. "Looks sexy to me, but then again, I think you look sexy first thing in the morning. And I don't see a burn."

"Give it time." She hooked her fingers in his pants pockets. "You look gorgeous, but I'm sure all the girls tell you that."

"Doesn't matter what the other girls say." He roved his gaze over her and bit back a growl. Damn, she looked good. "I'll have to beat the competition off with a stick."

The neckline of her baby-doll blouse dipped just enough to show her cleavage, and her jeans hugged her luscious curves. He'd have to work hard to keep himself in check throughout the date.

"Just a minute. I forgot something." She eased away from him long enough to dig around in her jewelry box. She turned and offered her neck. "Help me get the clasp on this."

Logan angled them both to her mirror as he draped the necklace across her collarbone. He fastened the tiny gold loop and planted whispery kisses on her exposed flesh. She giggled and sighed. He tried to sound nonchalant, but the tiniest bit of jealousy crept into his voice. Christ, his desire for her brought out the best and a twinge of the worst in him.

"Is this a gift from a former lover?" he asked.

Cass smiled at their reflection. "No. Les and I decided we deserved diamonds for Christmas a couple of years ago. She got earrings and I got a necklace. We picked out a bracelet for Maggie. She wears it all the time."

"Oh." He should've known. She wasn't the type to dwell on the past.

She kissed his cheek. "No worries. I haven't had enough boyfriends to warrant jewelry. Ray scared the bold ones off. Besides, he doesn't buy what he calls 'sappy stuff'."

Logan frowned at their reflection. "I'm sorry to hear that." He made a mental note. At Christmas, she'd get diamonds — as many as she wanted.

Cass grinned. "So? Am I beautiful enough for you?"

"I might just stay home because you look too sexy to take out into public," he joked.

Her eyes widened and her lips parted.

"I meant that in the most sincere way. You're beautiful."

She lowered her gaze. "I suck with compliments. I'm—"

"You don't have to apologize to me," he said against her lips. "I tend to suck at giving compliments. Now we've both got something to work on." He kissed her again then slipped her hand into his. "Ready?"

"I'm all yours."

He escorted her downstairs. Cass grabbed her keys,

phone and purse, then followed him through the garage.

He opened the door to his truck. "May I accompany you into town, m'lady?"

"For our date?" Cass blushed. She slid into his truck and settled in the middle seat. "I can't wait to see what you have in mind."

Hopefully, she'd like his surprise. He rounded the hood and climbed behind the wheel of the vehicle.

Cass twiddled with the stereo knobs. "This truck would look sweet with a lift kit and a set of straight pipes. Make the beast sound like thunder."

He engaged the ignition. A lift kit and off-road tires would look sweet as he tore down the road with Cass tucked safely in the crook of his arm. The engine roared to life, as did the radio. The band StrikeBox blared from the speakers. He glanced at Cass, expecting her to be offended or turn it down. Instead, she cuddled into his arm and sang along softly.

"Are these guys in your repertoire too?" he asked.

Cass looked at him. "Yes and no. No, we don't cover them on stage, but yes because Les likes them. Our last trip to Pennsylvania was one gigantic StrikeBox concert. The ride home consisted of nothing but the band Amazing Pain."

"Why Pennsylvania?" Logan scrunched his brows. He hadn't expected her to mention his birth state.

"Les has family in and around Erie. I did a library visit and a couple of book signings. Her mom is a big fan. Why? Have you been to good old PA?"

He rubbed his thumb along her knuckles. "I know my way around the place. I grew up there—Linesville to be exact." He could see the wheels turn in her mind. He also saw a dirty maroon vehicle pull into traffic behind him.

"Oh," she said and drew the word out.

He peered at the rearview mirror. The maroon sedan seemed to follow their movements perfectly. He accelerated down the main road. Blood thumped in his ears. The fact that the car rode his bumper was merely a coincidence.

Wasn't it?

Cass shifted. "What?" She shifted in the seat and he stomped on the gas. "You're doing seventy miles an hour in a fifty-five zone. Is Nikita behind us with another script change?"

He glanced in the mirror and saw the maroon car peel off onto a side road. "I wasn't sure what the limit was on this road." Not the greatest lie, but he didn't want her spooked through the date. This night was about them, not someone trying to butt in on their happiness. He turned down one of the country roads and away from the sedan. Once he was sure the car had disappeared, he blew out a long breath.

"It's fifty-five." She sat up beside him, but didn't scoot away. "So why did you go to Tinsel Town?"

He snorted. She could've read his story in a hundred articles, but the media never quite got the details right. For the first time in a long while, he wanted to talk about his past. "I came out to California at the ripe old age of twenty. I thought I was the shit and set out to set the film industry on fire. I had too much attitude for the small town. I'd been a jock in high school, complete with the atrocious grades and killer smile to go along with the asshat personality."

"Not you."

He chuckled. "Yeah, me. By the age of twenty-four, all I managed to blow up was my credit card bill. I bussed tables and stood in crowd scenes for television shows. Talk about an ego bust. Most people would've quit, but I wasn't that smart. Although, I did go home for a year to work on the farm. I had to lick my wounds and bulk up. Everyone wanted bigger muscles and I hate working out."

Cass shifted. "Muscles are good." She shrugged. "Why did you need to lick your wounds? I watched your early work. It's good. Did you have family issues too?"

Logan fought a lump in his throat. "I had great parents. Mom stayed at home and took care of me while Dad worked at the local bank as a loans officer. My grandparents had the four-hundred-acre farm and they worked me hard."

"Sounds idyllic," Cass murmured. "I bet it was heaven growing up there."

"I did have it pretty easy, but that's why I had the cocky attitude. I was a selfish bastard. I had this warped notion I was sexy, therefore I was entitled — to girls, to money, to stuff in general. I left disaster in my wake."

"Did you?" She put her hands up to her mouth in faux surprise. "I never would've guessed."

He kissed her head. "I'll make sure you get yours later."

She giggled. "Please do."

"Anyway, I went back to my grandfather's farm and bulked up by baling straw and hay all summer. It was a great time until... Well, it was good." He wasn't sure how much more he wanted to talk. He'd kept most of his private life quiet. He trusted her not to disclose his secrets, but the truth was he didn't want to dredge up the pain and heartache.

"What happened?"

Logan shifted in his seat. Cass had disclosed her prior life. Why was he any different? "My dad mismanaged loans at the bank. He turned to my grandparents and forged other loans to make up the difference. He couldn't bail himself out. I didn't ask and he didn't tell. But that last summer I worked my ass off at the farm, I loved it. Would've been the perfect summer except I walked in on my mother in bed with the father of one of my ex-girlfriends. Mom couldn't handle the stress Dad was putting them through and looked elsewhere for comfort. Dad's depression got the better of him and he took his life."

He gritted his teeth. Memories of the night he'd found his father came back in waves. No amount of suppressing would get rid of them. His eyes stung with unshed tears. Not now. He refused to cry.

"That's awful. I'm sorry."

"No one knew how deep in debt we were until they balanced Dad's accounts. We lost our house and my grandparents lost the farm."

He scratched his forehead and focused on the road. "The whole thing was a joke. She'd been cheating on him for years and he ignored the signs. I just wish I knew earlier. I would've stayed home. I wouldn't be the jerk I became. I'd have been a decent man—enough for them to work it out."

Cass rubbed his arm. "What they did wasn't your fault."

Maybe the cheating and stealing wasn't his fault, but the embarrassment of having to sell off the farm and hearing his father's name dragged through the mud in town had been more than he could handle. "They auctioned off the farm in ten-acre segments. It went at a loss and my grandparents were never the same. Grandpa died within three months and Grandma followed ten days later. I left for California the second time and never looked back."

Logan stopped at a traffic light. "So now you know. I've never shared those details with anyone."

"I'm humbled that you chose to tell me." She threaded her arms around his biceps. "What you lived through wasn't wonderful, but you're too hard on yourself."

Logan's ears burned. She was right and wrong at the same time. "I've got an attitude. I really do. Watch old clips of me on the entertainment shows. I thought I knew it all."

"You were young and brash. It happens."

"True. Now I'm older and I'm happy. When I'm with you, I forget all about me and worry about how to make you smile. You changed me into a good man, babe. My grandparents would have loved you, if you met them. They hated every single one of my girlfriends." God knew his mother would hate her.

Cass took another deep breath. "I think that decent guy lurked in there all along, but you needed a reality check to sort yourself out."

"If you say so," he replied. He wanted to believe her, but he knew the truth. He'd allowed his ego to run amok. Yes, the reality check of coming to Ohio helped, but he'd settled down because of her. If she hadn't been on the project, he wasn't sure what would've happened to him. He pulled into a parking spot. "Here we are."

Cass unbuckled her belt and gripped the dashboard. "No way. The surprise is Crawford Days? How'd you know I wanted to come up for this?"

He climbed out of the truck and rounded the hood to her door. He grasped the handle, but didn't open the door. "I thought you'd like to go on a date that didn't involve sneaking around your property or pissing off the boys in the band. Plus, I'm dying for some street fair food." He'd kept that tidbit of info under wraps too. He loved the food at the fair.

Cass climbed out of the vehicle and grasped his hand. "Thank you, sir."

Booths covered in bright yellow and white lights lined the city block. Vendors selling everything from fried food to arts and crafts shouted the worth of their goods. The screech of the various games of chance made quiet discussion impossible.

Cass fell into step beside him. "What's your poison?"

He paused. "Pardon?"

"Everyone has one type of fair food that they can't live without. I'm a sucker for the gyros," Cass said proudly. "What's your favorite?"

Logan stopped in front of a blue and green trailer lit with neon. "Fried pickles. Nikita would croak if she caught me, but I don't care. Get whatever makes you happy, as long as it includes me."

"I've already got you," she whispered. "Since you're ordering, I'd like a gyro, though."

"Done." He squeezed her hand. He hadn't known true happiness until he'd allowed her to invade his life. No, he'd been the invader. He'd pushed and prodded his way into getting what he wanted. Was he really that much of a better man? He wasn't sure.

"We can sit at the tables beside the band shelter. There's graffiti all over them, but they're sturdy." She pointed to one of the empty tables.

Logan dropped the food containers on the marred tabletop and snagged Cass on his lap. Damn. Life couldn't get much better. "Didn't know the best dates are the cheapest, did ya?"

She picked at the fries he'd ordered. "Any date is good as long as I'm with you, even if it is to a street fair. I haven't been out in public on a date in a long time. Usually Ray or Corbin insists on following along and then it's not a date. It's a lynch mob."

He'd assumed so. The guys seemed nice, but overly protective and he wasn't about to argue with her friends — not tonight. "Which is why I didn't tell them." He slurped from the gigantic cup of soda. "I wanted time alone with you."

She applauded. "I concur."

"I'm glad you agree."

He sat with her and ate in silence. No words were needed. The evening sun made her skin look like unblemished porcelain and brought out the red and gold in her dark hair. She stroked his libido with a glance and a smile.

Once he was done eating, he eased his phone out of his pocket long enough to check the time. "The real surprise starts in fifteen minutes, so let's get moving."

Cass stood and tossed the empty containers in the nearby trash bin. The light breeze toyed with her hair. "Oh. What's the next part?"

Logan nodded to the throng of people gathering around the band shelter. "There's a concert tonight and you're not singing." He patted her ass, then escorted her to the makeshift gate cordoning off the area in front of the shelter. He produced two tickets and handed them to the man guarding the roped off area. "VIPs, please."

"VIPs? Who are we seeing?"

"Didn't I tell you?"

"No."

"Then spill? Who is it?"

"You'll see." He led her to a place in the middle of the

crowd and he draped his leather jacket across her shoulders. She snuggled against him and rested her head against his chest. The first strains of the band blared over the noise of the crowd. When the performer, Vinnie Joel, triumphantly emerged at the back of the stage, she screamed.

She glanced back at Logan. "How did you know?"

"Your cover song repertoire." Logan pressed his groin into her backside and rested his chin on her shoulder. "Plus, I asked Les and Maggie."

Cass twined their fingers together. "I love it. Thank you."

She huddled against him and danced through the entire first half of the concert. She wriggled her ass to the beat and rubbed on his crotch, making it hard for him to concentrate. Entertainment buzzed all around them in the form of the music and the swaying crowd. She ignored it all and sang to him like this was their own private concert.

Without warning, the hairs on the back of Logan's neck bristled. He scanned the crowd and zeroed in on the man glaring. A woman shifted, blocking his view before he could imprint the stranger's face on his brain. When she moved out of the way, the man had disappeared. Logan inwardly cursed. Now what?

Logan scanned the throng of dancers once more. Nothing. The eerie feeling skating up his spine continued. His heart thumped faster than the beat of the current song. The idea of fleeing crossed his mind, but only for a moment. As of yet, no one in the mass of people seemed to recognize him. The anonymity thrilled him. This night was for the woman in his arms. She deserved every ounce of attention and devotion she could get. The more she rubbed, the harder he became.

Damn, life was wonderful. Thank God Vinnie happened to be playing Crawford Days. That fact made the evening even sweeter.

"Cass, I can't wait to get you alone," Logan rasped in her ear. His thick erection nudged her backside. "I want you surrounding me. Do you feel that? I want to make love to you all night long. I love you so much."

Cass turned and put his hands on her breasts under the protection of the jacket. Her nipples pebbled under his touch and her heart beat wildly within her chest. "Feel what you do to me, Logan." Her eyes closed and a tiny moan escaped her lips.

Logan caught it in his kiss, consuming her. He felt her deep in his soul. They bled into each other. He didn't know where he left off and she began and he didn't care. She was the woman he'd have for the rest of his life. He broke the kiss and tightened his arms around her. He'd never let go.

Vinnie Joel silenced the band and held up both hands. "This next song is for a friend. I hope it works because he put in a lot of effort."

"That's cool," Cass shouted over the first few notes of the song. "Wonder who the friend is. I didn't think he knew anyone around here. No one that famous knows anyone around here."

Logan grinned and kissed the top of her head. He knew her. Wasn't she famous in her own right? Sometimes the right amount of money and influence worked wonders—more so when the guy singing happened to be performing Cass' favorite song. "How'd you know?" She whistled and balled her hands in delight.

"I requested the next song for you as well." Logan held her with her back to his chest and sang to her. He pointed to her during the chorus. She danced in blissful oblivion, turning him on and his senses inside out.

"Logan."

He tugged her in closer and continued to sing to her. "You bring out the best of me," he whispered in her ear.

Cass pulled away from him. She kept her back to him while the rest of the crowd bounced along to the next song.

"Babe?" His curiosity piqued. Hadn't he been doing everything right?

"Can we go?" she asked. She folded her arms and refused to look at him. Her shoulders slumped.

"Sure." What had he done wrong? He escorted her through the crowd to the exit. And then to the truck. The longer she kept quiet, the more his heart sank. He stopped beside his vehicle. She might want to, but she couldn't give him the silent treatment forever.

"Talk to me. Everything was fine until I sang to you. Was it my singing voice? It sucks, I'll grant you. I haven't practiced in forever. Was it the words? You don't like dates?" He needed to know so he could improve for next time.

"I don't deserve this," she murmured. "I don't deserve you."

She started to pull away, but he caught her in his arms. Didn't deserve him? Well, yeah. She deserved a man a thousand times better. "You are the best any man could ask for."

"You should be with a woman who has the brass to walk the red carpet in slinky gowns. A woman who looks as good as she writes. A truly sexy woman with fewer curves. I'm mediocre. I'm—"

Logan kissed away her further protests. "Cass, you're gorgeous. You've got nothing to worry about with me. I adore you and everything about you. If you don't want to walk the red carpet, that's fine. I hate parading around like that, so you won't hear me protest if you don't want to do it either."

Her eyes widened. "Really? I thought every celebrity loved that kind of thing."

"Most do. I used to, but I'm tired of living under the glare of the media." Logan cupped her chin. "Truth is, I'll do whatever it takes to make you happy. I'd even quit acting if you asked. I'm tired of living a life of bullshit and booze. I want the peace and stability I've got with you."

She sighed and flattened her palms on his chest. "Stability? I'm a mess," she said. "Without the booze and bullshit, though."

"You're perfect to me."

Chapter Fifteen

On the drive back to the house, Cass snuggled close to Logan. Although she'd walked out on a perfectly good concert and expressed her doubts, he hadn't run away. He'd seen her rough sides and the better ones. She still didn't understand how she'd managed to turn his head, but she appreciated the affection. Life couldn't get much better than this. His warmth, his smell, his love wrapped around her. He made her feel safe and wanted.

"I have one more surprise," he announced and sped past her gravel lane. "I wanted some extra time alone, so we could talk, kiss or whatever. No constraints, no interruptions. I want to focus on us. On you."

She eased her hand between her legs and pressed her knees together. Her pussy heated and her stomach did crazy flip-flops. No constraints or interruptions? Sounded like the perfect end to the date.

Logan parked the truck next to the grove of maple trees and retrieved a blanket from behind the seat. "Wait here."

Crickets chirped and the wind rustled the leaves. The scent of licorice danced in the breeze from the multicolored leaves. In the dim light, she noticed him spreading out the blanket in the grass. He retrieved a cooler from the shadows. A shiver skittered up her spine. What did Logan have planned? The smooth muscles in his back flexed under the soft cotton with his every move. Even the jeans perfectly accentuated his tight ass.

He was her boyfriend? Unreal. She'd considered dating Ray, but he made her feel like she was with her brother, not a lover. Logan cherished, cared for and loved her. No brotherly affection involved. She warmed at the thought of making love to him again.

A moment later, he stood beside the truck. His eyes flashed as he opened the door. "May I have this dance?"

Notes from a country song played softly on the wind. She grinned and nodded. A quiet, slow dance under the stars? How romantic! He led her to the pavilion where they began to sway to the ballad playing on the little transistor radio. He held her close and she rested her head on his chest.

She noticed the blanket and the bouquet of daisies wrapped in paper.

Logan nibbled on her neck, sending more shivers through her body. "Sleeping on me already? I'm not that boring, am I?"

"No. I'm letting it all wash over me." Being in his arms, in his life was so dreamlike. "I still can't believe this is real."

"I know, but it is."

In that instant, she knew she'd never be the same. There was no going back from Logan Malone. He saw the real Cass. The girl who read widely, knew popular culture and could tactfully discuss politics. So she didn't have breeding or class. Underneath it all she was nothing more than a shy kid from a small town who dreamed big—but wasn't he just like her?

Logan held her and swayed with her for the next two songs. At the first upbeat tune, Logan stopped moving. "Think we deserve a rest?"

Cass leaned back to gaze into his eyes. "Oh, I suppose," she said and allowed him to coax her onto the blanket.

She leaned back on her elbows to stare at the swirling stars. The night, despite her misgivings about herself, was perfect. "I hear you like blush wine?" He handed her a glass. "Try this. Mags says it's your favorite." Logan clinked his glass to hers. "Cheers."

She took a sip and eyed him warily. Damn, she wanted to lick the wine right off those supple lips of his. She wondered what other parts of his body tasted like when drenched in wine? A ripple shot through her body. Yeah, she'd like to taste him. Everywhere.

Logan crossed his ankles and matched her pose. "If it weren't so chilly, I'd suggest skinny dipping. But then, I'll take any and every excuse to get you naked and nestled safe in my arms."

Cass could literally see the sparks crackling, not from the candle flames, but the fire in his hazel eyes. Heat and want simmered low in her belly, yet she cringed. She knew full well she wasn't skinny. So much for dipping. She tamped down her apprehension and swallowed hard. Maybe his opinion was the only one that mattered.

He set his glass on the top of the cooler. "I want to make love to you. Right here under the stars, I want to see you glow." He smoothed his hands along her body, pausing on her breasts. His voice dropped and his eyelids drooped. "Make love to me, babe."

Cass bit back a moan and shuddered. A vision popped into her brain. Her pulse quickened. She sat up to gulp oxygen into her lungs. Bits and pieces from the nightmare came back to her. She looked around, desperate to get away. Her niggling fear became too real to handle, with Logan or alone.

"Cass?" Logan grasped her shoulders. "Babe?"

Her breath caught in her throat. "I can't," she croaked and looked away. She rocked back and forth. This couldn't be happening. She saw the transformation between Logan and Dex as clear as day. Logan's light hold on her arm felt like a death grip. Dammit. Why did this stuff always mess up her life? *Because Dex has fingers everywhere.*

Logan let go of her and cocked his head. "Tell me what's on your mind."

She met his gaze and her chest ached. Celebrities didn't mix with civilians, especially not women who peeked around every corner, anticipating personal demons. She never should have believed she could get beyond her own past. It slammed into her present at every turn.

"This is too much like my dream, except you haven't turned into him yet." She stood. "I know I'm safe, but he makes me scared. Even in my dreams with him on the other side of the country, I'm scared."

He stood and held out both hands. He didn't try to grab for her, but he inched close to her. "Babe, we'll get past this. I won't make you do what you don't want to."

Cass shook her head. "I don't know how to get the devil out of my head. I'm scared all the time and worry too much. I—I'm not good for you, even if I love you."

"Slow down." He curled his fingers under her chin instead of retreating. "You have me. You'll always have me."

Tears streamed down her cheeks. She wanted to believe him, wanted to believe his happily-ever-after, but her worries and fears came back in waves. Dammit, she had to stop pushing him away when she wanted him close. "I'm messing up your perfect night. Logan, I'm—"

He traced her bottom lip with his thumb. "No apologies, babe. I understand you're scared. Hell, I'm scared too. I want to protect you and help you to forget the bad things in your past."

As much as she didn't trust herself, she trusted him. "The unscripted romantic language is better," she said and snuggled against his chest. "I like it more than the stupid scripts Nikita gives you." Tears slipped down her cheeks, but she felt safe in his arms.

He petted her hair and kissed her temple. "I'll protect you from Dex and the bastard stalking you. Sounds crazy, but my heart is in your hands—so is my life."

She paused. "Wait. You saw him too? In the crowd by the speakers?" So the guy at the concert hadn't been a figment of her imagination? That thought scared her more—she wasn't imagining the boogey man.

"Your sheriff friend was in the crowd. No one will hurt you while I'm around."

Her confidence lifted a bit, bolstered by his reassurance. He hadn't balked at her emotional baggage or breakdown.

Her faith in him wasn't unjustified. She grasped the front of his shirt and held on tight.

"Cass, I wanted you to enjoy yourself, preferably with me. I want that every night for the rest of our lives." He continued to stroke her hair. "We move at your pace. When you're ready, so am I."

"Logan?" She'd wasted enough time on people who didn't deserve her energy. Now she had someone who cared and she wasn't about to let him get away.

"Right here."

She nudged him back to the rug and straddled him. She wished the clothing wasn't in the way. "Make love to me."

He slid his palms over her ass and frowned, no doubt wondering what had brought about her change in attitude. A long breath escaped his lips. Desire bloomed in his eyes and brought out the gold flecks.

Logan stuffed one hand into her back pocket and slid the other hand along her side. He eased his palm beneath her blouse and cupped her breast. "Is this what you want?"

Cass licked and bit his bottom lip. "No. You're what I want."

He nodded. "For as long as you desire."

"Forever."

****

The next afternoon Logan rounded the corner of the cabin, only to freeze in his tracks. He'd heard the shouting clear across the set. He stopped at the edge of the cabin. Cass stood with her back to him and her stance wide. Nikita opposed her, with her lip curled in a sneer. He had no idea what in the world the two women would be arguing over. God knew they hated each other. Not that Cass didn't have a good reason. Nikita took cheap thrills in annoying her at every turn. He wasn't fond of Nikita, either, but in a way, he felt for her. Even if she could've been friends with Cass in another life, the situation between Cass and her brother made things sticky.

"I will not have the crew at this party. This is meant for the cast to bond," Nikita barked. "Got it?"

Cass stood with her hands on her hips. Her voice remained calm, but her volume increased. "Why are you shutting the crew out, Nikita? They did the bulk of the work on this project. They deserve the reward just as much as anyone else."

He gripped the cabin railing and stifled a whoop. She might be emotional at times, but Cass had a big heart. She only wanted the best for everyone.

"The dinner is a formal, catered affair. The per plate price is expensive and I'm not adding that to the budget. I mean, Jesus, they were doing their jobs—that's what they were paid to do. Besides, they wouldn't know what to do with a salad fork, let alone fine caviar." Nikita's sneer increased. "Probably never saw caviar before."

Logan nearly swallowed his gum. What the hell was Nikita planning? The wrap party was to celebrate the end of filming, not an awards show.

"I'll give them an idea what to do with a salad fork," Cass ground out. "You wouldn't appreciate it."

Nikita stomped her foot, leaving a deep impression of her boot. "I'm having an intimate gathering. Don't screw with my plans! Understand me? They aren't invited and neither are you."

"Whatever. I'm heading over to the pavilion so I won't bother you. Les and I have the burgers going already and the crew has been invited. Looks like the only one who wasn't is you and that's because you screamed at me before I had the chance to say anything."

Logan grinned. This was another reason he'd fallen in love with her. She cared about everyone—including her enemies. How could someone not like her? He shrugged and considered the source. Nikita hated anyone who got in her way.

"Are you fucking kidding me?" Nikita screeched. "They don't deserve it and you're butting in."

Cass nodded. "You're right. I butted in. I wanted a party and invited the crew who has been tromping all over my lawn for the last couple of weeks. I'm sorry if that offends you."

Logan leaned against the cabin and crossed his ankles. She had a point, but to him it sounded like the crew owed her.

"Well, don't expect your boy toy to show up. He's mine tonight!" Nikita snapped. "I already ordered the limo."

He frowned. *Boy toy?* Nikita had to be kidding. He wasn't that much younger than Cass and where did Nikita get off ordering a limo? Who was it for and when was she planning on telling him about the intimate party?

"You do what you want. It's a free country," Cass said. "If Logan wants to attend your wrap party for the Ohio portion of the shoot, then fine. He's entitled. I'm going to the barbeque." With that, she spun on her heel and gracefully walked away from the fight.

That was his girl, tough as nails and soft as fine silk. Logan doubled back around the porch to catch Cass. He caught up with her behind one of the makeup trailers. She ran her fingers through her hair.

"Of all the times for her to throw her weight around — not that she's got much, but still. It's only a party," she muttered.

"Hi, babe," he said. When she turned around and blushed, he smiled. "What brought on your argument with Nikita? Yes, I overheard. I'm pretty sure everyone within a hundred-mile radius heard Nikita scream."

Cass scrubbed her hands down her face and let out a long, tired sigh. "She's determined to undermine everything I come up with that's decent for the crew. I want everyone to enjoy the wrap party, not just the overpaid actors and a horny director/producer bent on having her way with a certain actor. She neglected to include Maggie!"

"Are you serious?" He snorted. "I have no lost love for Nikita. I'm not sure why she thinks there's still a spark." He draped his arm around her shoulders. "But enough about Nikita. How can I help out with your party? There's no way in hell I'd go to such an exclusive dinner party as Nikita's planned." He shrugged. "I heard an awful lot. Punish me later."

The corner of her mouth curled into a smile. "Can you dish food? Or do you want to man the grill?"

"I can do whatever you want." He fell into step beside her. This was romance, walking with the woman he loved. He cursed Nikita for causing so many problems, but the movie — even with Nikita involved — had brought him and Cass together. He kissed her temple.

"Speaking of whatever, I want to drag you behind the barn for a quickie."

"Logan." She jabbed him in the ribs. "Is that all you think about? Sex?"

"Yes." He tugged her behind a particularly thick maple tree. "What can I say? I'm addicted to you." He snagged her in his arms and slid his palms beneath the waistband of her jeans to pat her ass.

Cass leaned against him and rested her head on his chest. "We're out in the open. We can't do that, much as I'd like to and trust me, I'd love to take you up on your offer." She muffled her moan against his shoulder. "You'll make me forget what I need to do."

Logan mashed his erection into her abdomen. "My only thought is to pleasure you senseless," he whispered. "Babe, I need you." Although, he knew better. They were out where anyone could catch them and for all he knew, someone with a telephoto lens could be watching.

Cass sighed. "We'll finish this tonight, but right now… Les will kill me if she thinks I'm goofing off. She's very strict."

Logan rested his forehead against hers and kissed the tip of her nose. "I can grill, serve or take orders. You tell me what to do, and I'll do it, gladly." He winked. "Here or in bed."

Chapter Sixteen

Three hours later, Logan closed the lid on another batch of burgers. He glanced across the pavilion to Cass. She stood behind the table with the spatula, serving each crewmember in line. Never once did her smile falter. The breeze tossed her ponytail about, wrestling stray curls free and giving color to her cheeks.

In his old life, he'd thought women looked silly with their hair yanked high in an elastic. On Cass, the look was sporty and fun and damn, he wanted to run his fingers through the fringe of loose strands framing her face. Even in worn, curve-hugging jeans and the "I'm with the Crew" T-shirt — a gift from the gaffers — accentuating the swell of her breasts, she looked approachable and damned sexy.

"There you are!"

Logan closed his eyes and gritted his teeth. He should've known Nikita wouldn't stay away forever. He sighed and opened his eyes. Nikita, clad in painted-on black leather pants, stiletto boots and a neon pink halter, tapped her foot. Her short black hair stood in two-inch-tall spikes. The more he looked at her, the more he wondered what he ever saw in her in the first place. Probably the booze and lack of sex were the culprits. She'd be the right woman for someone, but not him.

He opened the lid to flip the barbequing meat. "Here I am."

Nikita notched her chin in the air and crinkled her nose. "Why are you frying things for these...these people?" She yanked down her designer sunglasses. "They stink."

"Good thing this isn't your dinner." He sneaked a glance

across the pavilion. Cass caught his gaze and shrugged.

At least Cass seemed to understand. He snapped the controls and cut the gas to the grill. He took the remaining hamburgers off the grates as the fire dowsed. Part of him wished Nikita would disappear. The rest of him knew better. She wasn't going to budge until she got what she wanted.

Les darted by to grab the plate of food, stuck her tongue out at Nikita and sped off before any retribution could take place.

He shook his head and laughed. When he turned his attention back to Nikita, he flinched. She irritated him so much. "Hey, I need to go over there." He wasn't sure where he needed to be, but anywhere looked better than standing with Nikita.

"These ingrates don't appreciate what you're doing." Nikita clawed his arm. "Look, the plan for tonight was for you to come along with me. We're having a wrap party, remember? You're supposed to be dressed—better than this. How can we celebrate when you smell like smoke and food?"

"Easy. You celebrate. I'll stay here and stink. At least one of us will be having a good time." He strolled across the lawn to Cass and snaked his arms around her midsection. "I want to eat you. Cass, I'm a starving man. What have you got that will sustain me?"

"I'm just a serving wench tonight, but I'll try to take care of you personally later." She laughed. "Or do you prefer someone a little taller?"

Logan nibbled on her neck. "I've got the person I want right here in my arms." He dragged his nose along her skin and sighed. He'd have to wait until later to have his way with her. "Did you get a chance to eat, love?"

Cass shook her head. "I waited until everyone else got through the line. Care to share the straw bale behind me?"

"I insist. Eat while the band plays so you can enjoy the food and the music." He handed her a burger and snagged a bag of chips. "We'll share."

She sat between his legs leaned back against his chest. "Nikita's angry," she said between bites. "Ray's mad at me and Maggie's grumpy. Any ideas how to make them all play nice?"

He took her hand and nipped the salt off her fingertips. "Make love, not war sounds good to me."

She shifted into him more and sent his fraying nerves into overdrive. Only a few more hours, then they could be alone with her stretched out beneath him, welcoming him, screaming his name. At this rate, he'd never make it.

She interrupted his fantasies. "Any better suggestions?"

Logan cleared his throat and shifted to release some of the pressure on his erection. "Well, going on the dirty looks I keep getting from your studly lead singer up there, I'd say he's undersexed and overstimulated."

Cass spit out a mouthful of soda and nearly choked. "What?"

He handed her a napkin. "Oh, babe. I'm sorry, but look at the guy."

Cass dabbed the soda from her shirt and tossed the trash in a nearby can. "He's one of my best friends. He's protective and doesn't trust you, but tonight it's like he's trying to punish me."

Logan rubbed her temple with his nose, filling his senses with her delicious scent. "I suppose I'm the reason you're being punished?"

Cass patted his knee. "You're either a bad decision, or the best thing that's ever happened to me."

"I like that answer."

"Will you give me a hand cleaning up?" Cass asked. "I'd rather not have to all alone."

"I wouldn't let you clean up all alone. Point me to the trash bags and I'm on it."

"In the garage. I left them on the counter along the back wall." She kissed him and hopped off his lap. "Thank you."

Moments later, he strolled outside with the box of trash

bags. He heard the arguing before he saw the individuals involved, but he knew the voices — well, one of them. Now who wanted to have it out with Cass? He stopped at the corner of the garage. He could step in, but Cass probably didn't want the intrusion. Logan stared at the man yelling. Ray. The guy stood over six feet tall, full of rock-hard muscle. She didn't appear to be backing down, but neither did Ray.

Cass rested her hands on her hips. "You don't know everything."

"I've got a better idea than you do right now." Ray folded his arms. "He's not...he's going to be trouble like the last one."

Logan gritted his teeth. He'd had enough of Ray's attitude. He strode out from his position by the garage and right up to Cass. He tapped the box on his thigh and wrapped his arm around her. "Am I interrupting something? I couldn't find you."

"For the love of..." Ray glared and his gaze burned. He clenched his jaw and his mouth formed a tight line.

"We were just arguing," she murmured. Cass stiffened in Logan's embrace. "It was nothing."

"It didn't sound like nothing from what I heard." Logan crooked one eyebrow. "You two could be heard clear back to the garage."

Cass shrugged out of his embrace and threw her hands in the air. "You know what? You two have issues with each other and I'm not going to be the intermediary any longer. Have it out. Do whatever you think you need to, but leave me out of it."

Logan folded his arms and watched Cass storm away. His mouth watered as he thought about how he'd like to tease, caress and lick her entire body.

"Malone," Ray snapped. He widened his stance and flexed the muscles in his arms. Damn, the man had one solid, wide chest.

Not one to back down from an argument, Logan matched

Ray's stance. Inwardly, he squirmed. Ray unnerved him, but he refused to let his twinge of fear show. "You wanted to talk to me, Ray?"

Ray clenched and unclenched his jaw. He looked like he could take on an entire army — by himself. "I have a thing or two to say to you."

Logan cocked his head. "I'll bet you do. About Cass?"

"She's taken a real shine to you," Ray said. "Thinks you might be the one. Somehow I don't buy it."

Logan narrowed his eyes and worked his slyest grin. "I hope so. I'm in love with her. Is it a problem?"

The color bled from Ray's face. "Really?"

Logan nodded and said nothing. Provocation? Absolutely. Retreat? Never. What exactly did Ray think was going to happen? He'd snap, growl and get Logan to come clean? About what? He loved Cass. Period.

"Don't get close to her unless you can handle her past." Ray sounded like he teetered on the edge of control. But it didn't seem like it took long for him to recover, based on the tight line returning to his mouth.

Logan bit back a groan. "I see you're close to her too."

"You have no idea, but this isn't the time to compete for her, actor," Ray snarled.

Logan's mouth formed a tight line. "Why's that?" God damn the man for being so hardheaded.

Ray averted his glare. "Because she's yours! I never had a chance. Trust me, I've tried. Lots of times, I've tried."

"Oh." Did Cass know about this competition? Or had she shut Ray down? "Guess there's not much of an issue then."

Ray balled his fist. "You do realize what she's been through, right?"

"She's told me enough," Logan replied, unsure of what else to say. She'd clued him into plenty of things in his life, but he had no idea just how much Ray knew. The longer Ray stared at him, the more he wondered if he really knew the entire story.

"So Les did tell me the truth. Huh." Ray shook his head.

"Did Cass open up about Dex?"

Logan bit back a growl. "Sure. I got to experience him up close too. The guy's a dick."

Ray kicked at an imaginary rock on the ground. "I'm surprised. She doesn't talk about him—ever."

"Not even when he shows up uninvited?"

Ray sighed. "The last time I knew he'd showed up, she had me come over. I stayed with her until he left. Guess I'm not needed now."

"I wouldn't say that." If she trusted Ray and saw him as protection, then Logan wouldn't argue. What if he couldn't be with her? He wanted to know she had someone who could take care of the situation.

"Cass doesn't offer up and Les said you made it easy. That's quite a task." Ray dipped his head. "You must be some guy."

If dealing with her nightmares, holding her as she talked through her problems and loving her like there was no tomorrow, then yes, he'd made it easy for Cass to open up. "You and Les care about Cass and I appreciate it. She's been through hell and needs good friends. I doubt she's told me everything, but what I do know isn't pretty."

Ray sighed with a hint of underlying frustration. Maybe a hint of softening? "Les and I worry about her and don't want her hurt again. I don't know everything that happened, but I know it was bad. What I saw was worse."

"That's not the half of it," Logan replied. "What'd you see?"

Ray's eyes burned with hatred. "I don't want to scrape her off the floor because you chose to use her, okay? I sat with her for too many long nights because she couldn't bear to be alone. She's not up to going through that shit a second time." Ray stood inches from Logan's face. "If you hurt her, not only will Les give you hell, but you'll have to deal with the race team and me."

Despite his frustration with Ray and the mention of the race team, Logan kept his mouth shut. He understood. If he'd been in Ray's shoes, he probably would've reacted the same way.

"I'm not only her neighbor, but I'm part of her race team. She doesn't advertise that fact—her owning a team—but she does and we all protect her. We take care of our own, like a big happy family. I bet you know nothing about that, being a permanent womanizer."

Logan gritted his teeth to keep from snapping back at Ray. He had a reputation and Ray wasn't wrong to call him out. Hell, everyone knew his track record. The difference now was he wasn't interested in being bad any longer. He wanted to be the man he knew he could be—the man Cass needed.

Ray sliced his hands thought the air in an X. "Remember, you will never be one of us. No way, no how."

Logan groaned. The testosterone fog was getting a little thick. "Ray, I don't know you and you're not making me like you too much, but I understand. I do. You're trying to keep her safe. It's admirable and I appreciate it, but the thing is, I'm not trying to own her or be like the guys in her past. I love her and want to make her happy. I won the jackpot when I met her."

Cass rounded the corner and stopped. She sighed. "I hate to interrupt this sappy moment, but the party's over." She poked Ray in the stomach before turning to thump Logan on the arm. "I'm not a prize, okay? I'm a person and even though I made some questionable choices in the past, I'm in a good place. I like the protection, though."

Logan wrapped his arms around her. "Sorry, babe."

Ray shot them both a death look. "If you want him, Cass, we'll put up with him, but I'm not impressed."

Cass groaned and shoved her hands into her pockets. "Ray. He's not perfect, but from what I overheard, he's not being a jackass."

Ray grumbled something Logan couldn't understand and blew out a long breath. "I'm warning you, he's trouble and just like Dex."

Logan closed his eyes and bit back a growl. Ray saw the parallel he'd been trying to keep contained. Damn it.

"I can handle myself. I know you're trying to help, but give me a chance. I might surprise you," Cass said. She turned to Logan as Ray stomped away. "I meant it for you too. Treat me like hell and I'll walk so fast you'll never believe it. I want a man who stands beside me. I'm not going through it again. I'd rather be alone than treated like that."

Logan bit back anger and almost through his tongue. His past would be the one thing to push her away, but he couldn't change what he'd done. He could change the future.

Her shoulders sagged and she let out a ragged breath. "Look, the team needs sponsorship money in order to race. I'm willing to give it. If they don't like you, I'm not happy, but we'll all adjust."

Logan grimaced, unconvinced and afraid. He didn't want to lose her, but he doubted he'd win over the race team. He'd kept his cool with Ray and hadn't changed his mind at all. "Really?"

Cass threw her arms around Logan's waist. "A very smart man told me something important once. He said, 'now that I've found you, I'm not letting go without a fight'. I agree."

He cradled her skull with both hands. She shifted against him, which sent blood rushing below the equator. He measured his words carefully. "I will make an effort to get along with your team."

"Fine. Let's dance. I've wanted to nibble on your neck to a slow song all night." Cass grinned and brushed her lips over his.

Logan's libido spiked. Too bad the gallon or so of water he'd drank needed to go somewhere. "Meet me by the cluster of oak trees in five minutes and I'm all yours."

"Deal."

Five minutes later, Logan strolled out of the cabin and toward the pavilion. Along the way, he noticed Maggie with her head in her hands.

"Come on," a male voice said.

Logan paused. He knew that voice. Ray?

"If you can't choose, then you can't have me. End...of... story," Maggie said. She wiped her face with the back of her hand and turned on her heel.

When she passed his position, Logan reached out to her. He put his hand on her shoulder. "You okay?"

She jumped and spun around. A tear trickled down her cheek. "Don't!"

Logan pulled back like she zapped him with static electricity. "Sorry."

Maggie shook her head and brushed her cheeks dry. "No. I should apologize to you. Logan, I'm fine."

She lied and they both knew it. Logan hated to see her upset, especially when he pegged her as a woman in solid control of her emotions. "If it makes you feel any better, I'm not Ray's favorite person right now, either." Not the best thing he could've said, but too late now.

"I appreciate it, even if that's not really the issue." Maggie patted his hand. "It's nothing a return trip to Long Beach won't fix." With that, she walked away.

He stood silent a moment, trying to figure things out. Cass sidled up next to him. "Why are you deep in thought? It crinkles your forehead, which must ruin your headshots."

Logan wrapped and arm around her waist and kissed her. "I saw something I'm pretty sure wasn't good, but it wasn't my business."

"Normally, I'd get involved, but this time I won't. Let her go." She sighed. "I've known Maggie for years. She'd tell us if she wanted help."

"I can't argue with your logic." He snaked his other arm around Cass and nuzzled her neck. "How about we focus on us?" He caught her up in a devouring kiss and she moaned into his mouth. She sagged against him, rubbing her breasts on his upper belly.

"Excuse me! I'd like to make an announcement."

Chapter Seventeen

Logan opened his eyes and froze. What in the hell did Nikita want now? Cass eased her tongue from his mouth. She wriggled from his grasp and brushed her hands on her jeans. Across the clearing, Nikita stood on a tabletop and waved a piece of paper.

"Shut up, folks. I have an announcement," Nikita growled.

Logan eased up behind Cass and rested his chin on her shoulder. "This will be bad."

"Hold still," she whispered. "Maybe she doesn't see us and we can fly under the radar."

Too late. Nikita's eagle-eye gaze zeroed in on their position. She pointed in his direction. "There you are. Logan! Front and center. I have a gift for you!"

He held his ground and Cass. "I don't want a gift!" Under his breath he added, "Not from you."

Nikita marched across the span to stand only a foot away from him. "Come on. I want to do this on the stage."

He shot her a look filled with daggers. "If I refuse?"

She grabbed his arm and tugged, pulling Cass along the way. "Don't challenge me, Malone."

At the stage, Nikita produced the paper once again and shoved Ray out of her way. He threw her a look that rivaled Logan's in terms of venom. Nikita seemed unconcerned. "Attention, everyone! Attention." She waited a moment for the noise to die down before proceeding. A wide, sinister smile curled her blood-red lips. "I had a small gathering in the cabin for the principal players in this production. Each principal received a token to show my appreciation. Since Logan helped over here, I'm hand-delivering his gift."

His eyes narrowed. A feeling deep in his gut said this would go far beyond bad.

Nikita handed him the paper and slid in close for the obligatory picture. "This is a very special gift, for a very special man." She put her lips millimeters from Logan's ear, making him shudder. "Since I'm taking over directing from here on out, you and I are taking a break first. We're going on a trip for two to Jamaica, leaving on Monday! Pack accordingly. I prefer you in nothing but that towel." She grabbed his ass. "Oh," she purred as she delivered a slap. "Still tight. Yummy." She pressed kisses to his neck and stuffed her hand into his back pocket. "Yes, I look forward to our vacation."

Logan groaned. The woman excelled at harassment. She had no qualms with screwing over her job in favor of her love life. From the corner of his eye, he noticed Cass' tight smile before she walked away from the stage. His heart shattered. Cass didn't deserve to endure that kind of treatment. If he truly loved Cass as much as he believed, then he'd better act—and fast.

Logan took the microphone from Nikita. "I have my own announcement to make."

"Are you serious? I've been waiting for this announcement forever," Nikita screeched and smothered him in a hug.

Logan balled his hand to keep his frustration in check. "You're right, Nikita. This is the exact announcement you want to hear. Cass?"

Cass paused. The color drained from her face.

Logan fumbled in his pocket and fingered the diamond ring. "I'm not running off to Jamaica with Nikita."

"What? Well, we can stay here. I know some people who can make things legal." Nikita clutched the front of Logan's shirt, crinkling the cotton fabric in her hands. Her bottom lip trembled. "That is what you meant, right?"

Logan faced the crowd and ignored the ferocious glare from Nikita. "Logan Malone is getting out of the Romeo business. I'm tired of being a fake. The celebrity side of me isn't me." He strolled across the stage to Cass's position. He wrapped his arm around her and kissed her temple. Her face flushed and she jabbed him with her elbow.

"Logan," she muttered. "What are you doing?"

"I decided a while ago I was going to be me — boring, goofy and not in California."

Nikita burst forward and shoved Cass. "Oh no. I didn't work this hard to let this crap happen!"

Cass clenched her fists. Her lips formed a tight, white line. "Stop."

Logan shook his head and stepped between the furious women. "Now, now, Nikita. Act like a lady." Now, about what he'd climbed onto the stage to do... He dropped to one knee and grasped Cass's hand. "Honey, I can't run off to Jamaica with Nikita when my life is here with you."

"I won't stand for this!" Nikita surged forward again, but Ray nabbed her. "Logan's mine!"

His heart was filled to capacity with love for her, but he couldn't vocalize his feelings. He'd sounded so smooth when he'd practiced his delivery the night prior. "You deserve better than a B grade actor, but you can't find a man who loves you more than me. I'm offering what means the most to me — my last name."

Nikita shrieked. "No!"

Logan gripped the marquis diamond ring between his thumb and forefinger. His hands trembled. He wanted the whole world to know how much he adored Cass. He was her man.

Tears streaked down her cheeks. The platinum sparkled against her porcelain skin as he slid the ring onto her finger. "Cass Jensen, I love you. I want to spend the rest of my life proving how much I need you. Will you marry me?"

Cass glanced into the crowd. She shrugged her shoulder at Ray, who shot back with a sneer. She bit the corner of her mouth and studied the ring. "I'm not sure I wanted to take this step, Logan."

His heart clenched. Oh shit. He hadn't planned on this.

"Cass? I'm dying here."

"I'm not sure you're dying, but you're overacting a little." Her chin quivered and a couple more tears raced down her face. "Yes."

Nikita whimpered in Ray's grasp. "Oh, hell no!"

Logan sank down onto both knees and raked his fingers through his hair. His heart pounded. "Cass, love, please say that again. I need to make sure I heard you right."

A wide smile blossomed on her lips and she laughed. "With all my heart, yes."

Logan gasped for the breath she took away and dipped his head. *Thank you, Jesus.* He eased her down into his embrace and kissed her. Her tongue tangled with his in a sensual dance and he groaned. He wouldn't trade this moment for anything. He held her close, ready to get out of the spotlight and away the glare of the media and everyone else.

Nikita wrestled free from Ray's death grip. "Oh, no, you don't! This wedding will never happen. Mark my words. Never," she screeched and escaped off the stage. "And you can forget that trip!"

Logan bit back a grin and shook his head. Trust Nikita to turn his private moment into a gigantic issue. Oh well. He had the woman he wanted and he'd spend the rest of his life proving he was her man. Moments later, he and Cass left the stage. The crowd nearly swallowed them in hugs and cheers of congratulations. High-fives and slaps on the back greeted Logan at every turn. He'd never felt such adoration, even at the height of his stardom. He didn't care about fame any longer. Pride swelled in his heart. She owned him, body and soul.

Maggie and Les nudged through the throng to meet them. Les dug her elbow into his rib cage. "Mind if we have a toast with her? You know, a girls thing?"

"Please?" Maggie whimpered. "We want to have fun too."

Logan smirked. They could have all the girl time they wanted. Hell, whenever she wanted. He didn't care as long as he had Cass's attention later on. "She doesn't have to ask me. Live it up," he said and smoothed his hand over his pocket. "I think my phone's ringing."

"How can you tell?" Les laughed. "It's so noisy from Ray's musical temper fit that we'll all need earplugs to recover."

"He is on a roll," Maggie said wistfully.

Cass smiled and kissed Logan hard on the lips. "Don't take too long on the phone. I want to celebrate with you too," she purred. "I want to taste you all over." She walked away with her friends, swaying her ass.

Without looking away from her retreating form, he retrieved the phone from his front pocket and swiped his thumb across the screen.

"Hello?"

"Logan, baby. How are you, my man?"

He shivered. The only time Carmine had talked like that was when he'd set up the awful television pilot with Carrie Greenfield, yet another ex. Carrie was clingy and emotionally fragile, which made it a bad experience from beginning to end. "Carmine."

"Logan, your new attitude and improved acting skills are paying off. I don't know what or who you're doing, but keep it up. The offers are off the charts."

Logan pinched the bridge of his nose. "How so?"

"Tamara Redmond has personally requested that you be her love interest in her video for *Vampire Love*. You don't even have to wear makeup. You just have to look beefy and fondle her. It's only three days of shooting. Not bad for two hundred grand."

Logan groaned. Beefy? That usually meant scantily clad. Besides, he wasn't beefy. He'd been working out, but hadn't built excessive muscle. He thought about the offer and groaned. Most highly acclaimed actors didn't have to participate in cheesy music videos. What did Tamara really want out of the shoot? To touch him and probably fall into his bed.

Hell, no.

"I don't think—" Logan said, but Carmine interrupted him.

"Oh, shut up," Carmine scolded. "It's good money. The video will run during football playoffs. Now, I also have a great romantic comedy lined up for you. It's a supporting role, but you get the girl in the end. You play a bachelor who has a big heart and a big wallet. He needs a date and falls for a simple girl who pretends to have money to compete in his lifestyle. When he finds out her truth, he falls for her anyway. It's a little over six weeks of work with the stunningly beautiful Petra Murdoch. You get a cool million and a percentage of the gross in the deal."

Logan pinched the bridge of his nose. If he was going to any of the jobs, he wanted to discuss things with Cass first and have a few stipulations added to the contracts. "Well, I—"

"Did I mention the invitation to escort Jade Weir to the music awards in a few weeks? I know how much you want her. Exposure, money and a career boost. Don't write it off, Logan. She's finally coming around. No more fooling around—you'll get a prime date."

Across the yard, Logan spotted the woman he wanted to fool around with, totting a large stack of serving trays. Les followed behind with an equally large stack. As they walked, Nikita threw a string of curse words that he could lip-read easily. Cass stole a glance to Les, who rolled her eyes. They both laughed, which made him smile. At least they took Nikita in stride.

"You know, Carmine, I'm not sure I want the role. I had other plans for the next few weeks. Why don't you—"

"Ditch the plans. These are opportunities of a lifetime that you can't afford to pass up over a woman you hardly know. Sex can be good, but the money you'll bring in will be so much better in the long run."

Logan squeezed the phone. Money and exposure weren't important anymore. "I'm planning on getting out of the business a while and marrying Cass Jensen. If you can work the schedules around my plans and give me time to talk things over with Cass, we might be able to make a deal."

"Are you kidding me? These are prime opportunities. I've already accepted the video. You've got to report to the location for the Redmond video In Los Angeles, Monday morning, sharp."

Logan felt the urge to dropkick something. He'd been so foolish and green when he'd signed on with Carmine. He'd given his agent the power to represent him when he wasn't in town. Shit. He closed his eyes and took a deep breath, but it didn't help much. The only way he'd be able to stay level would be to stay in Ohio.

Carmine's voice pierced through Logan's thoughts. "Did you hear me?"

Logan opened his eyes. "No."

"I'll repeat myself."

Logan cut in. He'd say his peace, even if it ended up short and sweet. "Binding or not, I'm not available right now. Give me a few weeks."

Carmine growled on his end of the line. "Why?"

"I'm staying in Ohio with my fiancée!" Logan snapped.

The growl turned into a string of curses, punctuated with words Logan knew didn't exist. "You're trashing good exposure. Logan, if you spend the time apart and she waits for you, then see how you feel. If you still want to continue the relationship, then go for it, but give it time. You aren't the binding together forever kind of man. You're a lone wolf."

"Enough!" Logan jabbed his thumb onto the screen to finish the call. Damn it. He'd just announced that his Romeo days were over and now he had to spend six weeks away from Cass in the heart of temptation with Jade, Petra and Tamara. He'd worked hard to prove to Cass he wasn't a playboy any longer. Would she still believe him?

He slid the phone into his front pocket and headed into across the pavilion to find Cass. This would take a lot of explaining. Like ten tons worth of explaining. He prayed she still trusted him enough to let him go, because he hardly trusted himself. Would her love sustain him? Was he still the cocky jerk he claimed to be?

Then there was Ray. He didn't particularly care for the way Ray butted into Cass's life. If Ray wanted to turn on the charm, he'd be hard to beat. Simmering in anger and self-loathing, Logan shuffled through the knots of people. Too many things seemed stacked against his creating a life with Cass. He hated himself for his past—a past he couldn't change, but he could make his own future. He loved her so much. She was so strong and full of heart. He was the weak link. Maybe talking to her would smooth his conscience and show him what to do with his future.

Chapter Eighteen

Once the party broke up for the night, Logan found Cass and headed to the house. He needed to feel her around him and craved being inside her. Did that make him sound like a horny bastard? He didn't care. He'd found the woman of his heart and he wasn't about to let her go.

By the time he collapsed on the bed, Cass had granted his wish — they'd made love on the sofa and made out on the stairs. He wanted to make love to her again, but damn, they both needed a rest.

Logan cradled her in his arms and she trailed her fingers along his chest then sighed. He loved the sound of Cass warm and satisfied, like the purr of a kitten. He could listen to the music of her being for the rest of his life.

"You're going to wear me out, babe." He tucked one hand behind his head and cradled her beside him with his free arm. "It's going to suck, though."

"Why?"

Her hair tickled his cheek. He blew out a long breath. Get it over with as soon as possible. "I got a call from my agent, Carmine. He's got a music video he wants me to costar in and a cameo on a TV show. It'll take four weeks easy. I wanted to tell you earlier, but we had no time together. I want you to come along. Will you? Come with me?" He held his breath, waiting for her answer.

"I can't."

He groaned. Damn. "I thought so." He should've known. She'd want to stay the hell away from Hollywood and Dex.

"Will you miss me while you're gone?" she asked.

Logan rubbed his cheek on her hair. "Miss you? I'll be a shadow of myself without you, love." Still, he couldn't deny the irritation. He wished he'd had more control over his life and hadn't allowed Carmine to put him in a difficult position. He'd fallen head over heels for Cass. She lit up a room with a simple smile and her energy was boundless. People flocked to her because she practically glowed. Then there was her amazing body. Dear God, the things she could do and the ways she made him react. Other women ceased to exist in his eyes.

"Just what I needed to hear," she murmured. "But I have some bad news."

"Bad?" Logan paused. "Like?" He thought they'd just discussed their future plans.

"I wanted to explain why I can't accompany you to California."

"Okay." Logan stiffened. She was the spark that lit his acting skills. Without his muse, he'd be a grouchy mess. So not cool. He closed his eyes and bit back a sigh.

"My editor called." Cass propped herself up on her elbow and spread her palm across his chest. "Don't flip out. It's nothing huge, but my editor appreciated having my short story in her hands. She was thrilled, but she needs the novel right away and I'm behind."

"I'll let you work — tomorrow." Logan smoothed his hand over her ass. He didn't have to like the separation, but he could completely understand. She only did what she needed to do to survive.

She kissed his lips, laving her tongue along his teeth. Warm. Wet. Damn, he needed to feel her surrounding him. She was sexy, wonderful and all his. Logan's dick rose to the occasion.

"The novel has a deadline that I'm going to miss, Logan. I need about four weeks of hiding in my cave to get it done and get a good start on the next one."

He frowned. Four weeks was a long time. Carmine said

he had at least six weeks of work contracted. Damn it. Maybe he'd get two weeks with her. Then again, once that was up, they'd have the rest of their lives together. Why didn't that seem like enough? Because she was part of him.

"I understand, but your cave?"

"My office." She shrugged. "It's where the magic happens. Can't exactly call it a palace."

Logan sighed and ran a hand through his hair. He hated his profession for what he had to do next. "I'm frustrated, but I don't suppose you can finish the novel with me pestering you all day?"

"No. I need to concentrate." Cass giggled. She drew lazy circles around his nipple. "There is email, the phone and video chat. I could always send a few risqué pictures to your email or arrange a couple of X-rated phone calls mixed with the pitiful missing you calls. Just don't go getting involved with an on-set hookup."

She knew him too well. He'd been a bad boy for so long. "Don't need to hook up with anyone else."

"Didn't think so, but trust isn't my forte." Cass settled into his arms once again. "I love you, Logan, so much."

Her breath warmed his skin and blood rushed through his body. How could he even comprehend six weeks away from her? Away from her smiles, away from her comforting arms. Phone conversations, no matter how X-rated, wouldn't suffice. Not by a long shot. He debated his next move. His thoughts swirled around Cass. She was so unlike all the other women in his life. The others wanted nothing more than the status of sleeping with him. They wanted his money and residual fame. Not Cass. She personified compassion. Her heart was so big and full and overflowing. She gave without wanting repayment or publicity, although she did have specific demands. She wanted his heart, his body and his love — things he never gave freely before. But, her insistence wasn't forceful. No. She was grounded, conventional and damned sexy just as God made her. He wasn't going to get on with his life if he let others choreograph it. He needed to let Cass in on his thought process and see what she thought of his decision.

"Babe, I'm gonna do it. I'm quitting the business so I can be here with you," he murmured and stroked her hair. "No more nude scenes, no more on-screen kisses, no more games or commitments where I can't be with you. I'm done with all that."

"Sounds wonderful." Cass rubbed her cheek against him. "But you're an actor and you need to act. As long as your heart is with me, I'm okay with you still being in the business."

"That's just it—I don't *need* to act. I want to be the one who does all the things you do because you have to. I want to do the yard work, tend to the animals and pamper you. I want to stay your other half and give you babies."

She sighed and snuggled in closer to him. "Sure."

"We'll marry soon. You can decide if it's an extravaganza or a simple barefoot ceremony on the back forty," he said. "Whatever makes you happy is exactly what I want. My only request is that you wear a white dress with a veil. You deserve a fresh start with all the past forgiven."

Cass stilled in his arms and her breath tickled his skin.

"Give me three weeks to sort things out with Carmine. He's got those short-term projects for me to finish and a guest appearance on a television show. But when that's over, I'm packing the GTO and coming home to you. No more lunch wagons or hairdressers, just you, me, the dogs and at least two children. That's the way life should be for the both of us."

His muscles twitched with the need to make love to her again. He'd never tire of loving her. With Cass, he felt at peace. He belonged. "I'll never let you go."

Her muddled hum of agreement was her only reply.

Logan rested against her and closed his eyes again. She draped her leg over his thigh and curled her hand on his chest.

He couldn't wait to get on with his life with her. He

couldn't see his future without her. "If anyone ever tried to hurt you, Cass, I'd give my life to keep you safe. I promise. You are my life. Mine."

* * * *

Cass replaced the phone in its cradle. She brushed a lock of hair away from her face and sighed. "Six weeks of hard work and more chocolate than I care to think about, but it's done." She stroked Elliott's fur. "The novel is done and in Naya's hands. I've got time to play when I see Logan tomorrow."

Elliott plopped his head on her thigh. Ever since Logan had left, the dog just didn't seem the same. If it were possible for a dog to look desolate, miserable and depressed, Elliott had them all down to a science.

"You want Logan to come home, don't you?" At the mention of Logan's name, Elliott's ears perked up. His eyes brightened. She knew the dog wanted his person home.

Cass scratched Elliott's ears and then idly caressed her own stomach. "I'm lonely without him too, but he says he's done with acting once these jobs are done. Who knows?"

In the space of a few months' time, Logan had managed to bust through all her defenses and become her closest friend. Her lover. Her other half. Just thinking about Logan sent heat and desire rushing through her body. Giddy excitement pooled low in her belly. What a hold he had on her. Whew! The need to touch him was that great. She walked downstairs and flipped on the television before retrieving a load of laundry. At least her stomach wasn't upset at the moment. She opened the front of the dryer and retrieved her clothes.

"Cass? Are you here?"

She looked up from the dryer. Ray stood in the doorway with his arms folded. His eyes blazed. Who'd pissed him off? Her? What'd she do now?

"What's wrong?" She retrieved the wet clothes from the

washer and tucked them into the dryer. When he didn't answer, she glanced over her shoulder. "Ray?"

He strode to the living room and fumbled with the remote. Changing the channel? He probably wanted to watch some race highlight show or something. She sighed and dropped the laundry basket, taking the remote from his hands. "What's the matter with you, Ray? What channel do you want?"

Ray moved in front of the television screen, but couldn't seem to look her in the eye. Cass shoved him aside and instantly wished she hadn't. A slender blonde dressed in a curve-hugging lavender halter dress flashed onto the screen. "Romeo Malone is at it again," a female news anchor said. "He spent time in the backwoods of Ohio, supposedly in the arms of author Cass Jensen, but our footage of the Calvin Leigh Music Awards last week tells a much different story."

She cocked her head and her stomach fluttered. An image of Logan waltzed onto the screen with Jade curled in his arm. His crisp black suit contoured to his every curve, while her barely there satin dress hid only the most essential parts of her anatomy. Logan smiled and laughed while Jade kissed his neck. A bright diamond sparkled on her left hand.

Cass bit the corner of her mouth and gripped her midsection. A clip from one of Logan's movies intermixed with the image of the announcer. In the scene, Jade knelt on the edge of the bed while Logan furiously pumped into her.

"No," Cass whispered. "He's not like that. He's not doing that any longer."

Despite her ramblings, the announcer continued to toy with her dignity. "Here is Romeo with his newest conquest, fiancée and the mother of his first child, according to our sources. After hitting the red carpet with Jade Weir, Romeo finished the graphic love scene for their new movie, *Brush*. Talk about bling for the mommy-to-be! Here's Jade showing off the four-carat pink diamond and her flat stomach. Her publicist, Rynne Reynolds, claims the couple is very happy and plans to wed by Christmas. The baby is due in early May. Now to other news..."

Cass curled her fists. Her heart and soul refused to believe Logan would betray her. To betray them. Something about the whole scene felt off. She could tell by the dim light in his eyes. She knew Logan at his best and this act in public wasn't it. Cass frowned at the television. "You know. I think it's a set-up, Ray. A scam. He wanted to fool the paparazzi. And if my math's right, the baby isn't his."

"Honey, he's not a good man. He's an actor, for God's sake." Ray sat next to her, but she edged away. She didn't want his consolation or pity. She wanted to change the damned channel.

"Where's my phone?" Cass wiggled her fingers. "I'm going to call him. Logan will tell me the truth. If there's nothing going on, then there's nothing to hide. Plain and simple." She pressed the keys and waited for Logan's voice on the other end of the line.

She frowned. "Welcome to Call-All Wireless. The number you are trying to reach has been disconnected. Please check the number and try again."

Cass stared at the phone in her hand. Disconnected? She spoke to him for over an hour the night prior. She shivered and placed the device on the counter. No, he wouldn't abandon her like garbage. She reached for her laptop and sent a quick email to Logan. Surely his email was still in service.

Within seconds of sending the email, a return notice arrived. Failure to deliver. Account closed. Mailbox nonexistent.

Cass trembled. Her entire body shook with her efforts to keep her emotions in check and stay calm. Logan wouldn't ditch her. He wouldn't make a fool of her in front of all those people. Better yet, he wouldn't trivialize the creation of his first child. She swallowed hard. Would he? She twisted the diamond ring around her finger and thought back to their last night together. *Just you, me, the dogs and a couple of children.* She never expected Jade to figure into their fairy-tale ending. Anger replaced her heartache.

Ray stepped to her position and smoothed his fingers through her hair. "Why don't you stay here and get the tears and anger out of your system, Cass?"

Elliott came over to lick her face. Paula nudged her hand to a cuddle. Cass shook her head and patted both dogs. She cleared her throat. Her stomach clenched. "Tears? I won't cry over something I can't confirm. Lies from a second-rate reporter don't count. Plus, Jade didn't look pregnant."

"I'll bet he's on his way here right now to set everything straight," Ray whispered.

Her brows knotted together. Was Ray serious? "You know, I think I'll try Maggie. She has his personal details in the records for the film. She'll know what's up with him."

Cass dialed her friend's number and waited. After four rings, Maggie picked up. "Hey, Maggie. How's life in sunny California?"

"It's raining, go figure, but I bet that's not why you called. Yes, I saw the clips from the Calvin Leigh ceremony. Logan made an ass of himself and I'm sure you saw it or you wouldn't have called. That kid can't be his."

Cass winced. "You're right and I'm sure it's nothing. By the way, do you have his number? I got a new cell and wanted to program the phone book feature."

Maggie chuckled. "I'll fork it over, but he won't answer. I tried him last night around ten and it said no service. Knowing that man, he probably didn't pay the bill on time or left it up to his derelict agent to do it."

Cass nibbled her bottom lip and wrote the numbers Maggie recited. The number hadn't miraculously changed overnight. "I'll try him again." With that, she disconnected with her friend. Cass turned to Ray. "Maybe there was a glitch with my email, but I know I programmed the right phone number into my phone."

She set the device to speaker and redialed Logan's cell phone number. Again the automated voice told her that the number was no longer in service. Cass disconnected the call. Something didn't add up. Why sever all ties? Did Dex get to Logan?

"Maybe he wanted to get a local number," Ray said and folded his arms. "Maybe he's trying to throw Nikita and Jade off his trail or to surprise you. Maybe he's driving in a dead zone where phone reception is bad." He crossed his ankles and leaned against the counter. "Look, I know you like him and I'm not going to give you hell about him any longer. Maybe it's a glitch and he's in the middle of working it all out."

Cass closed the laptop and ignored Ray, despite his change in attitude. She folded her hands as if in prayer. "Okay. No phone. No email. No problem."

"What?"

Cass slashed her hands through the air. "This isn't a problem."

"How?" Ray asked.

"I'll see him tomorrow. If he's at the airport like we agreed, then we can talk on the way to his apartment. If he's the decent man I remember and trust, then this is some sort of ploy. We'll get past it."

Ray pinched the bridge of his nose. "Cass."

She shook her head and raked her fingers through her hair. "What do you expect me to do? Put my life on hold because I don't know what's up with him? I can't reach him. For whatever reason, he's cut me out of communication." She laced her fingers together behind her head. "If he's moved on with his life, then I need to, too."

"Are you sure about this? I'll back you no matter what you decide."

"I'm sure there is a good explanation. We'll either get past this episode or that's the end."

Ray's shoulders slumped. "You know where I am if you need me." He brushed his fingertips down her arm, then left the room.

Once the door closed, Cass removed her engagement ring

and placed it on the china plate where she kept her other jewelry while washing dishes. "We'll get past this once I have some space," she mumbled and ambled upstairs to think. She wanted to believe Logan wasn't going back on his promises, but something didn't sit right with her.

Moments flashed through her mind—the concert as he sang in her ear, the quickie in the cabin, the way he brushed his hand along her bottom each time he passed. It all reminded her how much he loved her. How much she loved him.

She brushed away tears and shoved his clothes into an unused dresser drawer. Out of sight, where he belonged for now. His bathroom items, including his cologne and razor, went into the bottom drawer of the vanity. His razor reminded her of their tryst in the shower—she'd never had sex in the shower before him.

I'll always love you, baby, he'd said.

She shook her head, forcing herself back to the present. She looked around the room and missed his presence. She flopped on the bed. The olive-green comforter fluttered as she landed and Logan's scent wafted around her, bringing fresh tears to her eyes. The ticking of the wall clock sounded like bass drums pounding in her ears. Paula crawled on the bed beside her, but Elliott nosed the pillows. He barked, jarring her from her pity party.

Cass brushed the hair off her face. "What?"

Elliott got a good hold on the rumpled pillow and tugged it forward. There, bunched in between the mattress and the frame, was one of Logan's T-shirts. Elliott whimpered.

More tears pricked her eyes as Cass worked the garment from its hiding spot. Without thinking, she pressed it to her nose and breathed deep. His scent permeated her life.

"Oh, Logan. What are you doing to me?"

Cass tucked the shirt under her pillow. She shouldn't feel so awful about the situation. Just as he promised, he showed her that men weren't all pigs. He proved that love could be exciting and sex fulfilling. Logan showed her that her heart was big enough to love again.

"We'll get by, El," she soothed. "We will and soon we'll look back and laugh." Elliott rested his head on her lap. She understood the dog's pain. She loved Logan so much and didn't know the score.

A moment later, once she gathered her wits, she patted Elliott and Paula and stood up. She wiped her cheeks dry. "I've made a decision."

Elliott barked. His tail swished wildly. Paula jumped up and flopped over on the bed.

"That's right. I saw the clip. I've got a gig tonight and I'm going all-out. Those boys expect me to be one of the guys. Tonight they'll know I'm damned sexy and if Logan shows, he can explain himself because I won't go away without a fight. If he did nothing wrong, there's nothing to fight about."

She nodded sharply and headed into the bathroom to prepare for the concert. She had a job to do.

Chapter Nineteen

That night, Cass and Hillbilly Boots tore down the house. She'd never felt so alive in front of the crowd. For a little while, she not only forgot her problems but her cares too. After the third song, she stole a glance at Ray. Instead of approval, he glared at her. Why? Her clothing choices? The black tank and curve-hugging jeans weren't part of her ordinary stage attire. Who cared? The body glitter accentuated the girls a bit much, but so what? Wasn't she allowed to feel sexy and confident? Why did she think Logan had something to do with Ray's nasty attitude? Nothing else made sense.

"Thank you," Cass puffed into the microphone. "We need to take a breather, but we'll be back in about ten or fifteen." She took a bow with the band and raced off the stage. She strode straight to Ray's cousin, Ned, and grinned. "I believe you asked for a dance."

"I did." Ned stood up and tossed the hank of black hair off his forehead. Lanky and over six feet tall, he easily towered over her diminutive frame. He held out his hand and led her to the dance floor.

A ballad blared from the speakers, reminding her of her dates with Logan. She wanted to dance with him. Dancing with Ned seemed nice, but criminal. But where was old Logan to stop her? In California getting engaged to someone else. She shook her head and stared up into Ned's eyes. She'd deal with the Logan situation later.

Cass put her hands on Ned's shoulders, though it was a

stretch. "I forgot how tall you are, Ned Russell."

Ned laughed, tightening his chiseled jaw. "Must've been a growth spurt or you got shorter. I found your hips just fine."

Cass giggled. Other men said she had big hips. With Ned, she knew it was simply a blunt compliment. "So why are you here? Where's Drew? And why did you bring your mopey buddy over there? Am I boring you?"

Ned took a deep breath and nodded to his friend at the bar. "Ray asked us to catch the show. Drew got married about three weeks ago. Did the service myself, thank you very much. Jude's got a heart of gold and compliments him well."

"That's sweet. You're a good friend."

"As for Bret, I wanted to get the mope off the couch. He needs a woman, but I'll be damned if I'm gonna find one for him. I can hardly keep one of my own."

"I see," Cass lied. She couldn't see why Ned had problems finding decent dates, except that he went through women like water. She didn't know his friend Bret Cochran well enough to speculate, but both men were handsome in their own special ways. Maybe they didn't try hard enough. She didn't know.

A man she didn't know eased through the crowd to where she danced with Ned. "May I have this dance?"

Cass noticed the tip of a dagger, or was it a sword, under his dress shirt sleeve. Why did this man seem familiar? She stole a glance at Ned who frowned. She shook her head. "No thank you."

With that, the man glared and disappeared.

She rested her forehead on Ned's chest. "That was odd."

Ned touched her chin, bringing her back to the moment. "I hear you have a man issue. Wanna talk about it?"

Why did Ray keep butting into her business? And why did Ned think he could do the same?

"No. There's no issue, just a misunderstanding. It's over for now."

He crooked his brow. "Then kiss me."

Cass stopped cold. She looked into Ned's green eyes. This was Ray's cousin, not some drunk from the bar. He was a safe, sexy, upstanding citizen. Why did the idea of kissing him feel so wrong?

He wasn't Logan.

The corner of Ned's mouth turned up. "Kiss me, Cass."

Her lips parted, which was all the invitation he needed. He swooped in and brushed his mouth against hers. Cass's eyes fluttered shut, more out of respect than attraction. True, she liked Ned, but never more than as a friend. His late-day stubble abraded her cheeks, but there wasn't the shiver, the rush. In her mind, she pictured Logan. She wanted to cry. She missed the rawness and the raging desire. Correction.

She missed Logan.

"Well?"

Cass stared at the design on his dress shirt. "Well, what?" What kind of answer did he want? Based on the way he tipped his head to the side and the furrows on his forehead, Ned didn't seem to feel any sort of simmering passion between them, either.

"How did I make you feel?"

Cass pressed her lips together. Kissing him was nothing like Logan. When Ned kissed her, she felt like she just kissed her brother on the cheek or like when Ray tackled her during a touch football game and mashed his face into hers by accident.

"I thought so."

She met his gaze. "You thought what?"

Ned cupped her jaw in both hands. "Logan Malone had better figure out what the hell he wants and either let you go or keep his ass here. He's a fool if he doesn't want you."

"I never thought you were. But that man isn't here to defend himself."

Ned shrugged and let go of her. "You know, you might be surprised by what you get."

She frowned. More advice she didn't want. The song

ended and Ned led her to Ray's position at the edge of the stage.

Ray nodded over his shoulder. Frustration burned in his eyes. His jaw locked tight. "You have a visitor," he growled.

Cass rested her hands on her hips. "Who?" No one else she wanted to see would be at the bar that night.

"Me."

She whirled around to see a disheveled Logan waiting patiently by the stage steps. She sagged against Ned. What the hell? How did Logan get there? A lump formed in the pit of her stomach. If he was there, then he probably heard her songs. How did he feel, knowing she just poured her heart out? How did he feel about her dance with Ned?

"I need to talk to you," Logan said evenly. "Who's that guy?"

Cass looked at Ray before answering. "Ray's cousin, Ned. He's a judge."

"Why did he kiss you?"

Not wanting to back down, Cass volleyed a better question. "Did you screw around with Jade and father her child?"

Logan shoved his hands into his pockets. "I can explain everything. It wasn't what it looked like."

She narrowed her eyes. Logan's clingy black tee accentuated the muscles of his broad chest, while the butter-soft jeans molded to his legs like a second skin. Christ, she wanted him, even though she also wanted to rip him a new one. Had he lifted weights while back home in California? His body looked more like a statue than a real man. Not that it mattered if he did. She glanced down at his feet. Damn, he wore cowboy boots. Even his feet looked sexy. She swallowed hard.

"I think you better listen," Ray scolded. "Cass."

"Why? What do you know that I should know?" She forced her glare from Logan to Ray. A combination of love, lust and frustration surged through her body. She wanted to tackle Logan and the kick his ass for being such a jerk.

She also wanted to give Ray a piece of her mind for butting in.

"I called Ray," Logan murmured.

"What?" She bunched her brows. *Logan called Ray?* What next—pigs flying?

"I sent the jet to California to bring him back here," Ray said. He scrubbed his hand on the back of his neck. "You two needed to talk face-to-face and I didn't think you'd mind."

"I don't believe this." Cass stared at both men. *Sent the jet? Didn't think she'd mind?* Well, hell. She minded very much. Only Ray knew he could take liberties with her plane—with her life. But Logan... Did he really think he could waltz back to Ohio and push into her life after he'd created a baby with another woman? Not now. He'd never really left her life or her heart, but she wasn't going to break up a family.

Cass toyed with the hem of her tank top. Both men looked downright pitiful. The crease between Logan's brows deepened and sadness clouded his eyes. Ray stared at the ground and continued to rub his neck raw. Her stomach churned and fluttered. Even upset, Logan turned her on. She didn't know whether to want him naked or begging for forgiveness. Nothing made sense.

Ray met her gaze once again. "He didn't cheat on you. It was a set-up. Everything was a farce to get face time."

She ran the fingers of her free hand through her hair. Ray sounded credible, but then, he'd never lied to her. This all sounded dangerously like the truth. She poked Logan in the shoulder. "Lay this out for me. I want to know everything."

"I called Ray once I saw the footage of Jade and me at the show. *Delish* will publish anything to get hits on the website. They live for that shit because her old man owns the magazine. Cass, I didn't know what to do. I knew you'd be pissed. You should be, but you need to forgive me. I didn't father her child."

"I know," she replied.

Logan's shoulders sank, then he snapped his gaze to hers.

"Wait. You knew?"

Cass leaned against the closest table and kept her hands under her ass. She'd forgive him but not yet. She closed her eyes and pieced through what they'd said. She should've known the whole thing would be a joke.

"He called me for advice and help," Ray said. "Logan knew how much you meant to me and how much he loved you. He never wanted to break your heart."

Cass opened her eyes slowly. She stared at Logan while Ray spoke. The creases framing Logan's mouth deepened. Could men cry, even when the cameras stopped rolling? She seriously doubted it. All the bottled-up emotions and hormones raged to the surface faster than she could blot them out.

"So you two felt the need to double team me with this information? Come on. You're not giving me credit for having a brain." She shook her head. "Now I'm here, with a crowd of people possibly watching—who knows if there's paparazzi out there?—and you want to tell me how you're sorry? Excuse me if I'm having a hard time wanting to do that."

Apparently that sent the wrong message to Ray. His brows shot up and color rushed into his cheeks. Ray's eyes rivaled bowling balls. "Honey, you know that's not what we meant to do. We wanted—"

Cass socked him in the arm, hardly making a dent. "My heart and my life are not toys for you two to play with. I'm tired of the garbage and the smokescreens."

Logan reached for her, lightly brushing her shoulder. "Cass."

She gritted her teeth. She wasn't about to topple like a domino. Not yet. "You claimed you loved me," she bit out and fought hard against falling apart. "You claimed I was enough for you."

Logan's mouth opened and closed like a fish out of water. She had him dead to rights.

"I'm not pencil-thin and made up like the starlets you

normally bed, no question there. But, I got the impression that you appreciated the way I indulged you. Was that a lie too?"

Some of the dancers stopped to gawk and listen to the argument. The tips of her ears burned. Tears burned down her cheeks. "I spent too many nights crying with Ray, trying to heal my heart after what Dex did to me. I wasted too many evenings wishing that my prince charming would arrive. Like a fool, I gave too much time to you and your happily-ever-after, Logan. I know this was another set-up, but I don't think I'm strong enough to watch you parade around with other women just to sell pictures. I did that before and ended up alone and heartbroken. I won't do it again for anyone. I want all of you or none of you." Cass sucked in a ragged breath. "I won't settle for anything less."

She shook her head and went for the door. No more jokes. No more bullshit. She'd thought she'd found a couple of good men she could trust... So much for a fun evening.

"Cass, wait!" Logan called. When she didn't, he bit back a groan. Even angry, she turned his insides out. She had a great ass and a fiery spirit, no denying that. So why didn't she believe him? Because he came clean about his past and told her the God's honest truth — even the rough parts. He'd worked so hard to convince her that he'd changed and sixty seconds of film blew that all to hell.

Ray cracked his knuckles. The sound grated on Logan's frayed nerves. What a smooth team he and Ray were. So smooth Cass strolled right out the door.

"What do I do, Ray? I can't go on like this," Logan complained. Precious moments spent with her floated through his mind — their first meeting, the first night together, the first time they made love. Down to his soul, he craved her. "She's all I ever wanted and now she's on her way out of my life. I knew this would happen. I gotta go after her."

Ray took a deep sigh and slung his guitar across his chest.

"Why don't you stay with me until she calms down? I've got an extra room and my most recent roommate isn't real thrilled with me either."

Logan looked at his new ally. His curiosity rose along with his natural penchant for gossip. "Who and how? Gimme the dirt. Maggie?" He really hoped Ray meant Maggie and that they were going to work things out.

Ray looked away. "It's a long story that I don't feel like explaining."

Logan cocked a brow. Not explaining. He had to be talking about Maggie. "Hey, it'll get sorted out. I know." The way Maggie acted around Ray, they had to be in love — or seriously horny for each other He glanced back at the door. Cass was already gone and she had his heart. He puffed out a long sigh. "As for my love life, what should we do now?"

Ray restocked his shirt pocket with guitar picks. "Give her time to calm down and if she doesn't by morning, then we'll both grovel. I'm good at begging."

Logan pinched the bridge of his nose. "I'm game, as long as I can get her back." He didn't like seeing her kiss another man and could imagine how abandoned she felt. Hell, he never had a woman walk away from him until she came along.

He hoped the soon-to-be formed plan would work. It had to.

Chapter Twenty

Cass woke the next morning and stretched. Logan's scent drifted around her and she groaned. Why did she have to sleep in his stupid T-shirt? Because she missed him and wanted to be near him.

Why? The man she loved more than anyone turned out to be just like the fame-grubbing scum she'd divorced years ago. Well, not really. Logan needed to preserve his image — an image she didn't fit into. But wasn't that the problem? She wasn't the type of woman he needed on his arm. She could be cute as hell all day long, but the media and his image expected someone who wasn't her.

She wiped fresh tears from her face and forced herself to get out of bed. A hair clip and a baggy pair of sleep shorts would finish off a lovely outfit for a lazy, depressing day.

Cass trudged out of the room in her favorite kitty slippers. Despite the early hour, mint chocolate chip ice cream beckoned. Maybe even a call to the local Italian restaurant for lasagna at lunchtime. Why not? Nobody of importance would see her and she just didn't care.

The dogs twined around her feet as she made her way down the steps to let them out for the morning. "Don't trip me, kids." She clipped their collars to their runs and closed the door. "Ice cream."

She headed back to the kitchen to locate the ice cream when she heard the doorbell. She grabbed her cell phone from the counter and swiped her thumb across the screen in an attempt to figure out where the sound came from. The barking of the dogs alerted her to the door. Oh yeah, the doorbell. Wow. She was out of it.

She braced herself, expecting Logan or even Ray. She knew darn well Ray would simply barge in and Logan had a key. Neither needed to ring the blasted bell.

The doorbell broke the relative silence in the house again. "Just a minute!" she called and smoothed out the rumpled T-shirt. God, she felt like hell warmed over and knew she probably didn't look much better. She opened the door and nearly jumped a foot. She stared at the slim woman sobbing on her porch. Well, hell.

"Are you Cass Jensen?"

Cass fumbled a moment. Where had she seen this girl before? Damn, she looked familiar. The girl swiped the tears from her face, effectively smearing her thick makeup. "Are you Cass Jensen?" she asked again.

"I am. And you are?"

The girl collapsed into fresh tears. "It's my fault!"

Cass stared at the woman. Who was this girl and why did she claim something was her fault? What the hell? She sighed. "Who are you? I think I missed your introduction."

The girl smoothed away more makeup and a couple of stray locks of blonde hair. "I never gave you my name. I'm Jade Weir. You saw me and my boobs in all those photos with Logan. It's all a lie, and it's all my fault. I'm so sorry," she said in quick succession. Her shoulders slumped and she started to cry again. Jade's body looked frail, like her bones could snap in a stiff breeze. Dark roots showed under her bleached blonde hair. She looked younger than the tabloid assigned age of twenty-one years old. Actually, she looked damned tired too.

Cass raked a hand through her tangled hair and replaced the clip. "Come in and sit. We'll talk this out." She led Jade to the living room and found a half-full box of tissues. "Wipe your tears, honey. We'll figure this out. What's the story?"

Jade slouched and kicked out of her high-heeled shoes

while Cass tucked her legs under her body. Jade took the tissues and attempted to make herself more presentable. She smoothed her hair behind her ears and took a deep breath.

"Please promise you won't throw me out, even though I deserve it," Jade whispered. She sounded more like a child than an adult. "I'm a bad person."

Cass patted Jade's knee, like an older sister might. "Tell me the story and we'll figure out what to do."

"I had an affair with Dex."

Cass gulped air. "Oh." She never saw that coming. She'd expected Jade to admit to the affair with Logan.

Jade looked down at her hands. "I met him on the set of *Sunset*. He seemed like a nice enough kind of guy and he kissed pretty well. Not great, but he told me I was appealing and that he wanted to 'see' me. Said we'd make beautiful children together."

Cass nodded. He'd told her those exact words years ago and, like Jade, she fell for it, hook, line and sinker.

"We only made love in my trailer and it made me wonder. What was wrong with his place, you know? So I went to his trailer, expecting to find him with another girl."

Cass gritted her teeth. *Here comes the big one. Wait for it…* "And?"

Jade shook her head, but wouldn't meet Cass's gaze. "It wasn't a woman in the flesh, it was a hundred or so pictures — of you. But you know, I didn't care because I was having his baby."

Cass shivered. Fear and disgust ran the length of her spine. She wanted to wretch. "He's the father?"

"I wanted to be with him because I loved him. He's the father of my child. So I told him that if he got rid of those pictures, I'd do whatever he asked. I figured he'd want kinky sex or partners or something. I knew his reputation. Everyone does. But that wasn't what he really wanted."

Cass braced herself once more. "What was it?"

"He found out you and Logan were involved. He wanted

me to split you up. If I did, then he'd marry me and take care of the baby. And I was stupid enough to do it because I thought a family would change his mind. Dex used me. Fucking stupid!"

Cass sank back in her seat. The man was good. He could spot a sucker a mile away. Jade was nothing more than a puppet for his sick desire. It still made no sense, why Dex wanted her back. The silly excuse that he hated to lose? That seemed ludicrous. What else could she possibly have? He hated to see her happy with anyone else.

"How did Dex know?" Cass asked. "We hardly ever went out in public. There wasn't time."

Jade's hands fluttered in the air. Her voice came out choked. "Spies. Nikita gave him the info and I used Logan. I had the paparazzi get those pictures and hunt him down for that publicity event. Once Nikita told me to hit it hard, I called in a favor or two."

Cass leveled her shoulders. "Who wrote the headline on that picture in Logan's trailer?"

"Nikita got my lipstick shade. She made Ania do it so you wouldn't recognize the handwriting. She also made Ania break your window. That poor girl just wanted to become a director one day. She'd do anything for Nikita."

"So you all wanted to make my life with Logan a living hell? Why? To get me to leave him alone? That's ridiculous." Although she'd seen people do lesser things just to get into their partner's good graces.

Jade fumbled with her hands. "It wasn't supposed to go down like that. That's why Ania got out. She wouldn't do the dirty work any longer."

Cass remembered the comments she'd shared with Ania. The girl had seemed rather pleasant. They'd even sort of bonded. Hopefully Ania would be able to find her true path in life, away from the clutches of Nikita and Dex.

"I mean, I did like Logan for a while," Jade said with a sniffle. "Hell, it was fun to watch him chase. He always gets what he wants and I liked knowing he wanted me, but that's in the past. He wants you, not me. Me wanting your ex is what screwed this all up. Help me make this right. You and Logan belong together." She collapsed in sobs once again. "I'm so sorry."

Cass rubbed Jade's back and processed her words. Too many of Jade's statements were eerily true. "What about that *Delish* clip of you two at the awards? You staged that, didn't you?"

Jade nodded and wiped her face once more. "Yeah. I tackled him and flashed the camera crew to get them to pay attention. I made up the story that Logan was the father to get air time. Logan got pissed, but played along sort of, until we got into the auditorium. When he found out the lie, he lit into me in the bathroom and left before the award show officially began. He said I screwed up his only chance at happiness. He was and is right."

Cass scrubbed a hand down her face and comforted Jade. "Then what about the baby? When are you due? Are you taking care of yourself?"

Jade sucked in a ragged breath. "I was never pregnant to begin with. My period was late due to stress, not a baby. When I found out, I wanted to get even with Dex for using me and didn't think about how you'd feel. I'm sorry."

"Oh hell." Cass balled her fists. Dex finally had someone just as devious as he was. He deserved the trouble he'd created. "I don't suppose you know about the shooting, then?"

Her eyes widened. "Shot? Someone…"

Cass teetered on the edge of control. Her voice cracked. "Yeah. Someone shot at us while we were in my house. Whoever it was had shitty aim, thank God."

"Dex wanted to keep an eye on you, but I never wanted him or you dead." The color bled from Jade's face. "I wouldn't have helped him with that. Promise."

"Okay, Jade. Okay." If her life had to go to shit, then why not go whole hog? Cass picked up her cell. Ray would have an answer. Or at least he'd help her figure out what to do.

On the third ring, Ray answered, but not as she expected. "Talk to Logan."

"You don't even know the problem." That's why she never called Ray in the clutch. He jumped to conclusions and gave quick answers.

"He's here and waiting for you," Ray said, his voice strong.

Cass nearly fell off the couch. She bit her tongue as she fumbled for what she wanted to say. "Waiting for me? He never left—even after I gave him a piece of my mind?"

"Yeah, the poor fool really loves you."

"Are you thinking clearly, Ray? You took him in?" She reeled and rubbed her jaw. This wasn't right. Jade on her furniture crying and Logan at Ray's house? What next? Dex at her door with another ring, professing his undying love? She hoped not. Not today.

"My thinking is crystal clear," Ray said quietly. "We bonded."

Cass smoothed her hand over her stomach, forcing it to calm. She felt like the world suddenly hit the brakes. Men like Ray and Logan were too alike to work together. "Bonded? You and Logan?"

"We have some common interests," Ray replied.

Cass rolled her eyes. Same interests? "Really? Come on, Ray."

"He loves you and so do I. We can't bear to see you hurt," Ray said. "Logan never meant to for this to happen. He's willing to do whatever it takes to win you back."

"I know," she whispered. She believed Ray and Logan, despite her misgivings. They wouldn't be working together for nothing.

It was Ray's turn to act stunned. "Wait. What?"

Cass paused. "Jade's here and I know everything. He was set up—by Dex. There was no baby, just a lot of spite and hate. This is so screwed up."

"We'll be there in ten minutes." With that, Ray clicked off the line.

Cass sighed. Logan never left and they both demanded answers. Time for the soul-searching talk they should've had the night before. Her heart skipped a beat. He still wanted her. She preferred to melt into the floor or climb under a rock and hide. Instead, she walked into the dining room to decompress.

* * * *

"Ray, I can't do this. She's been through enough," Logan mumbled and mashed himself into the passenger seat of Ray's truck. "She won't take me back."

Ray steered the rusty truck into Cass's driveway. "You don't know what she'll do until you let her do it."

Logan crossed his arms. He made a mistake. Leaving her alone killed him slowly and managed to ruin all the good he'd built with her. "How is she going to trust me? Even when I'm not trying to fuck up, I still fuck things up."

Ray brought the truck to a screeching halt in the gravel next to the garage. Two sedans sat in front of the garage. A shiver ran along Logan's spine. Had she replaced him already? But still… Two cars? Everything felt wrong.

"Something isn't cool here." Logan gripped the door handle. Jade's words rang in his ears. *You don't want a girl like her. She's pure. You're filthy. I claimed you as the father of a child that doesn't exist to make the papers.* Nikita's words slam burned a hole in his stomach. *'You're so above a woman like Chunks, Logan. Give up the charity case. Cass just plain broke his heart. I can't watch you parade around with other women. I did that before. Not again. Was our love all a lie?'*

Ray cut the power to the engine and looked out the window. "If she wanted another man, she'd call me. But I doubt it because I'm stuck with you. Now what's not right about this situation?"

Logan stared at the cars a moment longer. Maybe the red car belonged to Les or another friend, but the light blue one had him riled. Something felt very wrong. He threw Ray a

236

dirty look. "Look, just because we're getting along doesn't mean I won't kick your ass to rescue her." He'd die for her, no questions asked.

"Put it back in your pants, Malone." Ray scratched the slight growth of hair on his chin. "Cass and I have a special bond, like a sister-brother thing. She told me that if she never found the man that made her whole, she'd choose me. It's too late for that. She found you and I'm damned proud."

"Proud? Ray, I'm touched." He climbed out of the truck and stood in front of the vehicle. The two extra cars still bothered him.

"I want her to be happy. You make her happy. I just seem to boss her around."

Logan rubbed his palms on his jeans legs. "Shit. I haven't had a chance to shower. I look and smell like the bar, even though I only had two beers."

Ray grabbed Logan by the collar. "Fight for her, you ass. Stop being a pussy. She won't care if you had a couple of drinks last night. Now, get in there and apologize for your Hollywood crap before I have to beat it out of you."

Logan raked his fingers through his hair, standing it on end. His nerve endings sizzled. Blood surged through his body. Yes, he would fight for her. Absolutely.

Logan followed Ray into the house. The silence bothered him. When they reached the kitchen, Paula and Elliott rushed to them. Paula sat quietly while the male dog chewed on his jeans cuff. Logan noticed Jade sitting on Cass's plaid couch. Christ, he wanted to die. Sure Cass said his ex was there, but seeing Jade in the flesh rocked his shoddy nerves. He felt like a heel for the way he'd treated Jade. Even more so because he wanted to be with Cass. "Where's Cass?"

Jade sniffled and turned around. "She's in the front room."

Logan stood directly in front of Jade. Primal instincts drove him to push harder than needed. "What's this about? Tell me everything."

Jade blew her nose and recited her story. As she talked,

Ray clenched his fists. Logan scrubbed his hands on his face. He noticed Cass quietly listening in the doorway. The sloppy sleepshirt and pants made her look adorable. Logan longed to tug her into his arms. Good grief, he needed her. He'd beg, steal or kill for the opportunity to redeem himself. If she listened, then maybe they still had a chance.

"Is that everything you know?" Ray demanded.

Jade nodded. "Yeah. Logan, I'm sorry."

Logan glanced back at Cass. "That's a nice gesture, but it's not what I think that matters. It's what Cass is willing to accept. I can't change your mind, love, but I can hope that we'll move past this. My heart hasn't given up."

Cass folded her arms and puffed out a long sigh. She stared at the ceiling for a few tenuous moments. Fear crept into his brain. Too much bravado would push her away. A lie would slice his remaining hopes to ribbons. Logan thought he'd die waiting. Did she need the words to tell him to get lost? The longer she stayed silent the further his hope plummeted.

"I think I need time to think this through. Logan, I trust you, but I've heard so much this morning. I'm not sure what to believe anymore." With that, Cass stepped past the three of them and went out onto the deck.

Logan surged forward to catch her, but Ray stepped in his way. He followed her onto the deck, leaving Logan and Jade alone together. "I have a really bad feeling about this. Jade, did you come alone?"

She stared at him. "Yeah, why?"

Logan felt the color drain from his face. He remembered the extra car in the driveway. He thought of the smashed flowerpots and the scattered cigarette butts. Someone else was there. He racked his brain.

Who?

"Shit!"

Jade looked at him with a startled expression. "What's wrong?"

He burst forward through the kitchen. A ripple of fear

shot through his body. Dex was there to collect his expected due — Cass. "Jade, call nine-one-one. Shit just hit the fan. Dex is here."

* * * *

Cass gripped the railing. Footsteps thumped on the wood planks behind her. "Ray, I'm fine."

"Move one more inch and I'll do it, Cass."

The air rushed out of Cass' chest. She knew that voice. Dex. Oh God. The devil came to Ohio. She wanted to slap herself. She never should've come outside alone. Something cold pressed against her temple. Dex's thick, sweaty arm closed around her throat. Hot breath smelling of stale cigarettes burned her ear. "I can't face life without you."

She needed to be calm and rational. "Dex, please let me go."

His grip tightened around her neck as he moved them off the deck. "No can do, Chunks honey. You got away from me once. I'm not letting it happen again. Get in the car and we'll take a trip to the airport. Let's go home."

Cass closed her eyes. This wasn't happening. It couldn't be. For crying out loud, she was still in her pajamas! His cologne wafted around her like a thick fog. She wanted to throw up and run. Running sounded like a good idea, except for the fact that the lunatic had a damned gun and his arm locked around her. "I am home, Dex."

"I can't let you throw away what we had. I tried to catch you over at the Hawthorne and then at the library. This won't continue. We're going back to our home in California." He shoved her down the deck steps and across the yard to the garage.

Tears streamed down her face. "Let me go and we can talk this out like adults," she whispered and gripped his forearm. She fought hard to stay calm because he fed on her fear. "I won't try to escape. Those other times, I wasn't sure it was you and I was afraid. You can trust me."

239

"Cass, now really." Dex pushed her forward and tightened his grip around her neck. "If I can't have you, then no one will. I won't surrender and give up on you this time."

Cass grimaced. Bile crept up her throat. "You don't give up. Ever."

"He won't be that stupid again." Nikita held a bright pink handgun, aimed at her. Go figure. Only Nikita would accessorize her weaponry with her outfit. Cass ground her teeth together. How the hell was she going to reason with two crazies and stay alive?

"He's not letting you get away to marry Romeo Malone, either." Nikita snorted and waved her gun. "Dex has class and you need some. Dex, go before they come out here. I already took care of Ray. I don't want to hit anyone else and get blood on my gun."

Cass gulped for air. Her thoughts ran as wild as the dogs barked in her kitchen. They wanted to protect her and probably eat Dex alive. Elliott's guttural growl thundered over the pounding of her heart. She had to think fast and stall Dex and his sister. "Wait, Nikita. Where's your minion, Ania? Aren't you grooming her to be your protégé?"

Dex relaxed his grip the tiniest bit. "Yeah, where is the mouse? I'd like to thank her for her assistance. She's good with rental companies."

Cass snuck a sideways glance at Dex. Son of a bitch! If he were the man watching her at the bookstore and library, she'd be willing to bet his size thirteen shoes made the footprints outside her house.

Nikita sneered at her brother and Cass cringed. She didn't particularly want to be in the middle of a sibling argument, especially not with a couple of guns involved. Where in the hell were Ray, Logan or Ronan? Duh. Ronan left once the film crew departed and Nikita claimed to have whacked Ray with the butt of her gun. Then where was Logan?

Nikita waved the pink firearm in the air nonchalantly. "I fired her. She wasn't competent," she replied with a sugary sweet smile. "I'm sure she'll do just fine on the unemployment line."

Cass's jaw dropped. "Nikita. That's evil."

Nikita's eyes narrowed. "I never claimed I was a nice person. But enough about me. It's time to get rid of you."

Dex's grip around her throat contracted. Cass coughed and choked and he laughed. "No, no. I'm taking her home. I won't let her within an inch of Malone. He's got her all mixed up."

The gun pressed tighter against her temple. With every trembling step her cotton and faux fur slippers felt like lead boots. Oh, God. She needed a miracle. Logan, anyone... please?

"You're right. She's not marrying me."

Cass's eyes widened as she recognized Logan's voice... but he did not just say... She wished she could see him. She needed the reassurance he was lying or whatever.

"That's right. Cass won't marry me. I cheated on her. She's nuts to want me." Logan ambled over to Nikita and slung his arm across her shoulders. "I wanted to announce this later, but" — he smiled lovingly down at her — "I really want to marry Nikita. She's more like me in every badass, fucked-up way."

Cass bit her tongue to keep the cry at bay. His acting skills weren't award winning, but they weren't awful either. Was he trying to confuse Nikita? If so, it worked. She glanced over Dex's arm at her house. Elliott jumped against the French doors, rattling the glass. Too much longer and he'd break through. Why not? She needed the help and moral support.

Nikita lowered the upraised gun and curled into Logan. "I knew you'd come around, baby boy. Ready for that trip? I had the travel agency leave the dates open."

"And not a moment too soon." Logan took the revolver from Nikita and tucked it in his waistband. "We can use this for role playing tonight. You always did like cops and robbers." He wriggled his eyebrows and clicked his tongue.

Nikita blushed. "I do."

Cass rolled her eyes and chewed the inside of her cheek to keep from shaking her head.

Logan nodded at Cass. "I was stupid to fall for Cass when I wanted you all along."

Cass clenched her teeth. Even if he wasn't interested, Logan didn't have to lay it on quite so thick. She spotted Ray at the corner of the garage. Blood streaked down his shirt and he winced, but otherwise seemed to be okay—not that she could help him.

Dex's grip loosened and he looked away. "Oh, please. That's my baby sister you're mooning over. Get out of here and get a room."

That moment of laxity was enough. Ray charged at her like a wild bull. He shoved her to the ground and under his large body. "Stay behind me," Ray insisted through his teeth as he stood. "Go to hell, Dex, and take your sister with you."

Cass plastered herself to her friend's back. What the hell just happened? She peeked over at Dex who lay on the ground, gasping for air. She didn't see any blood. Maybe her ex really was a sissy after all.

"Stay put, Cass. He's not playing with a full deck," Ray warned under his breath. He forced her back with his strong arm. "Please?"

Cass rubbed the muscles along Ray's arm. "Logan's not thinking straight either. He's going to get himself killed."

"Shhh. Trust us," Ray bit out.

Nikita giggled in Logan's arms. Her voice came out in a shrill childlike tone. "Logan, I need to help Dex. That bully just knocked him down. Shoot him or something."

Cass peeked out from behind Ray's massive frame once more.

"Logan won't do anything to hurt you," Ray muttered and patted her hip. "Trust him."

"I do," she muttered.

"Ah, let Ray handle it," Logan replied. "I never really wanted Cass, but he sure does. Let them fight over her."

"Wait a minute!"

Cass inched out farther to see Jade scream and the dogs bounce off her as she jogged across the concrete sidewalk with her high-heeled shoes in hand.

"You can't have him, Nikita. I have the engagement ring right here." Jade stuck out her hand and shoved it under Nikita's nose. "I won't let go without a fight. Sorry about the dogs, Cass. They pushed past me before I could catch them."

Cass dug her nails into Ray's skin. She'd trained the dogs to stay on the run, not necessarily in the yard. Now she had to hope they wouldn't run away before she could corral them.

Dex groaned from his position on the ground. "That bastard hit me!" he shouted. He stumbled trying to stand up. "That son of a bitch hit me. Somebody shoot the motherfucker."

"I'm busy," Nikita shouted. "I had him first, bitch."

"Please. He can't stand you," Jade snapped. "Told me he never wanted to see you again."

Logan disengaged from Nikita and grinned at Cass. His eyes flashed and he mouthed, *It's a set up. Trust us.*

Cass clutched Ray's shirt. She wanted to believe Logan, but everything was a little too scary at the moment.

"He's mine!" Nikita snarled.

"I had him first." Jade buffed her nails on her shirt. "I'm not sure I'm willing to back down so easily."

Logan yawned and reached down to scratch Elliott. "Let me know when you decide, girls."

Nikita's eyes narrowed. "I had him first! You got him as a cast-off."

"You didn't treat him like an adult," Jade spat and folded her arms.

Cass noticed the gun lying in the grass a few feet away from the grumbling Dex. Edging out from behind Ray, she made a break for the firearm. Luck wasn't on her side – Dex grabbed it first along with a thick lock of her hair.

"Thought you were smarter than me, didn't you?" He tugged at her hair to remove it from the grip of the gun. "Remember your place, Cass. You're not that smart. Give up like Jade and realize I'm in charge here."

Cass fought off a shudder and nodded. Pain seared her scalp. His groin pressed into her hip. He had a God damn boner. She wanted to throw up.

"Nikita, get in the car," Logan commanded.

Cass turned in the direction of his voice. A different light flickered in his eyes. Hatred. Possession. Determination. The dogs both froze in their tracks. Elliott sat up a litter straighter and his ears perked. Even Paula took notice. She parked herself by Cass.

Logan spoke to Nikita, but his eyes never left Cass. "I don't want you to get hurt."

A shiver surged along her spine, but she felt oddly safe. Logan might not stick around for long, but he'd never intentionally put her in harm's way. She knew he'd work like hell to keep her that way.

"But I don't—" Nikita whimpered.

"Do it!" Logan shouted. "Now!"

Cass shivered again. Logan's voice reminded her of thunder, like he could split the heavens with his rage. He probably could. Nikita did as told and got into the blue sedan. She folded her arms and huffed like a child. "That ass thinks he owns me, does he? No fucking way. Bastard."

Logan stepped up to Dex and held out his hand. "Give me the gun, Dex."

"Oh, shut up, all of you!" Dex pressed the gun to Cass' temple and used her as a human shield. "This ends here, Cass. You and me. I told you, if I can't have you, then no one will. That's a promise."

Ray stood at his full height next to Logan. "Hurt Cass and you'll have to go through me too. No more games."

Dex narrowed his eyes and aimed the gun. "Fine. I never liked you hanging around her anyway. Too clingy." He clicked the trigger and everything around Cass went silent, but she felt the impact deep in her soul. She turned to see blood seep from Ray's shoulder. Realization hit hard. This was her fault. Her friends, her dogs and her lover were all at risk. No more.

"Dex! You shot Ray!" she screamed and punched Dex in the chest. Her fists met the unforgiving iron of his abdomen, but she didn't care. She continued to dish out her aggression with kicks to his shins. "You shot my best friend. You asshole!"

Dex whacked her with the gun, connecting with her temple. "Shut up!"

Cass bit her tongue as she landed on the ground and clenched her fists to block out the pain throbbing behind her eyes. Elliott charged, snarling and spitting at Dex. Her ex-husband lashed out, trying to kick the determined dog off his pant leg. The screech of expensive cloth tearing and the low growl from the animal meant Elliott wasn't letting go.

Dex tackled her and aimed the barrel of the gun back at her forehead. "Now it's your turn, my sweet Chunks."

The air seemed to split in two. Her life flashed before her eyes as a mass struck her body, pinning her to the ground. Grass and the scent of Ray's aftershave drifted past her. The wind rushed out of her lungs.

What the hell just happened? She shoved against the body on top of her. *Ray.* The rest of the scene unfolded without her really believing what she saw. Blood drenched Logan's shirt as he wobbled on his feet. His eyelids drooped and he tumbled backward.

Nikita screeched and locked the car doors with a loud click. "Logan!"

Cass dug her fingers into the grass for support. Sirens blared and flashing lights bounced off her house. Sheriff Mackenzie charged from his cruiser and began shouting orders to Deputy Cross and the other officers. "Where's Ronan Levine? I need my sharpshooter. Levine!"

Jade cowered behind the nearest police vehicle. "Get

him!"

Cass allowed Ray to pull her into his embrace. Logan panted to catch his breath. The color drained from his face. He met her gaze and half grinned, then winced.

"Cass, I'm sorry we didn't get out here in time to get rid of that ass," Ray whispered and stroked her hair. He rocked her in his embrace. "I love you so much. Are you okay?"

Cass heard Ray's words, but couldn't fathom the meaning. He loved her, indeed, but more like a sibling, not a lover. Her tears wetted his shirt. "I know, Ray. I know. I'm scared, but, Ray, you're bleeding! You need to stop bleeding." Her lungs constricted. She couldn't breathe. The sticky crimson seeped onto her shirt. "Please, stop bleeding."

Ray shook his head. "Calm down, Cass." He stroked her hair some more. "Calm down. EMS is here. I'm good. He just grazed my shoulder with that first bullet and Nikita just clocked me. There's nothing in my head to hurt, so don't worry about me. I'll be fine."

She shivered, unsure whether to laugh or cry. This wasn't right. Ray shot, Dex lay still in the grass…and Logan…she wasn't sure where she stood with him or if he was even okay.

Cass stared at Dex's prone body. Blood poured from the single hole in his chest and seeped onto her grass. She reached down to check his pulse and found none. She shivered and wiped her hands on her shirt. Paula trotted to where Dex lay and examined him for a moment.

Cass was about to call her away when the dog sniffed the man's body and snorted. She reached out and the dog willingly came to her. "Good girl," Cass murmured.

"Cass, baby, it's over," Ray said and rubbed her shoulder. "It's all over."

She turned to scan the area, needing Logan. Where was he? "Where's Logan?"

"I'll take you over there. The paramedics are working on him." Ray escorted her across the lawn to the ambulance. Logan lay on the stretcher, talking to the sheriff's deputy. He handed over Nikita's pink gun. Elliott watched at Logan's feet, offering protection. A paramedic cut through his shirt to bandage the wound on his shoulder. Logan nodded at Cass and smiled weakly.

Cass felt numb. Her world turned on its ear. Without thinking, she reached over to scratch Paula's ears. The action soothed them both. Like she was stuck in some sort of magnetic field, she walked right into Logan's outstretched good arm.

"Babe—"

The paramedic elbowed Cass out of the way and loaded Logan into the waiting ambulance. "We got the bleeding to slow, but we need to extract the bullet from your shoulder. Let's go."

Cass grabbed the hem of Logan's shirt. She couldn't leave him in his present condition. The paramedic patted her arm. "Ma'am, you can ride along. We'll need to check you out too."

She stole a glance at Ray. He nodded. "Go. I'll put the dogs in the house," he called and cornered Paula. "I'll follow behind in the truck."

"Me too! I'll help," Jade added and grabbed Elliott's collar.

Before Cass could change her mind, the medic closed the doors and the ambulance sped off. She shook her head and buried her face in Logan's torn shirt. Tears fell fast and furious, stinging her cheeks. Even damaged, he still smelled masculine, earthy and all Logan. Desire sizzled through her veins. Great now she was angry and horny. What a combo! She barely heard the beeps and buzzing coming from the machines or the conversation of the paramedics. Logan's battered body filled her senses.

He held her palm tight and stroked the back of her hand with his thumb. "I thought I lost you. I couldn't deal with you gone from my life, baby."

Cass wiped her tears with a tissue. She wanted to punch him in his good shoulder for all the drama he caused. "You idiot! You put your life in danger. Why did you shoot Dex?

He would've killed you without a second thought and I can't be angry with you if you're dead."

"I didn't shoot Dex," Logan said softly. "Jade called the sheriff, but Ronan got there first. I couldn't kill the bastard, even though I wanted to. I'm a horrible shot."

"I don't understand." Cass's throat constricted, making it hard to breathe again. "How did you see Ronan?"

"I recognized his truck off by the barn. When I talked to the guards, I talked to him too. He's an expert marksman. I'm not thrilled he had to leave when the production did, but I trusted him with your life."

She stared at her hands. "How did you get hurt?"

"Dex had his finger on the trigger. When the bullet struck him, his arm jerked out. The trigger on that gun must be touchy. I caught the bullet intended for you."

"So your proclamation to Nikita was scripted?" *Please God, let it be scripted.*

Logan tilted her head to look into her eyes. "I played the toughest role of my life, sweetheart. I had to get her to think I was over you. That was the only way I could maybe get you out of the line of fire." He sighed and gripped his injured arm. "I came back for you because I love you. Ray went to help before I could get a plan sorted out. When I saw you out there with Dex, I couldn't hold back. I told you I wouldn't let him hurt you ever again. I don't lie."

Cass stared blankly into space, words escaped her. The image of his blood staining her grass permanently etched itself in her mind. He nearly killed himself trying to protect her and she'd doubted him. How do you repay someone for kindness like that? A voice jarred her back to the present.

The medic opened the rear doors of the ambulance. "Come on inside. The doctors want to check you out, Ms. Jensen."

She turned and nodded. The chaos of the emergency room overwhelmed her. High-pitched beeps and mechanized noises blitzed her senses. The scent of antiseptic churned her weak stomach. Too many shouts from frustrated doctors and nurses combined with the chatter in the waiting room overwhelmed her. She needed to see Logan. After the unreality of the morning, she needed to know that he was still okay.

"I'm sorry, Ray. So sorry." She huddled against him as he draped a jacket around her shoulders. "Nothing makes sense."

"It will." Ray hugged her tight. "Logan asked for help. That's when I knew for certain he loved you."

She was safe, but the fear wasn't totally gone. "What about Dex?" She eased her arms into the sleeves of the jacket.

"Sheriff Mackenzie took custody of the body for now. That ass can rot in the morgue for all I care." Ray led her to a chair. "They'll release him to Dex's folks, I suppose. He's not your worry any longer." He snorted. "Sorry about the jacket. It's all I had in the truck. Didn't exactly have time to get you something to change into."

"This is perfect." She slid her hands back into the sleeves for warmth. "That's what I get for coming downstairs in my jammies."

"Honey, you had no idea what happened would happen." Ray kissed the top of her head and side-hugged her tight.

Deputy Marlon Cross ambled across the waiting room. He wore his dark sunglasses perched on the top of his head and his muscle-hugging uniform. The gun accentuated his toned waist. Two nurses turned to drool as he passed their position. "She was one wiggly little girl," Marlon remarked. He strolled up to her and Ray and stuck out his hand. He shook hands with Ray.

"Who?" Cass asked.

"That Nikita Cline woman," Marlon replied. "She nearly got out of the cuffs and then threatened me with her lawyer. Freddie's got her on unregistered firearm charges, disorderly conduct and resisting arrest. He wants her held without bail too. She can't claim the body from jail, but she did call someone's parents. I got confused when she explained how she and Mr. Rose were related."

Were. Dex was really dead. Cass rested her head on Ray's chest. She needed time to process and to just exist. The man she'd once called lover was dead and the one she currently loved was in surgery.

"You okay, Cass?" Ray smoothed his hand over her back. "Need something?"

Need something? A few seconds with no guns, no glamorous women parading around and no crazy ex-husbands. A moment where the man who owned her heart wasn't injured and possibly on life support. Yeah, she needed time — and maybe a stiff drink to wash it all down. "I'm — well, I'm not okay, but I'll be fine." Cass looked up. "It's just been a long day."

Marlon nodded. "I need a statement from you both, but you can wait until tomorrow. Just don't forget. By the way, have you seen Ms. Weir? I need to talk to her as well."

Apparently overhearing her name Jade stepped from behind a curtain. "I'm here, just hiding."

Cass stood up and crossed over to the younger woman. "Jade honey, are you okay?" She grabbed Jade in a hug. "I was worried about you."

"You shouldn't worry about me. I'm no one important." Jade smoothed her hair through her fingers and smiled. "I'll be fine." She shook her head. "I see it now."

Cass cocked her head. "I don't understand."

Jade touched Ray's shoulder and ran her fingers over his snug T-shirt. "I don't know about this guy, but I know Logan would never risk his life for me. You two really do belong together."

Ray shifted uncomfortably. "I'm sorry?"

"She's lucky to have a friend like you." Jade sighed. "My friends worry more about the designer clothes I'm wearing than whether or not I've been shot. They don't even know where I am. Daddy only cares as long as I create news for the magazine."

Cass smiled and brushed a tear from Jade's cheek. The girl had every photographer in America clamoring for her image, sycophants fawning around her in droves and oodles of money, but no one who honestly gave a damn. All she wanted was to matter to someone. Behind the hairspray, makeup and spray-on tan was a scared, scarred little girl wanting decent, scrupulous attention.

"I worry about you," Cass said. "I do."

Jade's eyes widened. "Why?"

Cass nodded. "You're a decent woman who just hasn't found the right path in life." Jade tucked her hair behind her ears, probably trying to rationalize Cass's words. Cass continued. "You're welcome to stay here and be yourself, whenever you want. I don't mind."

A smile blossomed on the young woman's face. Tears shone in her eyes. "Thank you."

Cass grinned. "Any time."

Jade glanced at the trio and dipped her head. "I've gotta go. I've taken enough of your time."

Cass opened her arms. "Be careful."

Jade turned her attention to Marlon. "Deputy, I'd like to make my statement tonight, if I can. I have a life to work on in the morning."

Marlon's eyes widened, but he regained his poise within seconds. "Right this way. You can follow me to the station."

Jade wiped away her tears. "Bye, Ray. Cass, I'm good. Stay cool." With that, she followed Marlon out of the emergency room and out of sight.

Cass hugged Ray tight again. He gave her the tiniest smile. The man was a true blessing decorated in tattoos and muscle.

The doctor pointed to a recovery room. "Ms. Jensen? Mr. Russell? You can come in now. Mr. Malone is stable."

Cass turned, but barely caught what the doctor had said. "I'm sorry, what?"

Dr. Lawrence smiled clasped his hands together. "I'll let you talk to Logan."

"Thank you." Cass gasped when she entered the private room. Logan's normally tan face was pasty. His hair lay in damp hanks around his face and his eyes opened only half way. The hospital gown fell across his chest and a thick white bandage covered his shoulder. A round stain of blood seeped through the gauze. He half smiled and sighed. "Hi, babe. I'm sorry I got myself shot."

"Hi yourself," she replied in a whisper. She wanted to cradle him, to make the nightmare and the wound go away.

Ray cleared his throat. "Umm… Well, I bet you two want some time alone. Anyway, I gotta meet someone." He shuffled his feet. "You've got a lot to talk about."

Cass took a deep breath and then wrapped her arms around Ray's middle. "It'll work out, Ray. Go."

Ray dipped his head and disappeared.

She watched her friend leave. Ray was a grade-A, dependable, devoted man. He deserved an equally worthy woman — someone who didn't treat him like a sibling. Cass knew the right woman was right under his nose and waiting to pounce. First, he'd have to give the woman a chance.

Cass turned her attention back to the man in the hospital bed. The steady beat of Logan's heart monitor cut through the thick silence. She wanted to curl up next to him and breathe him in.

Logan bowed his head and pinched the bridge of his nose with his fingers. "Cass, I'm not all right."

Cass stroked his forearm. The sprinkling of dark hair tickled her fingers. The black writing near his shoulder caught her eye. When did that get there? She tipped her head to get a better look. Calligraphic letters that read, *Cass*. Oh good Lord, he had her name inked into the tight skin enveloping the thick muscle of his biceps. But instead of looking garish, like Ray's skull and dagger tattoos, this looked…pretty. Well, maybe not pretty, but manly and sexy. She gently touched his skin where the letters decorated it. Damn, the tattoo did add to his appeal. A lot.

"When did you get a tattoo?" she blurted.

"I need to tell you a few things."

Cass eased onto the edge of the bed and patted his thigh.

"Go ahead."

"I got the tattoo to mark myself. I wanted all the cute little starlets to know I belonged to someone. No more cheating, no more lies. Even if you don't belong to me, my heart will always be yours. I'm your man."

Cass took a deep breath. "Okay."

"I don't want you to think that I'm like that monster. If you didn't want me, I'd still want you, but I wouldn't chase you all over to prove my point. I'd let you go and let you decide what you wanted. Before you walked, I'd make sure you knew I'd wait for you. Even if that wasn't what you needed, that's what I'd do."

Cass looked away and bit back a smile. True, his words sounded a lot like Dex, but something way down deep in her gut knew for certain that he wouldn't end up treating her the same way. Ever. What he felt was real and honest. He'd let her fly and wait when she decided to land. Her head and her heart were in agreement—she still loved Logan. Always would.

"Will you grab my jeans? I need to show you something," Logan said and broke her concentration. He pointed to a blank plastic bag on the hospital chair.

Cass grabbed the garment in question and sat back down on the edge of his bed. "You aren't going to flash me, are you?"

Logan forced a feeble smile and produced the diamond ring from the front pocket. It looked so small and delicate in his large hands. "I know you took this off because of that shit, but I want you to have it. This ring is yours to do whatever you want."

She put her fingers on his lips. "It's over."

Logan shook his head and a tear slipped from the corner of his eye. "No, it's not." His voice cracked. The blood pressure monitor spiked and screeched. "I don't want us to be over. I need you, babe. I did everything I promised. Please give me another chance."

Cass stared at the jewelry. All the promises he made

remained intact. He'd even nearly died for her. She rubbed his thigh, inadvertently stroking dangerously close to his dick. Her gaze zipped straight to the growing bulge, so warm and inviting. Logan was so much a part of her that Cass wasn't sure where she ended and he began — even if he was a hornball.

Logan sucked in a ragged breath. "You better watch what you're touching." He nodded to the tent in his hospital gown. "That's liable to go off at any minute. I'm on a hair-trigger. I've missed you too much."

"I missed you too."

"Cass, I'm done," Logan said, turning serious. "I'm out. Carmine had stuff lined up for me and I refused. I have a new job waiting for me here in Ohio, which is the reason I disconnected my phone and deleted my email account. I wanted a fresh start with you."

She blinked. This didn't sound right. "But acting is your life."

"Don't you remember? I told you this."

She stared at him in disbelief and tried in vain to remember ever hearing those words, any words like that. Nothing came to mind. "Are you sure? Did you hit your head? You never said anything about a job in Ohio."

"You were asleep," Logan murmured. "No wonder..."

"Logan?"

"I'm moving to Ohio to work with Ray on the dirt team. I'm doing their public relations and working on adding sponsorship dollars so he can focus on the cars and Levi can focus on driving. We even have Noel Liamson's company, Prep Productions, on board for next season. When I called you the other night, I used my new phone."

Cass swallowed and looked around blindly, trying to process his words. "When did you decide this?"

Logan brushed her hair from her face and cupped her cheek. "I talked to Ray last night when you walked away. But the other stuff...when we were still...I fired Carmine and sold the condo four weeks ago. The GTO's in storage until I retrieve it. I'm out of show business for good. I tried to tell you my plans the night before I left, but you must've fallen asleep."

She continued to glance at the nondescript walls, letting his words become coherent sentences in her brain. *Out of the business for good? Fired Carmine?* "But you love acting. It's all you've ever wanted."

"That chapter of my life is over. I can't be the celebrity I'm expected to be any longer." He held the ring in his palm. His brows furrowed and the worry lines etched his forehead. "I love you and still want to marry you. Do you—love me?"

Cass bit back a sob and a lump formed in the back of her throat. This was the way life was supposed to be, together. Nothing, not Dex, not Ray or even a bullet could keep her and Logan apart.

"What?" Logan's face lost the little color he started with. His blood pressure monitor went berserk again. She expected a doctor or, at very least, a nurse to rush in to check his condition. He gripped her hand tight. "Honey?"

More tears fell. He did exactly what he promised. He came back and he nearly lost his life in the process. And now with the new details, how could she possibly turn him away?

"Well, being married makes everything so much easier," Cass replied. His eyes grew to the size of saucers. "Say again?"

She needed to tell him—not that she would've kept this kind of secret from him for long. She dragged a breath in to fortify her nerves, then exhaled. "I don't want my child to grow up without both parents." She parted the jacket, placed his hand on her belly and nodded.

A smile blossomed on Logan's face and his eyes lit up. The color filtered back into his face. "When?"

"About seven weeks ago, or thereabouts," Cass replied and twined her fingers with his. "I go to the doctor next Thursday morning, but the pregnancy tests were very pink and very positive."

Logan kissed her knuckles, then paused. "Tests? How many did you need?"

The tips of her ears burned. "Three."

Logan's laugh echoed in the room. "Babe, I'm so happy and relieved. This is the best thing that's ever happened to me. You're the only woman who'll carry my children. But why three tests? Were you scared or embarrassed?"

She shrugged. "I dropped the first one in the john and needed the second one to actually take the test. The third was just insurance in case I did it wrong. I'm lousy under pressure."

Logan's hand caressed her stomach under the sleep shirt. "There's a little Malone in there. Well, I'll be…"

"I wanted to tell you tomorrow after a romantic dinner. I had it all planned out. Trust me, I wanted to look better than this." With the sweep of her arm, she gestured at the oversize jacket, wrinkled shirt and muddy slippers. "But that doesn't matter right now. I just hope you want to be a husband and father to our child."

Without missing a beat, Logan slipped the ring back onto her finger. "I love you. I'll be the best father and husband I can be. I want that more than anything."

She nodded. "I love you too."

Logan eased her into his half embrace. "My baby's having a baby," he murmured. "My baby."

Cass laughed. She'd take that as agreeable.

"Christ. I want out of here so badly. I'm not wild about hospitals as it is and now I've got two sweet reasons to celebrate."

"If the doctor allows it," Cass replied and rested her head on his good shoulder. So Logan's acting skills weren't Oscar-worthy. At least her life would always have laughter and excitement. He cared about people besides himself and wanted to make their lives better. She'd never be alone and she liked it that way. "Once you're one hundred percent, we'll do all the celebrating we can," she murmured and closed her eyes. "But first I have to call Ray and Les to bring the truck. We don't have a ride home."

Logan clicked the call button. "Oh, Doc?"

Epilogue

Two months later, Logan stood at the front of the little stone church tugging at his collar. He wasn't keen on tuxedos and usually only wore suits to award shows or premieres. But this event was special. The chilly November air blew in from an open window and swirled around him. He admired the smattering of candles decorating the small turn-of-the-century sanctuary in the tiny church. She wanted quaint and managed to find the perfect church for her desires.

He tugged on his coat. He had desires, too — all of which included Cass naked. At the thought of his bride open and waiting for him, his mouth watered. Yeah, she was beautiful in anything — especially naked. His cock thickened behind his zipper. Shit. He had a hard-on in a church.

"I will pay you back for making me dress up," Ray snarled and took his place beside Logan. He fidgeted with his cummerbund. "I hate these things."

Logan shook his head. He should've known when he asked Ray to be his best man that the guy would hate wearing the tux. "I'm not wild about them, either, but she insisted." Logan clasped his hands together.

Ray elbowed Logan, jarring him from his daydream and deflating his lust. "Nervous?"

Logan tugged at the aggravating fabric once more and willed his thumping heart to quiet. "I've been married four times — all in the movies. I've never done this for real. Yes, I'm scared to death."

"You should be." Ray chuckled. "There's only two people on your side of the church. Where are your legions of friends? Family?"

"We wanted to keep this private," Logan said and hoped he sounded confident. Truth be told, he didn't have any family left to attend — short of his mother and he doubted she'd show up. He doubted she cared about him any longer.

Ned leaned in and broke up the nervous conversation. "Ready to get married?"

Logan nodded. "Stoke it up." Having a judge for a friend sure made the whole quick wedding business go a lot smoother.

Ray chuckled again. "You aren't funny."

Logan shrugged and focused on the back of the church.

He noticed Maggie and Les coming down the aisle, but the moment he saw Cass, his breath caught in his throat.

The empire-waist gown showcased her breasts and minimized her growing belly. Deep love, admiration and desire flooded his heart. Cass was definitely his lifetime love. Holy shit! He was about to marry the woman of his dreams. She joined his side and smiled.

Logan laced his fingers with hers. "You're beautiful," he whispered.

"So are you."

Logan nodded. Life would have its ups and downs, but their love was rare and perfect. Yes, he was a lucky man and ready to face any challenge because they'd do it together.

Once the ceremony concluded and the photographer snapped the last shot, Logan backed up as Ned kissed the bride. He shook Logan's hand. "This was a beautiful ceremony, kids."

Cass dipped her head and smiled. "Thank you, Ned."

"Yes, thank you. Are you sticking around for cake?" Logan wrapped his arm around Cass. The thought of cake did nothing for him. No — he'd rather hurry through the reception in order to get Cass alone and naked.

Ned's smile widened. "Nah, I'm getting out of here. First Drew and now Cass. This wedding business may be catching."

Cass laughed. "You mean you found someone?"

Ned blushed from his hairline down past the collar of his dress shirt. "Well, there is this woman I want to get to know."

The laugh bubbled in Logan's throat. He'd been in Ned's shoes, but luckily he ended up with marital results. "Get to know? You? The Casanova of the judicial system?"

"Let's just say, I'm trying to catch her in my hallway so I can meet her," Ned replied. "She's a sweet girl who deserves a second chance."

Logan cocked his head. "Oh, so you know her?"

Ned grinned once more. "Not yet, but I will. See you later."

Logan kissed Cass's temple as Ned strolled away. *Good luck, man.* He hoped the judge really had found the woman of his dreams and was ready to hold on for the ride of his life.

Cass began to laugh. "He's a charmer."

Logan clutched her close. "So are you, babe."

Cass smoothed her hand over his chest, then nodded to the pews. "Who's that woman sitting in the back row? I've never seen her before. She's giving me the willies. Tell me you know her and she's not a member of the press."

Logan glanced over his shoulder and the wind rushed out of his lungs. He knew the woman all right. Thin bone structure, professionally styled bottle blonde hair, too much expensive jewelry and stiff posture — yeah, he knew exactly who she was.

"Logan?"

He opened and closed his mouth, forcing himself to speak. "That's...that's my mother." A thousand memories rushed into his head and his heart ached. The woman who'd abandoned her family, cheated on her husband so many times he lost count and claimed she never loved her child or his father was at his wedding. What was he supposed to say to her? I'm sorry seemed hardly enough and what was he apologizing for? Keeping her away? She'd done that herself. Did she need money? He had no idea.

Cass rubbed his shoulder, soothing the healing injury. As always, she was the rock that steadied him. "Want me to hang around, or should I leave you alone?"

Logan shook his head again. This was something he didn't want to deal with alone. Ever. This was his version of staring down the devil in a frilly lavender dress. "No, we're a family now. We'll deal with this as a family."

Cass nodded and squeezed his hand. "We will."

The woman looked down at her lap, as if she knew they spoke about her. Logan walked the few feet to her pew.

"Coralline?"

The woman tilted her head to match his gaze. A tiny smile curled her overly plumped lips. "You remembered."

Logan gripped the end of the pew and held on tight. He hated that smile. "Can't forget the woman who gave me life."

"I bet you want to talk," Cass said. "I can go."

"No. Stay." Coralline offered her hand. "My son chose well. I'd like to meet you formally. My name is Coralline Malone Carothers. You must be Cass Jensen. Well, no, now you're Cass Malone. The pleasure is mine."

Pleasure his ass. She wanted something, but he didn't know what. "How did you find me?"

Coralline stared at her hands, toying with the enormous diamond ring. "It wasn't hard. You're in all the papers. I did Internet searches on you and your bride. Cass was actually easier to find. She led me to you."

"You've been out of my life for almost fifteen years and the day I get married, you show up. What were you expecting? A happy, greeting card ending? I'm not sure I can do that right now," he managed. "You walked out on me."

Coralline smoothed invisible strands of hair from her face and straightened her narrow shoulders. "You seem to have turned out all right," she snapped.

Logan gritted his teeth, but stayed quiet. Nothing she could say would ease his pain and loss. There was too much long-term damage done.

"I don't want a full blown, huggy-kissy relationship with you. Too much time has passed for any chance of that. All I wanted was to see for myself what kind of man you turned out to be. You're the only natural child I have and the spitting image of your father. I'm proud of you."

Logan rolled his eyes. Spitting image of Dad? Proud of him? What the hell was she thinking? "I don't believe this."

"Logan, I'm sorry." Coralline offered her manicured hand once again. "Cass, you're very lucky. He's a good man and he's blessed to have you."

Logan pinched the bridge of his nose with his thumb and forefinger. "Explain to me why you're here. I can't wait to hear your ridiculous justification for showing up out of the blue."

"Not now," Coralline growled. "This is a happy day."

"My life got screwed up because I didn't think I had anyone who cared!" Logan thundered. "Now is the perfect time to explain this to me."

Coralline straightened her spine. "Your father's job always came first. You were second in his heart. I came last. When he lost everything, I broke down. Then we lost your father." She shook her head. "You have to understand, when I looked at you, I saw your father and all the things I did wrong in my life. I got out to escape my pain. It had nothing to do with not liking or not wanting you."

Logan shook with anger. He let go of the pew and clasped his hands on top of his head. "Why do you want me now? Because I was famous? Because I've got a little money? Tell me. I'm not going to be your meal ticket, Mother."

"Okay." Cass nudged him away from his mother. "Stop. Please."

Logan grimaced. He needed to calm down, but come on. Hurt like that wouldn't go away in an instant. "Why?"

Cass' smile faltered. "Because this is a happy day. Because you still have a mother. Because you will be a father soon." She smoothed her hands down his shoulders and over his silk lapels. "If I learned anything over the past few months, it's that you have to forgive and move on. Accept her apology, as contrived as it may be, and move on. The scars won't heal right away, but they'll never die if you don't deal with them."

Logan fumed and blew out a long sigh. As much as he didn't want to hear it, she had a point. *Fuck.* "I'll do it for the baby, and for you."

Cass smiled. "Now go. I'll be right here beside you."

He needed to hear one more thing. "Promise?"

"Forever."

Logan kissed his new wife once more and sighed. He crossed the room to where his mother waited. "There isn't going to be a perfectly scripted ending here. I forgive you for leaving, but I'm not ready to let you back into my life."

Coralline whimpered and allowed more tears to fall. "I understand. I don't agree, but I understand."

"There's a lot of hurt here. It's not going away simply because you showed up and I said those three words." He exhaled and his chest ached. "Look, come to the reception. There's going to be plenty of food."

"Thank you." His mother blotted her tears with a lace hanky. "You'll find that having a child changes your perceptions."

"Sure does." Logan stared at her. "How'd you know?"

"I listened." Coralline stood and patted his arm. "You're going to be a good daddy, I know."

Logan nodded as his mother walked away. She'd turned her back on him once because she couldn't handle him and now because he couldn't handle what she'd done. Some things didn't make sense, but he would worry about those things after the honeymoon.

Cass eased up beside him and slid her arms around his waist. "You did good," she whispered.

"I've got you." He squeezed her tight. "That's all I need."

"That's good to hear."

"Now, let's create material for your next alpha male," he

263

murmured in her ear. "I could be a great example."

She gave him a quick kiss. "You already are."

He shivered as they walked out of the now vacant church. Life was definitely sweet being her man.

Between Us

Excerpt

Chapter One

"Where are a couple of farm boys when I need them?" Channon Kennedy brushed her horse, Peaches, and rested her head on the side of the large animal's neck. She liked being around the horses. She could talk to them and not have to worry about someone arguing with her. She'd done enough arguing in the last year for a lifetime.

"I don't know how I'm going to manage," she said. She stopped brushing the horse and looked Peaches in the eye. "I'm one person with three horses and a hundred acres. That's a lot for one person to keep things going."

The horse snorted, then shook her head.

"I get it. We'll figure it out." She sighed and surveyed the stall. According to her father's notes, there were two farm hands living on the property. She hadn't seen anyone, but the state of the stall said otherwise. Someone had cleaned it out recently. She'd need to shovel out the muck and add fresh straw, but it could've been worse.

Not knowing who lived on the farm was her own fault. She'd been at the house for three days, but had only ventured out during the last hour. Between the guilt over not being home when her father died and mourning the loss of him, she hadn't wanted to be out in public. She grieved for the end of her relationship with her former boyfriend, Jack, too. The bastard had cheated on her and dumped her for a younger woman. She shouldn't have been so upset. Getting rid of him should've been a relief, but it wasn't. Seven years was a long time to be with someone, only to be shafted.

Channon climbed the side of the stall and sat on the wooden planks. She leaned against the divider bars between the stables. "I miss the boys the most." She gripped the shelf along the wall. "I could use their help, yeah, but I miss their friendship. Brian and Shaun were here when no one else cared."

Peaches shifted around and bumped her head against Channon's side. Channon hugged the horse. "I miss them. I shouldn't because we're horrible when we're together. I still remember all the times we got into trouble, but it was fun."

She glanced over at Herb, Peaches' brother. "You're eating well. Looks like you're exercising, too. How about you?" She turned her attention to Brutus, her father's horse. "I'm not sure how I'll be able to keep you all exercised, but I'll try."

She paused, listening for anyone else in the barn. She hoped Brian or Shaun would stroll around the corner, but no. Nothing. She blew out a long breath and hopped down from her perch.

"Oh well." She patted Peaches again. "I'll be right back to clean out your stall." She wasn't sure why she'd explained herself to the horse, but whatever. She headed out of the barn. The sunshine blinded her for a moment and heated her skin. She liked the peace of the farm. Loved the privacy and not having to worry about who would show up. In the distance, she heard the hum of a tractor.

Who had a tractor on the property? One of the farm hands? She noticed the red machine moving across the hay field. She shielded her eyes to better see the man on the tractor. Her breath lodged in her throat. Shaun? Couldn't be. He would've told her he was there — wouldn't he?

The man on the tractor steered the machine to the edge of the field and stopped when the mail truck zipped up the driveway.

Channon ran across the lawn. She needed to get a dog to help intercept intruders and so she wouldn't be alone. A dog would alert her to visitors, too.

She stopped in her tracks when the man in the mail truck left the vehicle. "Brian?" she murmured. No way. Someone who either was Brian or looked one hell of a lot like him strode across the short strip of grass. The man on the tractor met the mail man at the fence. She could've sworn Shaun stood on the other side of the barrier. If it wasn't them, then who was intercepting her mail?

"Hey," Channon called. "That's mine." She stopped again when both men turned to her and smiled. "Brian? Shaun?"

Shaun whipped his ball cap off his head and wiped the sweat from his brow. "She remembered us. Only took her three days, but she did."

"Well, we are hard to forget." Brian opened his arms. "Give us sugar."

"Sugar? You're holding my mail." She yanked the letters and magazines from Brian's hands. "Since when did you become a mail man?"

"Chill," Shaun said. "We get our mail here, too."

"What?" She leafed through the letters and, sure enough, some had Brian's and Shaun's names on them. "Why? Are you dodging an ex-girlfriend who wouldn't or couldn't handle the both of you?" Brian and Shaun's girl-sharing hadn't been lost on her. She'd dreamed of being the woman in the middle of their man sandwich plenty of times, but they hadn't been interested in her. They probably still weren't and had a girl waiting for them, wherever they were living on the farm. Still, Channon could dream.

Shaun and Brian exchanged glances. "You're done for the day, aren't you?" Shaun asked.

"I'm through with my route, yeah, but I'll have to do my end of the day stuff." Brian folded his arms, then turned his attention to Channon. "I work at the post office during the day and help Shaun the rest of the time. It's worked nicely for five years."

"Oh." In the last seven years, she hadn't really considered what her former friends had done with their lives.

Shaun wiped his hands on his pant legs. "I need to finish the second cutting in the front field, but I'm almost done. Shouldn't take me more than another hour."

"Sounds good," she said. "Do you have plans tonight?" She probably shouldn't have been asking, but she wanted to know. She wasn't sure she wanted them to be with someone. Truth be told, she wanted to keep them for herself, now that she knew they were still on the property.

"How about we make dinner for you tonight?" Brian grinned and leaned against the fence. "Our cooking skills have improved since high school. I can even boil water."

When he flexed the muscles in his arms, he could've been the poster child for hot mail men. She wondered how many women on his mail route fantasized about him. She did. She wanted those arms wrapped around her.

"Channon?" Shaun tipped his head. He had dirt on his cheeks and smeared across his T-shirt, but he had the rugged style going for him.

Where Brian worked the clean-cut and professional angle, Shaun still had his rough edges. She wanted his arms around her, too. Who was she kidding? She couldn't decide between them. God, she was screwed up.

She met his gaze and shivered, despite the early summer heat. "I'm sorry. I bet once you get *cooking*, you're probably unstoppable." She rolled her eyes to hide her embarrassment. They wanted to make her food, not come on to her. *Jesus.* They probably just wanted to be nice to her, too…and maybe keep her happy so they could keep their home on the farm.

"Well?" Shaun tipped her chin to meet his gaze again. Despite the strength in his body, he had such a light touch. His sweaty shirt was glued to his chest and showcased his taut, muscled frame.

Channon's knees weakened. She widened her stance to keep herself upright and bit back a groan. Either she needed sex or needed him—correction, them—more than she realized. Maybe she'd gone too long without sex and was horny. If they were feeling the electricity too, they weren't showing it.

"Channon?" Brian stood beside Shaun and touched her arm. "Are you in there? Or is Shaun's hot body mesmerizing you?"

"Huh?" She should've been paying attention, not getting caught ogling them. "Sorry. Sure. Dinner sounds good. What time and what would you like me to bring? Where do you want to meet?" *How about my place, my bed tonight and all night long?* Oh man. She couldn't say all that. Not now.

"How about at the guest house?" Shaun asked. "Your dad allowed us to live there if we worked for him."

She stared at them. They lived in the guest house? That explained why she hadn't seen them. She hadn't ventured to that part of the property in years. "I didn't see either of you when I drove in three days ago. Haven't seen you working ground or anything."

"You haven't set foot outside the house in that time," Brian said. "I take the truck out before the ass crack of dawn. Shaun's been working in the barn and on the back forty. It's pretty easy not to see us. We keep out of sight."

"With someone, I'm sure." She wasn't sure why she'd said that. She didn't want them with another woman. She had no claim on them, but still.

"We're alone," Shaun said.

"Really?" she blurted.

Brian sighed. "How about we have a nice dinner tonight and get things sorted out? Yes?"

She shrugged, unsure of what else to do. "I'd like that."

"Good." Brian climbed behind the wheel of the mail truck. "I'll be back in an hour." He drove off, leaving her alone with Shaun.

Channon turned her attention to Shaun. "Okay. Spill. What's going on here?"

"Nothing that I know of." Shaun leaned on the fence. "We want to treat you right tonight."

"Because?" God. Being with Jack had made her quick to question every nice thing in her life. She needed to shake that bad habit and fast.

"Just because." Shaun shrugged and tipped his head. "We want to."

"You two never do anything because. Your wanting to always has a proviso." Her lack of trust in almost everyone was showing more than she wanted.

"We're doing it because we want to." Shaun smiled. "You deserve a nice night."

For a split second she could've sworn he said *because we want you*, but she knew better. Still, she didn't trust them. "Oh, well. Thank you."

"We want *you*." Shaun grinned and tugged her into his arms. "Have for a while." He kissed her hard on the lips, then let go of her and strolled to the tractor.

Channon stared at him in stunned silence. She trusted her hearing this time. He'd said they wanted her. Really? She hoped it was real, but her second-guessing came back to haunt her. She hadn't heard him incorrectly, but she doubted they'd want her for long.

Shaun glanced back at her and grinned, then climbed into the tractor.

Channon grabbed the fence post for support. She wasn't about to try to figure Shaun or Brian out. She knew better. She'd tried before and only ended up with a broken heart.

She needed to move forward with her life and focus on the future. She had a farm and three horses to take care of, and no time to worry about how her farm hands made her body sizzle.

She forced herself away from the fence and headed back to the barn. She tossed the mail onto the storage box just inside the building. When she'd left Jack in Cleveland, she'd cleaned the shit out of her life. She picked up the shovel and strode to the first stall. Not the glamorous life, but she loved being back on the farm and close to Brian and Shaun.

More books from
Wendi Zwaduk

There is always fun in the club, but taking the fun outside and into life might be exactly what's needed for a lifetime of passion.

Find what you need at the Store Front. Blood, sex…we have it all just for you.

A topless dancer plus a cynical cop doesn't equal a lifetime love…or does it?

She's the one he wants, he just doesn't know it yet.

About the Author

I always dreamed of writing the stories in my head. Tall, dark, and handsome heroes are my favourites, as long as he has an independent woman keeping him in line.

I earned a BA in education at Kent State University and currently hold a Masters in Education with Nova Southeastern University.

I love NASCAR, romance, books in general, Ohio farmland, dirt racing, and my menagerie of animals. You can also find me at my blog

Wendi Zwaduk loves to hear from readers. You can find contact information, website details and an author profile page at https://www.totallybound.com/

TOTALLY
BOUND

Home of Erotic Romance

www.ingramcontent.com/pod-product-compliance
Lightning Source LLC
Chambersburg PA
CBHW021518240626
47154CB00002B/681